CIRCLE'S END

by

J.A. KAY

Grosvenor House
Publishing Limited

This book is published by
Grosvenor House Publishing Ltd
Link House
140 The Broadway, Tolworth, Surrey, KT6 7HT.
www.grosvenorhousepublishing.co.uk

A CIP record for this book
is available from the British Library

ISBN 978-1-80381-282-3

Other books in this series:

Rory MacSween and the Secrets of Urquhart Castle incorporating *The Story of the Mythical Highland Haggis.*

Rory MacSween and the Rescue.

Circle's End.

Dedication

This book is dedicated to the memory of my friend and illustrator, William 'P' Petherick, who has now joined his true love, Freda, in the afterlife.

Preface

Rory was a very unusual young man of 16 years. He was physically very striking with his highly developed muscular six-foot-four-inch frame and square-jawed handsome face framed by his shoulder-length red hair. He was the epitome of a highland warrior in his full one-piece MacSween tartan kilt with his magic longsword strapped to his back. But his appearance, although intimidating, was not what made him special. He possessed the Hagpipe, made from the right-hand tusk of the first ever haggis, which gave him all its mystical, magical properties, including increased strength, speed and intelligence.

His own abilities, which were numerous, were also multiplied by the power of the Hagpipe in accordance with his age until his 33rd birthday. Among its many magical properties, it imbued him with healing powers, which he had already used to cure his mother from imminent death and, in the process, burn his soul pure. One of the more unusual features of the Hagpipe occurred when it was blown; it gave Rory the ability to command the Mythical Highland Creatures of Scotland and to open the Time Travelling Portals located on the ley lines. Hag the Haggis, Ben the Great Scottish Eagle, and Nessie the Loch Ness Monster were his friends with whom he could mentally communicate. They could travel with him through the natural, ancient portals to any time and place where they connected. He had already called on the assistance of his creature friends to save his father from the Vikings and reunite him with his dying mother.

Now he was being ordained by St Columba to save the world by recovering the Grail Box, a direct link to God, from impending capture by evil forces intent on its destruction. The Grail Box was the resting place of every Holy Relic, including the Grail Cup and death shroud of Jesus, along with the Ten Commandments and all the original, complete religious scriptures which could reunite or destroy mankind.

It could only be touched by the Pure One!

The great evil, embodied in human form, was out to destroy it and remake the world into a hungry place of hate without love or compassion. It had a plan to make Rory despair and to crush all that he loved.

Hag, Ben and Nessie had aided Rory in the past, but could even their awesome power help him this time?

The ultimate confrontation between good and evil was imminent, and Rory might have to fight this battle alone and also save his daughters, who were lost in time. The fate of the whole human race and that of his little girls rested in his hands.

Read on as Rory begins his most important adventure to date. Can he square the circle in time and defeat Evil itself?

About the Author

J.A. KAY was born in 1960 and raised on the west coast of Scotland, where he completed secondary education at Greenwood Academy in Dreghorn. He was fortunate to have the author William MacIlvanney, the Scottish novelist, short story writer and poet, as his English teacher in the 1970s. His success inspired him to put his own stories to paper. Other notable pupils educated at the Academy during this time and thereafter include the actress Julie Graham, singer-songwriter Eddi Reader and the First Minister of Scotland Nicola Sturgeon.

The author served as a police constable for 30 years in Scotland and decided to write as a hobby on his retirement. His interests include freemasonry, rugby, martial arts, real ale, and spending time with his two adult children and three grandchildren, not necessarily in that order.

His background of dealing with and experiencing emotional and sometimes traumatic, life-changing experiences was highlighted when he was run down by a car while on duty. He was subsequently diagnosed with PTSD, which sparked his stories into life as a mechanism for dealing with this condition. This was balanced by a good sense of humour that all the emergency services develop to deal with the unpredictable, stressful situations presented to them, which is evident in his writing. With these life experiences providing valuable background information, and the ale acting as a catalyst for his imagination, these stories were developed.

The author has travelled extensively in Scotland and abroad and has been aware of the cultural and mythical stories of the creatures from the Highlands of Scotland since childhood. Loch Ness has been visited by him both as a child and adult, where the stories of the Monster and the Wild Haggis were implanted in his mind.

He became aware of the history of the Druids and the power of the ley lines when serving in Kilwinning, where the police office is adjacent to the ancient abbey and 'Lodge Number 0', which is reputed to be the first Masonic Lodge of Freemasons in Scotland if not the world.

He learned at this time that all the ley lines passed through both Stonehenge and the Kilwinning Abbey and has witnessed this power seeping out, affecting the local area. He was stationed in Kilwinning when a piece of masonry fell from the abbey through the roof of a colleague's car. He had researched the ley lines and raised his fist, and voiced his disbelief in the magic contained within the ruins of the building. He never recovered from this shock and retired from the police service as a result.

Much of what is written is factually correct, but it is up to you, the reader, to decide what to believe or dismiss. But in either case, enjoy the story.

J.A. Kay

Thanks

I would like to thank all my followers on my Facebook Page @ scottishjakay, Twitter @ScottishJAKay and on my web page at ja-kay.pageonpage.com for their kind words and encouragement and support through this process, and I hope you enjoy this third book in the Rory MacSween Series. Just follow the QR link to my web page for all of my free stories including my children's tales of Santa Claus and his grandchildren.

To Bill Petherick, my illustrator, as he tried to get into the mind of J.A. Kay to complete his artwork for my books. A special thanks goes to Liz Martin and Martin Papworth for their patience in correcting all my grammatical errors in editing this book.

I must also mention my, 'handler' as I call her, Melanie Bartle from Grosvenor house publishing for her expertise in putting this book together.

Lastly, to my long-suffering wife, Ann, and my friends and family, who have persevered with my tales over the years.

Most importantly to the wee wild haggis of my grandchildren who make this old man laugh.

Chapters

CHAPTER 1

Mason Knight Templar

The local St Columba senior priest (well, the only priest), unusually named Mason Knight Templar, lived at the nearby but remote Kilmory Chapel, situated along the bleak hill road from Castle Sween towards the west coast sea, known as the Sound of Jura. Mason was a very fit, mysterious, medium-built man in his seventieth year. He stood tall, unstooped at six foot (1.82 metres) in height, and moved with a stealthy gait.

He was named after his great grandfather, who had been a Knight Templar on the ill-fated Third Crusade to Jerusalem with Richard the Lionheart. Mason was a young man when he joined the Order of the Knights Templar, following in the family tradition, and he knew all of the order's secrets. Now an old man, he was the society's highest-ranking member and the guardian of the graves of the Templar Knights, all of whom were buried at Kilmory Chapel, including his grandfather.

He was exceptionally pleased this Christmas Day to see Rory and his parents, the new Laird and Lady of Knapdale, arrive for this special service following their recent ousting of the treacherous John De Menteith the Younger at Castle Sween. (Refer to Book 2 *The Rescue*.)

The chapel was rectangular in shape with a thatched roof. It was small but very sturdily built with the local Keil rock. It was the perfect place for worship as a Keil, translated as a church. A wall of the same Keil rock surrounded the full graveyard and the chapel with a central path leading up the slight incline to its single sheltered door, facing east, away from the sea and Loch Sween.

Mason watched carefully as the congregation arrived and saw Rory go white in the face as he stepped into the hallowed ground of the chapel. It was obvious to Mason how disturbed he was looking, as if he was walking on his own grave. He approached Rory, exchanging a warm and very secretive handshake with him and his dad, the new laird, welcoming them to the chapel.

Mason knew how special a person he was greeting, and he was looking forward to having a private word with the 'Great One' at the Christmas ball in Castle Sween, to which his father, the laird, had just invited him.

He concluded the Christmas Service in a very timely manner and was the first to publicly give his blessing to the new regime in charge at Castle Sween in front of the whole congregation within the chapel.

More importantly, he privately forwarded Laird Ruaidri a Christmas present of a very substantial credit note that he had received that very morning by the interdoonet (carrier pigeon post) from Abbot MacCallum at Castle Urquhart, vouching for the wealth of the MacSween! The monks of St Columba were the nation's bankers, and their credit notes could be redeemed wherever they were based. The physical assets of the MacSween's were under lock and key in their vault at Urquhart Castle.

Christmas was a very joyous affair in Castle Sween, and Laird Ruaidri and his wife, Lady Mary, had been waiting for this day since they first returned to Scotland with Rory as a child. At long last, they were home, with all their assets restored. They were very happy and very generous to all who attended the grand feast that had been hurriedly prepared for the Christmas ball in the communal hall of Castle Sween, which was a lot smaller than the great hall of Urquhart Castle. It was jammed full, with no room to swing even a cat, never mind to carry out a jig (dance), but everyone seemed to manage.

It was fortunate that it was a very well-designed castle, which even had a privy on its top level. This was much appreciated by the guests because of all the free drink that was flowing. The only thing missing, Rory thought, was Heather, his fiancée, and he stood apart from all the guests doing their thing on the dance floor and having a great time. He was concerned about his visit to Kilmory Chapel earlier that day, and he spoke or rather shouted above all the noise to Mason Knight Templar, arranging to meet the St Columba priest there the next day. Rory wanted to find some explanation for the strange feeling and the perception of his own death that he had experienced on stepping on this holy ground.

Everyone wanted to speak to Rory, who kept being called "Great One", much to his annoyance. It was sometime later that he managed to escape from the party and get to his bed in his new chambers, near to his parents, who had moved into the luxurious rooms occupied by the previous laird, John De Menteith the Younger.

Rory arose early, looking for answers, making do with leftovers on the feasting table for breakfast as he stepped over the drunken guests sleeping where they had fallen in the hall. It would be some time yet before these sleeping beauties would be awake and able to function, going by the loud snoring coming from them. There was enough food and drink lying about unconsumed, and they would just start partying again.

He made his way to the stables where Jet, his horse, greeted him warmly, looking for a special treat. Fortunately, Rory had lifted some preserved apples left on a table at the feast, which Jet enjoyed as a Christmas treat while being saddled over a blanket for warmth. It was a cold morning, the temperature having dropped to minus ten overnight, and the surrounding hills were white with frost and snow, while the edges of the loch were beginning to freeze.

Rory rode to Kilmory Chapel through a winter wonderland, and he could have been the only living person on the planet as he took in the beautiful scenery around him. He saw and smelt the peat fire burning in the small stone thatched cottage next to the chapel and knew that Mason Knight Temple was up and expecting him. He had left the party early the previous night, knowing that Rory would be visiting him.

The ground crunched below Jet's hoofs as he rode him down the slight slope on his left towards the chapel. Rory wanted another look around the graveyard prior to speaking to Mason, feeling that was something there that he had to see!

As soon as he passed through the metal gate into the graveyard, he again felt as if he was walking over his own grave. The ground was heavy, with white frost covering everything. Several large flat stones, about seven feet long, were placed on the ground, covering the graves below them. Rory could see nothing because of the frosty covering on them and bent towards the nearest one on his left, touching it to brush away the frost. An electric-like shock surged up his left arm, causing him to recoil from the stone, which began to steam, melting all the frost from its top.

Rory looked at it!

Engraved on its surface was the image of a giant of a knight, holding a full-length sword identical to his own. The grave was weathered, but Rory recognised the unmistakable Nessie-shaped hilt on the sword grip. He nearly jumped out of his skin when a voice behind him said, "Yes, it's you."

He turned and saw Mason standing behind him, dressed in his heavy brown habit, tied at the waist with a stout cord.

No one could walk up on him on this crispy ground surface without Rory hearing them, but Mason had done it! His enhanced hearing should have detected him, Rory thought, but he had been distracted by seeing his own grave!

Rory realised he was dead and was shaken to his core, knowing that all his plans would fail!

Mason said, "Come into the cottage to the warmth, and I will tell you what I know."

Rory turned and walked with him to the cottage, still shaken at the vision of his own mortality!

A metal kettle was steaming above the fire as Mason poured them both a mug of tea. He began his story of his great grandfather, returning from the Third Crusade to recover the Grail Box with the coffin of this knight and several others they had managed to recover, following the events which had unfolded after the Battle of Arsuf on 7 September 1191.

Saladin's Saracen forces had suffered heavy losses at the hands of the Templar Knights in this battle and were forced to withdraw. After the Battle of Arsuf, Richard moved his forces towards Ascalon. Anticipating Richard's next move, Saladin emptied the city and camped a few miles away.

When Richard arrived at the city, he was stunned to see it abandoned, its towers demolished. The next day, when Richard was preparing to retreat to Jaffa, Saladin attacked his army. A furious battle took place where his great grandfather and King Richard I, the Lionheart, barely escaped with their lives. This was due to the bravery of the Templar Knights, including the one buried outside, who had fought furiously to defend them.

Richard managed to save some of his troops and retreated to Ascalon but not before many of the knights were wounded or killed. This was the last major battle between the two forces. All military attempts by Richard the Lionheart to retake Jerusalem thereafter were defeated.

Richard only had two thousand fit soldiers and 50 fit knights left to use in battle. With such a small force, he could not expect or hope to take Jerusalem from the bolstered, multiplying numbers joining Saladin's Saracen army.

Although Richard got near enough to see the Holy City, he had no other option, being vastly outnumbered, but to return home to bury his dead.

Mason Knight finished his story, stating, "This was passed down to me in records written by my great grandfather who brought the body of this knight home to be buried here, where he originated."

Something just didn't feel right about this to Rory!

The fact that he was dead and buried outside just didn't make sense. Rory wanted to see inside the grave. He knew he could not meet himself, living or dead, as he would be interfering with time. As a result, he would cease to exist, but he was sure he was not in the coffin!

He asked Mason for a shovel. Mason was not happy at all about the grave being desecrated. He took a deep breath and thought, *What a crazy position to be in. If you are alive and want to check your own grave to see if you are in it, then surely you can, but as soon as you step into the grave, you will be in it?* The whole idea seemed preposterous as he handed Rory a shovel, rubbing his throbbing head from thinking about it.

He watched Rory return to his own grave. The ground around it was soft, following the defrosting caused by Rory's touch. He easily lifted the seven-foot-long, enormously heavy gravestone with his image carved on it, standing it against the stone wall surrounding the graveyard to replace it later.

Rory's image looked down on him as he dug down through the soft earth for about six feet until he hit the top of the still preserved, heavy wooden coffin. He cleared the soil away from its lid, revealing a burnt mark on its surface, showing the eight-pointed Templar Cross of St John the Evangelist.

Mason recognised this cross and identified its significance to Rory, advising him that the occupant within was a Knight Templar. Rory felt the Hagpipe tingling against his skin below his shirt as he carefully prised open the coffin lid with the shovel.

It was empty!

No skeleton or any bones at all! Well, it was not quite empty. In there was a grey wrapped cloth in its middle looking in remarkably good condition.

Rory reached inside and lifted the surprisingly heavy bundle of cloth from the coffin with his left hand as an electric bolt passed between him and it. It was as if a connection had been remade, as if a switch had been thrown, turning on a light.

Rory, with his Hagpipe-enhanced physical abilities, easily jumped up and out of the grave, landing beside Mason Knight. He was more shocked than Rory to see the grave empty and was very curious as to what had been so important to be concealed within.

Rory saw his interest in the bundle he was holding. Mason was the guardian of the graveyard. Rory knew it was his place to unwrap it and handed the bundle to him. Mason was taken aback at its weight, carefully unfolding the grey cloth to reveal a large grey cloak with an attached hood. Inside was a pure white tabard, marked on its front with the Red Cross of St John.

Rory watched Mason's face go white with shock as he opened the cloth, revealing a shiny brass triangle with the shape of an eye in its middle. Mason felt unable to hold it, sitting it on top of the wall of the graveyard. He joined his index fingers and thumbs together, making them into the shape of a triangle, and raised both hands up to his right eye. Looking through it, he bowed towards the brass triangle on the wall. *This is very strange behaviour indeed*, thought Rory, as Mason picked up the triangle and walked back to his cottage with it, holding it close to his body like a prized possession.

It was time for whisky, not tea, as Rory quickly reinstated the grave with his super speed and strength and watched in amazement as the ground refroze over the gravestone as he replaced it. One could not tell that it had even been disturbed as Rory joined Mason in his cottage. A large whisky was waiting for him as Mason started on his second, the brass triangle laid out on the wooden table in front of him.

Mason asked Rory to sit next to him as he explained what he had recovered. "It is the symbol of the Order of the Knights Templar containing all their secrets, created by St John when he founded the order to protect the Grail Box in AD 45."

Rory remembered this from his school lessons on his eighth birthday when he had found the Hagpipe. They were both born in a leap year on the summer equinox on the 24th of June, the only difference being that Saint John had been born in AD 15.

He was a disciple of Jesus and had written the Gospel of St John and the Book of Revelation in the Bible! Mason explained that, without this symbol, the Knights Templar would not exist to protect the Grail Box that St John had hidden in Jerusalem. No one knew how St John had come into possession of it, but Rory was starting to understand why he was here and what he had to do.

But first, he would have to know what all the symbols and letters on it meant?

CHAPTER 2

Knight Rory

Mason told Rory that what he was going to explain to him was a Higher Degree from the one he had received when he became a Warrior of HAGI. (* See Appendix.) He had to know this information as Mason was in no doubt that Rory was the 'Pure One'. On completion of his instruction, he would knight Rory, making him a Knight Templar.

Rory was intrigued as Mason showed him the front and back of the brass equilateral triangle. The front had what looked like an open eye in its middle, a perfect circle offset to look oval with a dot in its centre, Mason explained that it depicted the All-Seeing Eye of FIRE!

The front triangle's sides were marked with equally spaced grooves, giving the impression of a stone wall to contain the Eye of Fire. At the pinnacle of the triangle, above the eye, was an M-shaped engraving in the shape of a bird, symbolic of the Great Scottish Eagle, the most powerful creature in the sky! It corresponded to the engraved letter 'W' in the same position on its reverse side, which referred to the power of the WIND!

The bottom left corner on its front had an inverted 'U' that looked like a mound of soil which Mason explained representing the power of the EARTH! On the same spot, on its reverse, was the letter 'H' referring to the haggis, the most powerful creature on Earth!

The bottom right corner, on the front, had three squiggly lines like a 'W' representing waves, similar to the three humps of Nessie protruding from the water.

On the reverse, on the same spot, was a very strange back to front letter 'N' referring to Nessie, the most powerful creature in the sea and the Power of Water!

When combined, all four symbols on the front represented the powers of creation and the planet: EARTH, WIND, FIRE AND WATER!

The reverse middle of the triangle was blank, symbolic of endless possibilities. The letters around it were very strange looking and Mason could see the quizzical look on Rory's face as he said, "Hold it up to the mirror!"

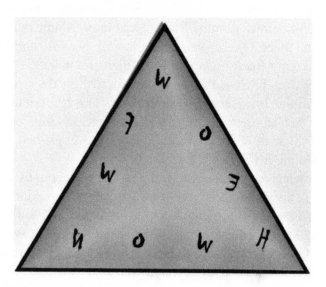

All of the letter became clear as some moved position and became readable. Between the bottom left letter, 'H' for Haggis to the top letter 'W' for Wind were the letters 'E' and 'O' and on the right side, between 'W' for Wind and bottom 'N' for Nessie, were the letters 'F' and 'W'.

On the base of the triangle on the rear between the 'H' for Haggis and 'N' for Nessie were the letters 'W' and 'O'.

Rory could see no pattern to these nine letters, which in the mirror read from the top W, F, W, N, O, W, H, E, O. Mason explained and showed Rory how to rearrange the letters, which now read NOW, FOE and WHW!

"NOW and FOE represent the power of acting in the present and to be constantly aware of the evil enemy," said Mason. The last three letters WHW were random and made no sense to Rory. Mason saw the confused look on Rory's face and said, "These are the most important letters of them all and means, When Hope Won, in reference to a great battle that is to come!

Mason continued his instruction and explained the sign of identification between fellow knights, which was only to be disclosed in private. "On seeing this symbol, complete the actions you saw me perform at the graveside." Mason raised both hands, with his index fingers and thumbs joined together in the shape of a triangle up to his right eye, looked through it and gave a slight bow.

Rory was rapt with attention, recording every word and action to his enhanced memory!

Mason continued, "The grip of identification is the same as the Warriors of HAGI, taking hold of the right hand, pressing three fingers into the palm while squeezing the top of the hand with your thumb. You always cover the right hand with your left, so no one sees what you are doing."

"The password is the letters 'E', 'W', 'W' and 'F' for Earth, Wind, Water and Fire. You give a letter each to the person you are interrogating who replies with the next letter until all four are exchanged."

"This is all you need to know to be identified as a Knight of the Temple," said Mason Knight Temple as he finished, "but there is a token of identification."

Mason reached into a concealed pocket in his habit and removed a gold triangular object no larger than a palm-sized penny coin. It was a miniature version of the brass symbol, except the rear of it was not blank but engraved with the cross of St John.

Mason stated, "You must keep this on your person at all times, and it can be used to redeem a favour from any fellow knight."

He noticed the quizzical look on Rory's face and continued, "You can take this pure gold with you through the portals, as it comes from the MacLeod's gold mine where you recovered the elements to repair your magic sword, and the powerful symbols on it will aid its passing."

Rory was dumbstruck. How did Mason know so much about him? Abbot MacCallum and the monks of St Columba must have been talking to him. They were keeping secrets from him still!

Mason continued, "There is a specific way you must exchange this to ask for a favour until you can repay your debt and have it returned to you."

He showed Rory how to conceal it under the three fingers of his right hand as if he were giving the grip with the thumb on top and how to pass it into the palm of the knight whose help, he wanted.

"When you have paid your debt and want your token back, the process is reversed," he instructed Rory. "I will have a new one made for you and trust you with mine until you have completed your task and return it to me."

Mason then asked Rory to put on the white tabard and cloak. They fitted perfectly as if they had been made for him. Rory knelt in front of Mason as he raised his sword and knighted him, dubbing him Sir Rory, Knight of the Temple of St John.

Mason raised Rory to his feet with that special handshake and explained that he now possessed a great deal of information that he would have to know before embarking on his quest to recover the Grail Box. He asked Rory if he could return to see him over the winter for further instruction which was vital as it explained the origins of the Christian Religion as currently practised. He suspected Rory had played or would play an integral part in past events leading to its development.

Rory suspected the same, with one of the main points being that he would travel far back in time to make the brass triangle for St John and give it to him to start his order to protect the Grail Box. He agreed to return over the winter and planned to start his quest to see St John on his seventeenth birthday on the 24th of June. He wanted as much power as possible to fulfil his task. He knew he would get another boost to it on this date following the summer equinox increasing its supply to the Hagpipe. The right tusk from the first haggis would, he knew, continue to increase his abilities until his thirty-third birthday. This was a new adventure for him, and he did not believe in coincidence anymore. He was sure everything had a plan, albeit one that he could not understand!

The first thing Rory wanted to do, he thought on his ride back to Castle Sween on Jet, was to visit the Castle Blacksmiths. He wanted to practise his skills and make a copy of the brass triangle from his memory of it. He knew he would have no trouble finding brass in the time of St John. It had been in existence since prehistory in the Bronze Age, in the third millennium BC. It was easy to make, being a copper-zinc alloy, which was very durable and easy to cast. He could not take any metal object with him except Hans, his magic sword, and his sgian dubh, which both contained parts of the left first haggis tusk. Also, he could now take Masons gold token.

But there were problems!

He did not want to leave his token in the past, using it as money. The monks of St Columba had not been in existence that far in the past, so he was unable to rely on them. He would have to acquire gemstones which were small and valuable for currency. As he rode, deep in thought, he hardly noticed the sky grew grey, and the wind picked up from the north. It was the first major storm of the winter, and being caught in the open was not a good idea!

Warlock Stan, alias John Grant, was embracing his newfound power and experimenting with it. He sat in the middle of the pentagram in the cottage of the Grant Witch, looking into a saucer of black ink. It cleared into an image showing Rory on horseback travelling along the high single-track dirt road at the left side of Loch Sween. Stan saw the storm and decided to give it a nudge taking hold of his black evil-filled crystal around his neck. He projected the evil contained within it into the storm cloud with an instruction to make Rory its target!

The grey cloud turned black and cut the light from the sky instantaneously, as if a solar eclipse had occurred, plunging Rory into darkness. Jet began to rear and prance about, feeling this unnatural storm as it hit Rory with a full blizzard. The snow struck, covering him as if a white sheet had been thrown over him.

Rory dismounted and took hold of Jet's reigns, talking softly, to calm him. He, too, could feel the unnatural element in the storm, which was the same as when he had rescued St Columba as he travelled to Scotland. (*See Appendix.) Rory was blinded and could not discern in which direction he was facing on the road. He was in grave danger of falling off the track and down the hillside into Loch Sween. He knew he would survive, but Jet would not! He held onto his horse, who was beginning to froth at his bit in fear.

Evil Stan 'Was the Man', he laughed at the vision of Rory in distress in front of him and at how easily he could manipulate the storm. He conjured up a lightning strike and thunderbolt to throw Rory's horse over the edge. The sky lit up, letting Rory see how close to the edge of the road he was. He braced himself, holding onto Jet, waiting for the thunderclap, which he knew would send Jet into a frenzy. The air vibrated with a clash around him, but Rory easily held Jet with his enhanced strength. However, if this did not stop, he would be the one injuring his horse, holding him down as he struggled.

Rory had to do something. He pulled the Hagpipe out from below his shirt by its thong around his neck. He raised it to his lips and visualised a white light as he blew it towards the black sky. The shrill screech of the Hagpipe vibrated through the air, taking on the physical appearance of a pure white light as it expanded out in waves towards the black cloud. When it connected with the blackness, it pulsed and vibrated, turning it back to the natural grey of a normal winter storm. The clouds throbbed, beating the evil black backwards, increasing in speed until the whole sky was clear.

Evil Stan was unprepared as the saucer mirror of ink exploded in front of him as his spell recoiled on him. A blizzard of snow and ice blew out of it like a tornado, covering him and the whole interior of the cottage with snow, burying him as if he were under an avalanche!

That would cool him down for a while!

Jet calmed down at the removal of the malevolence from the storm as Rory walked him back to the castle and a warm stable. The storm did not abate, and the whole area was soon a winter wonderland covered in deep snow.

It was going to be a long, very cold winter!

CHAPTER 3

St Paul and Constantine

Spring eventually came as Rory sent the last pigeon that Mason Knight Temple had to Castle Urquhart and to Abbot MacCallum, the head monk and banker of the monks of St Columba. It contained his fifty-pound credit note, which he had given him all those years before in exchange for the six haggis tusks. One of them had turned out to be very valuable indeed, being the left-hand tusk from the first ever haggis and now comprised the grip of his magical sword 'Hans', which he had remade.

The interdoonet system comprised carrier pigeons connecting all the St Columba chapels and monasteries in the country. It worked very well but required a constant update of newly trained pigeons to be taken great distances and then released to return home quickly when required. This meant that when spring arrived with the ability to travel, the roads becoming easy again, there would be a constant traffic of monks, moving pigeons and other larger valuables about. Attacks on them were rare due to their renowned fighting ability but more so due to the secret society protecting them as it was considered taboo to interfere with them. Anyone doing so was quickly hunted down and summarily dealt with. A one hundred per cent success rate was guaranteed, and it took a very stupid bandit to attempt to steal from the monks.

It was a bright, crisp, clear-skied morning as 'Pooie Doo', the nickname given to Brother Patrick Doogan, the brown-robed

Irish teaching monk who had a shaved bald patch on the middle of his head, arrived at Castle Sween. He was in charge of the doocot at Urquhart Castle, and due to that fact, he was always covered in pigeon droppings. He drove his two-horse-drawn cart, full of pigeons segregated in their location-marked carrier boxes, through the castle gates into the courtyard. His cheery smile ignited one on Rory's face when he saw him, and to readers who know of the character Friar Tuck from Robin Hood, he could have passed as his twin. He was always ready with a joke or witty comment and was very popular. He was welcomed warmly by all, and he was soon holding a frothy pint of ale in his hand. Rory waited until the excitement of a visitor bearing mail and messages from relatives in Castle Urquhart had subsided before he approached Pooie to receive his messages. Heather had sent a bundle of letters basically reiterating her love and concern for Rory to be careful, though she seemed to be withholding something on which he could not quite put his finger.

Pooie went to the rear of the cart as Rory quickly scanned the letters, reading them in super-fast time. Pooie selected a pigeon box from the middle of the cart and removed it, sitting it away from the rest. As Rory watched, Pooie opened it and inserted his hand into the box. Shooing the pigeon aside, he opened a hidden hatch covered in doo poo below the pigeon, a secret place that no thief would have ever found! He removed a small, leather thong-bound bag from the concealed compartment and handed it to Rory.

He took it, emptying the contents onto his large open left palm, which then sparkled in a multicoloured array as the sun reflected off the gems and diamonds. Rory's mouth dropped open. This was a very special credit rate which he had received. What he was holding was at least 10 times more valuable than the worth of his credit note. What did Abbot MacCallum know, when he was giving him this amount of money for his journey into the past?

Rory spent his time until the summer equinox and his seventeenth birthday studying his condensed *Book of St Columba* (*See Appendix), which had been given to him by Abbot MacCallum. There were some very strange pictures contained within this book, which Rory had committed to his enhanced memory. One showed a ship, wrecked on rocks in a large bay off a hilly, tropical-looking island in the middle of a fierce black storm. Rory knew by now who was good at making them!

The picture next to it was a cross of light in the sky above a long stone bridge. What was that about?

Rory intuitively felt that his time to find out was drawing near as he polished and practised with 'Hans', his magical sword that leapt into his hands from its leather reinforced sheath that was strapped to his back. The sheath was very distinctive, being embossed with the image of Nessie swimming in Loch Ness. He was sure if he called his sword, it would fly to him, and he decided to test his theory, placing it on the far side of his bedroom.

It was his birthday tomorrow, and his power, supplied by the Hagpipe around his neck, would multiply his natural abilities by another year. He held out his right hand and called out to 'Hans' in his head. The sword lifted from the ground and flew 10 feet through the air, hilt first, straight into his hand! He could feel the onset of the additional power flowing through him.

He prepared his clothing for the next morning. This comprised his shirt, with his sword and sheath strapped to his back, full highland kilt and leather sporran containing the gems. On his feet, he would wear his long woollen socks with his sgian dubh concealed in the right one and his sturdy leather boots.

Over this, he would wear the pure white tabard marked on its front with the Red Cross of St John. All of this would be covered by the large grey cloak with its attached hood. He knew from experience that he could not get too hot or cold, as the Hagpipe around his neck automatically adjusted his temperature according to the conditions he was experiencing.

He was ready!

Rory was not the only one making plans for the summer equinox. He was being carefully watched by the old Grant Witch and Evil Stan, who had refined his skills as a Warlock under her tuition.

They sat together inside the pentagram carved in the middle of the stone floor in her cottage. It was in the centre of the stone circle hidden in the forest of the Parish of Glen Moriston in the vast Urquhart Estate, which reached from Loch Ness to the mountains far to its west.

The cottage was situated on a major ley line and was a place of great power, feeding the evil force with which they were consumed. It was channelled into the black crystals on the chains they wore around their necks. Both of them looked into the inky black of the saucer in front of them, watching Rory prepare for his journey as they discussed their devious plans against him.

Stan decided he was going to travel to the Keil Cave at Southend on the Mull of Kintyre to ambush St Columba in AD 563, therefore, preventing Christianity from coming to Scotland and giving their evil full reign and changing the whole of the history of Scotland. (*See Appendix.)

The Grant Witch planned to attack St Paul even further back in time in AD 60. She would attack St Paul as he travelled by ship to Rome when her power would also be boosted by the summer equinox. She would ambush St Paul at Malta, stopping him from establishing the Christian religion. His death here would change history and affect the development and fortification of Malta with the aid of the Order of the Knights of St John, the guardians of the Grail Box. She knew if she was successful, Christianity would be stopped in its tracks before word of it travelled to the west and would make the job of destroying the Grail Box and the Christian Religion a certainty!

* * *

Rory awoke before dawn, having made his goodbyes to his parents the previous night. He dressed and had a good breakfast before climbing up the stone staircase to the top turret of Castle Sween. He had landed here after jumping from the back of his Great Scottish Eagle friend, Ben, just before Christmas in the retaking of Castle Sween from the Menteith's. (*See Appendix.)

The sky was clear and brightening from the east as the sun's light illuminated the horizon in a display of pinks, purples and reds prior to its appearance. Rory sent out a mental message to Ben the eagle and Nessie, calling them to him.

As if anticipating his call, Nessie emerged from below the waters of Loch Sween, looking up to him as Ben descended, changing from being a black dot in the sky to a huge eagle, the size of a jet plane, silently hovering above the castle.

Rory communicated his plan to them to travel back in time to see St John as a young man of 20 years in AD 35; he had to try to convince him to create the Order of the Knights of St John. This had to be achieved to protect the Grail Box, which he would afterwards conceal with the help of Joseph of Arimathea following the crucifixion of Jesus.

Nessie telepathically replied in her motherly voice that she would travel with him into the past in case he needed her help as the booming male voice of Ben volunteered to carry him. Rory was very grateful for their help and still amazed at the intuitive connection he had with them, as if they were a part of him and not just his friends.

The power of the Hagpipe was flowing through Rory now as the sun eclipsed the horizon, bathing him in its early morning red light as the multiplication of his 17 years boosted its power. He felt the additional strength flowing through his body as he jumped into the air, soaring 30 feet into the sky as easily as if he were stepping off a kerb and landing on the back of Ben's neck, who swooped below him as he began to descend.

Rory removed the Hagpipe from below his clothing and blew it as he faced the dawn of a new chapter in his life.

The red glow of the sun enveloped and expanded around Ben, Nessie and himself, surrounding them. It was as if they were in a large ball, which went from the sky and down below the water to Nessie.

The extra year of additional power now meant that Rory did not need to pass through a portal or a stone circle to connect to the ley line network to travel along it to his destination.

The red ball of light encompassed all three of them as Ben flew along Loch Sween towards the sea, and Nessie simultaneously swam at the same speed below them. The power of the Hagpipe was flowing through all of them; as Ben picked up speed, it was equally and effortlessly matched by Nessie.

They travelled down the west coast of Britain towards the Atlantic Ocean and France, continuing to pick up speed and distance as they began to travel into the past.

As Rory looked down, he could see major cities on the mainland disappearing brick by brick, taken away by ant-like people moving backwards until only open ground remained.

Once over open sea, nothing seemed to change as waves were waves, but the clouds were all moving backwards at incredible speed. Nessie remained in the bubble and seemed very happy as she was carried along inside it.

The French coastline was on the left now as it joined the now Spanish Kingdoms and Muslim States of the past. They completed a left turn into the hot waters of the Mediterranean Sea dotted with small islands, now popular holiday destinations, towards the jutting foot of the Roman Empire.

Ahead was the Holy Land. A black cloud obscured Rory's view as it sat stationary over the small hilly Island of Malta. Rory could feel the evil extending from it towards him but could do nothing about it due to the speed at which they were travelling. The bubble struck then burst, exploding in white light.

Rory and Ben were expelled from the bubble, thrown away from it, tumbling forward in time and backwards in direction.

The last glimpse he saw below was Nessie, struggling against giant waves near a ship being hurled towards rocks jutting from the main Island of Malta at the land mass of Minstra at Selmun towards two smaller islands, protecting a large bay.

The mental connection between Nessie, Rory and Ben was broken as she saw them disappear. Time was running at a normal pace now and Nessie was stuck in a strange sea in unusually very warm water. A major storm was in full force, but it was a normal storm now as the evil directing it had ceased at the same time as Ben and Rory had disappeared and the opposite forces had collided. Nessie was used to storms and more than capable of dealing with them but the ship on the crest of the giant wave next to her did not have four powerful flippers to control it. In a few seconds it would crash onto the jutting rocks in front of it and be totally destroyed!

Nessie did not even consider her actions, moving with her maximum speed towards the ship and, as with the ship of St Columba, positioned herself below it, inflating her three humps like airbags below its hull. She stabilised the ship, steering it away from the rocks towards two small islands protecting a calmer half-circular bay. It had very deep water, which dropped dramatically away in shelves from the rocky beach.

* * *

The occupants of this prison ship, which was conveying St Paul to Rome for trial, could not believe their good fortune and were unaware of Nessie as she nudged the ship onto low rocks between the two small islands but still a considerable distance from the shore. The impact caused the ship to tear apart in the storm, but this provided plenty of wood for the prisoners and the entire crew to cling onto for their long swim to the rocky shore of the large calm bay in front of them.

Nessie was pleased with her good deed and gave a short blow out of her antennae, clearing them of water, causing a horn noise to be made. This was copied by a group of people on the shore who thought this was a signal from the ship, which they were watching in disbelief as it tore apart in front of them. People from it were taking to the water, clinging to anything that would float as the storm blew them towards the shore, helping carry the survivors to safety.

St Paul was one of the first thrown clear out of a rent in the hull of the ship, and as he got close to land, he heard the town leader blow a horn which, unknown to him, was the method of communication with friendly ships.

He heard someone call out from the shore in Arabic, saying, "Do you come in peace?"

St Paul heard this and understood the language, calling back in the same language, "We come in peace."

The leader replied, "Then come in peace."

All were helped from the water and taken to a bonfire that the locals had been gathered around to warm them from the chill night air of this the 10th of February AD 60!

Roman guards and slaves together huddled around the fire to heat up from the cold winter water. The ordeal of St Paul had not finished as an adder emerged from the bottom of the drying wood pile next to the fire, sprung and latched onto his left wrist. All the townspeople watched in disbelief as he shook it off into the fire where it died. The townspeople believed that the man they had saved would surely die from the adder's venom.

They waited and watched, but St Paul suffered no ill effect from the snake bite, and as a result, he was venerated as a God by the superstitious locals. He subsequently went on to bless the Island of Malta and to heal the sick there.

From that day to this, it is remembered in the history of Malta that all snakes on the island lost their venom, becoming harmless. And it is still reported that any poisonous snakes being brought to the island also lose their venom and become harmless!

The stories told by the old men in the bars and taverns of Malta today state that the venom had to go somewhere and that it went into the tongues of the Maltese women!

Believe what you wish!

The site of these events is remembered and easily found today as a church to St Paul was built on the site of the bonfire, and is known today as the 'Church of the Bonfire' or 'The Church of the Shipwreck' and the bay was renamed as St Paul's (Pawls) Bay! Malta would be fully converted to Christianity and, in time, become English-speaking.

Unknown to her, Nessie had put history back on track as she swam off to try and find Rory!

The ley line network was very busy that equinox morning as Evil Stan disappeared from the middle of the pentagram in the cottage, holding his evil-filled crystal as the dawn sunlight came in through the window, illuminating him in a blood-red light. The old hag, Isa Grant, then sat in the middle of the pentagram with a saucer of black ink bathed in the sacrificial red, holding her crystal as she searched the images flashing in the ink mirror, looking for St Paul arriving in Malta in AD 60. It did not take much of her influence to give the already vicious tropical storm a push, directing its full force towards the ship sailing towards the island.

She cackled in delight at her plan being fulfilled as a red ball flew into the storm, exploding in a white light. The saucer shattered and exploded upwards, covering her already ugly features in black ink as she was thrown backwards out of the pentagram.

* * *

Rory held onto Ben's neck as he somersaulted through the air in recoil from the collision with the evil storm. He focused all the power flowing from the Hagpipe into Ben from his hands to give him strength and stabilise him.

They were thrown through time, their bond with Nessie broken in the sea below. The protective red time bubble had been shattered, replaced with white light that was emitting from the Hagpipe, and Rory bent it to his will to ensure his and Ben's survival.

As he and Ben tumbled through the air and time, Rory was sure he saw the image of John Grant, his stepdad and now Evil Stan, with black inset eyes, laughing at his peril as he flashed past him on the ley line network, on his way to confront St Columba. If Rory knew this was where he was going, it would be him that was laughing.

The whole future of Christianity was still in jeopardy as Rory and Ben materialised at sunset, calculated in time from the point of the collision, it was now 252 years into the future in AD 312. Below them was the stone Milvian Bridge which crossed the Tiber River in Rome. It was the evening prior to the battle that would define the Roman Empire. This was between Constantine the First and Maxentius, the two armies facing each other on opposite sides of the river. (*See Appendix.)

Rory clung to Ben's neck as they tumbled head over tail feathers forward, totally illuminated in a blinding white light. The outline of Ben's wings was fully extended, and his rigid body and tail feathers were jutting out as they stopped falling and hovered above the tent of Constantine the Great. He was standing watching the opposing army while considering his battle plan. The red background of the sunset sky suddenly lit up in front of Constantine. The shape of a white cross appeared as the excess power from the Hagpipe sparked off Ben's feather, emitting 33 white stars like the shapes of the four points of the cross. To the sight of Constantine, they formed into the shape of letters I, H, S, and V, which meant in his language, "In This Sign You Will Conquer"!

Constantine had received his sign from God, and he was instantly converted to Christianity, ordering a battle flag to be made, showing this very image in the sky above him.

The Christian soldiers in his army who had previously been concealing their beliefs came forward to him; the first two letters of Christ's name were painted on their shields along with a red cross. The next morning, they went to war under this new banner in the first religious war, routing the army of Maxentius.

Rome and its Empire was now Christian!

CHAPTER 4

St John

Rory saw the two opposing armies on the ground on either side of the snaking Tiber River and knew he was far from where he wanted to be. He clasped the Hagpipe to his chest with his left hand and asserted his full will, visualising St John in AD 35. The brilliant white light surrounding him dulled to the colour of the setting sun, and he and Ben vanished from the watching eyes below. He could feel something very important had happened, but he did not have any influence over it. Not for the first time, he realised that he was unable to control his own destiny or actions, and he felt like a pawn in a game of chess being played by a higher being.

Time moved backwards again as Ben flew away from Rome out over the Mediterranean Sea towards the Holy Land. Rory looked down as he passed Malta to see a familiar shape in the sea, swimming backwards towards the island. He realised that as he was going backwards in time, he would see Nessie moving in reverse since she was moving forwards in real time. He was pleased that she had survived the storm and was looking for him, but he was unable to communicate with her without stopping in real time.

Rory knew he could blow his Hagpipe and stop in real time, thus being able to call out to Nessie. She could again travel with him, but he decided to leave her to have a holiday. *She would quite like all the new species of fish in the warm*

Mediterranean waters, he thought. Nessie could find and open a portal anytime she wanted to travel home.

He was going to an area of land in any case, and she could not help him there. Ben spoke in his head, agreeing with his thoughts. Rory had forgotten about the openness of his telepathic connection with his friends. It was safer not to try to keep secrets but to be honest and truthful at all times.

Rory felt the pace he was travelling at slowing and pushed his upper body up from Ben's neck, his grey hood up over his head.

He was in the time of Emperor Tiberius now as he and Ben entered normal time, looking for landmarks to lead them to Jerusalem and, hopefully, to find St John. Legions of Roman soldiers were marching below, the sky was clear, and the sun shone behind Ben and Rory. The Great Scottish Eagle was the largest bird ever to inhabit the planet, and even from one hundred feet in the air, they were visible to the naked eye of the legions below.

As they marched towards the sun, they stopped in their tracks. Hovering in the sky in front of them was the black silhouette of an enormous eagle with two heads. From this day forward, history would record versions of this image that was imprinted into the memories of the soldiers who had seen the first two-headed Roman eagle. Thereafter it would be used on the flags of numerous countries throughout the world!

Rory looked down, and he could see the commotion he was causing below. If he were to find St John, he would have to do it on foot!

St John (* See Appendix) was still a young man of 20 years and not yet a saint in title, but he exuded a holy spirit which sparkled from his wise, compassionate eyes. He was just beginning to write and preach his Gospel following the crucifixion of Jesus two years before. The nature and beliefs of all who had witnessed the events of that day had irrevocably changed them forever. The world had been cast into darkness for three days with an earthquake destroying the second

Temple of King Solomon in Jerusalem, rending the veil of the Holy of Holies, leading to the most secret inner part of it, containing the two stone tablets of the Ten Commandments, given to Moses from God.

To say there was panic was an understatement. Even the views of Pontius Pilate, the Roman governor, who had washed his hands of stopping the crucifixion, were changed. He now realised the truth and was converted to this new religion.

It was a time for cool heads as St John spoke with his fellow disciple, young Paul, and his good friend and fellow Christian, Joseph of Arimathea, a very rich local businessman who had the ear of the governor. Joseph had, without thought, surrendered his own burial vault for the body of Jesus, assisted in the cleaning and wrapping of his body in the white linen shroud, and covering his face with a linen napkin.

The tomb was sealed with a huge rock and protected by two terrified Roman guards, authorised by Pilate. For three days, the new Christian community worked together in darkness, preserving everything to do with their Master.

The cross he was crucified on was removed and made into a coffin-shaped box, six-foot long by three-foot wide and three-foot deep. It was made from local acacia wood, having two holes in the planks on opposite sides where the nails had been driven through the wrists of Jesus and one on the bottom panel, where his feet had been nailed. The top panel, comprising the lid, had been stained red with the blood from the crown of thorns on the Messiah's head. The movement of his blood-stained head on the cross had formed a shape of the first perfect cross of St John, as it would be known, with its distinctive eight points denoting the Beatitudes quoted by Jesus on his Sermon on the Mount. (* See Appendix.)

All the disciples were amazed at the sight of this cross, which all revered as another sign for them from their Master.

It was the night of the third day when they inserted a rod through the two holes at the front and a shorter one at the rear, lifted the completed Grail Box*(Reference at the end.)

and carried it to the remains of the temple, now abandoned by the priests who had fled in fear of their lives. The procession of believers led by St John went to the Holy of Holies, where they recovered the undamaged stones bearing the Ten Commandments and placed them within the Grail Box along with the Grail Cup, which St John had retained following the Last Supper he had shared with the disciples and Jesus.

It was filled with the dried blood of Jesus, which Joseph of Arimathea had collected after Jesus had a sword thrust into his side as he was crucified. The cup was wooden and had been made from the same acacia tree that was used to make the cross on which Jesus was crucified. It was the only container that could withstand this potent blood and would come to be known as the Holy Grail. It was told, and become an historic myth, that a sip from it would bestow everlasting life!

The earthquake had rent a tear in the ground at the rear of the Holy of Holies, opening up a chasm and revealing the top of a stone arch with a keystone at its top. (* See Appendix.)

St John knew what this was, as did the rest of the disciples. They could hardly contain their excitement as this doorway had been searched for since the first Temple of King Solomon had been destroyed by Nebuchadnezzar II after the Siege of Jerusalem of 587 BC. It was his secret chamber and was reported to contain vast treasure and, more importantly, all the original Old Testament Text (Torah) depicting the history of man and his relationship with God since the time of Adam and Eve!

The information contained there could reunite all the religions on the planet and create world peace or, if used irresponsibly, end it! (* See Appendix.)

The tight-knit group of friends, now Christians, knew this discovery must be kept secret, and it was also the perfect place to keep the Grail Box secure as they added artefacts and the new gospels they were compiling to it.

Joseph was aware of how guilt-ridden Pontius Pilate was, and Pilate took little persuasion to commit to protecting and rebuilding this religious site with the best and most modern fortifications around the ancient city, using the trusted stonemasons, under the supervision of Joseph, of course!

The morning of the fourth day saw more artefacts for the Grail Box as St John and Joseph were called to the tomb of Jesus, where the huge stone sealing the entrance had been rolled away, and the terrified guards nowhere to be seen.

The world had been restored to light with blinding sunshine illuminating the burnt landscape and the cavern-like tomb. The body of Jesus had vanished, leaving his burial shroud on the stone slab where he had been laid. The napkin-like cloth that had covered his face was neatly folded and sitting a short distance away. Both men looked at the napkin, knowing that when eating, if the cloth is folded and put down when the person leaves the table, the meal is not finished and the diner will return.

St John, St Paul and Joseph were shaking as they entered the tomb and recovered the shroud which was embossed with the perfect image of Jesus. The significance of the folded napkin nearby was not lost on them as they recovered both items and placed them in the Grail Box!

* * *

Rory was literally dropped off by Ben the eagle in a remote area away from prying eyes, a short distance from the city of Hebron (translates as 'Friend') which was nestled in the Judean Mountains located in the Southern West Bank nineteen miles south of Jerusalem. You cannot conceal a bird the size of Ben, but you can try, and this was as good a spot as any for Ben to hide. Hebron dated back to the early Bronze Age and was the perfect place for Rory to make the symbol for the Knights of St John, which was going to encourage St John to start. The first thing he had to do was pick up the local language, and the three shepherds he had spotted would be perfect for this. He stealthily sneaked up to them until he was close enough to hear and see them. Their language was alien to him, but he was no ordinary person, and he was very gifted at languages, especially as his mental abilities were boosted by the power of the Hagpipe.

Rory was soon confident he could communicate with them as he left his hiding place and casually walked towards their campsite, wrapped in his one-piece full-length cloak not dissimilar to that worn by the shepherds. He soon struck up a conversation, stating he was a travelling pilgrim and was invited to share a meal with them. Rory very quickly gleaned all the information he required about where to go in Hebron to make the symbol.

The heat did not affect Rory as he thanked the shepherds and left them the next morning. The Hagpipe was cooling his blood like a personal air conditioning system as he broke into a run once out of view. It was a long time since he had tested his speed which seemed unlimited as the countryside whizzed past, and he leapt over rocks, thoroughly enjoying himself, rediscovering this super ability. He pushed it to the limit just to see how fast he could go as the surroundings appeared to be standing still around him. A walled city came into view in front of him with a dusty road leading to it. He had passed a loaded cart being pulled by a donkey with a single elderly man leading it towards the city, and before he realised, rocked it with a blast of air as he zoomed past.

Rory realised he was going so fast that the old man hadn't even seen him, and he willed himself to slow down. He felt great, with the blood pumping through his veins under the addictive power of the Hagpipe, and he had to calm himself, restraining himself from running more under its intoxicating effect.

Hebron was an ancient fortress of a city and it had been no stranger to conflict, as Rory saw by the scars on the stone walls surrounding it. He greeted passers-by on the way through the city gates, who warmly replied, confirming it was a city of friends.

It did not take him long to find the industrial part of the city as he recognised the distinctive noise of a hammer on an anvil.

The blacksmiths' shop was very old-fashioned compared to what he was used to, but the wiry old, bearded owner was welcoming when Rory explained he was a craftsman who wanted to hire his forge and buy some brass to work. The payment of a small gem saw the old man run off, leaving Rory in charge of his premises as he left with a big smile on his face to exchange it for some local currency.

Rory saw a cauldron of bubbling brass which looked of very high quality with few impurities, and he quickly set to work, making a triangular clay cast for it. He had repeatedly practised this procedure at Castle Sween and, in a very short time, had made and engraved a perfect copy of the symbol of St John that he had first seen when he recovered it from the grave at Kilmory Chapel. A thought crossed his mind as he polished the finished brass symbol that would ignite a fraternity of future Masonic followers.

Was this really a copy, or had he just created the very item that he would hold again in the future?

CHAPTER 5

Revelations

As luck would have it (If you believe in it) or, in Rory's case, divine intervention would be more appropriate, St John was visiting Hebron, preaching the new Gospel and converting hundreds from Judaism to the new religion of Christianity. Everyone wanted to hear the story first-hand, and his sermon on how everyone could obtain everlasting life was very appealing to the crowd.

A hooded Rory heard the crowds of people talking as they passed by, heading to the city square to hear the prophet. He kept his head covered as it was sensible to be protected from the sun but also because no one had his hair colour, and he did not want to draw attention to himself. He followed on, not believing in his good fortune, feeling the weight of the symbol safe in his concealed sporran.

There was a heavy presence of Roman soldiers patrolling the area in groups of six, who did not look at all happy about such a large group of people in one place, wanting to hear this prophet. Rory saw one group of soldiers who seemed more agitated than the rest and very antagonistic towards this still new religion. They had spotted a lone woman in a red dress walking from a quiet side street towards the main road and the safety of the large group of people assembled there. Rory's enhanced eyesight saw that the woman was very beautiful, and she looked just like his beloved Heather. She was the fairest among thousands and altogether lovely. His heart leapt at the sight of her, but it was not the hearts of the aspiring centurions that were leaping as they ogled her.

He watched the group of soldiers spread out in a line at the mouth of the lane and walk down it towards the woman. She saw them and realised their intent. Clutching her wooden cross to her chest, she turned and ran from them, back down the lane. The soldiers were too quick for her and pursued her, pinning her to a wall with the largest one pulling the cross from her neck and trampling it into the dirt with his boot.

The woman was distraught and terrified as she scrambled in the dirt, lifting the cross from it and clasping it to her breast, while looking upward to the sky with her eyes shut, praying for deliverance from the fate she was about to endure.

Rory was having none of this, thinking, *What if my Heather was put in this situation? Then what would I do?* No one else in the area was paying any attention to the terrible situation that was unfolding in the lane. With his super-speed, he ran down the lane and, with six quick blows to the back of their heads, laid the entire troop of soldiers out cold, unconscious in the dirt at her feet.

By the time this important elected woman of her local community opened her eyes after hearing six thuds and had found the courage to look forward, Rory had gone. Her prayers were answered, and so the story of Electa (The Elected Woman) would become part of the annals of history.

Rory had been taught many bible stories at church, but only now did he realise he was the reason for this one as he re-joined the crowd to hear the sermon from St John.

The abbot of the monks of St Columba in Urquhart Castle had talked about St John many times in his sermons, but Rory was hearing him first-hand as a witness to the actual events. He was as awestruck as everyone else in the huge crowd as he joined the queue at the end of the sermon to be blessed and christened by St John.

He held back to the very end, making sure he was the last person waiting to be seen as the sun set and the crowd dispersed to their homes to eat. An exhausted St John, still smiling, requested Rory to kneel in front of him. Rory obliged, but his huge frame still stretched up to almost the same height as St John as he reached out his right hand and pulled down Rory's hood. There was an audible gasp from him as he saw his first ginger man. Rory's long red hair tied in a ponytail dangled down his back where it met the carved shiny ivory monster handle on Hans the Sword, strapped there.

Rory lifted his head and looked into the kind but slightly fearful eyes of St John as he stood and loosened his cloak, revealing his tabard emblazoned with the Red Cross of St John.

This caused a second gasp from St John, who had last seen this sign two years previously on the lid of the Grail Box.

"We have to talk," said Rory.

St John was returning to Jerusalem the next day, and Rory joined him on the journey that was passing through the Judean Mountains on route. Rory had tried to explain to him the reason for his presence, but once you had seen your friend resurrected from the dead and become a living God, a time-travelling ginger Scot was a bit farfetched.

Rory knew things that St John could not explain, and although he had the Red Cross on his clothing and seemed genuine to him, he was used to getting his answers replied to directly from his prayers. As they reached the mountains, St John excused himself from Rory's company, saying he was going to climb up the slope to pray in the peace and quiet.

Rory sat on a rock, wondering how he was going to reach St John. It was not like it was with St Columba, who had pictures of him in his book and who could compare them with his in the abbreviated book Abbot MacCallum had given him. (* See Appendix.)

As he contemplated what to do, Rory heard a familiar voice in his head. It was the deep voice of Ben, his eagle friend, asking Rory to come up the mountain and help the wee man looking at him. Rory sprung to his feet and, nimbler than a deer, ran up the mountain to see St John standing with his mouth open, staring at the biggest eagle the world had ever known, sitting on a rock and eclipsing the top of the mountain in front of him.

St John was in shock, unable to move as Rory walked past him and began tickling the giant bird at the back of the neck to its obvious delight as it squawked in pleasure. This bird could easily kill them both but sat like a pet budgie that enjoyed being petted.

Rory turned to St John and signalled him to come forward. He was praying frantically to himself but appeared to be finding his answer as he walked up to Rory and Ben. "He is my friend," Rory said and showed St John where to tickle Ben behind his ears.

A huge smile spread across the face of St John as he petted Ben, the greatest of God's creatures. "OK, what do I need to do?" he asked as he turned to face Rory.

Rory showed St John the brass symbol he had made and explained all the marks on it to him. St John had some difficulty in comprehending the size and strength of Nessie, and the description of Hag the Haggis confused him, but he could see Ben in front of him and accepted that they were real. The lessons of the triangle and All-Seeing Eye of Fire were easier to fit into the parameters of his religion, and he knew the Grail Box would have to be protected for a very long time. Rory taught and tested him until he knew as much as himself and gave him the brass symbol.

Rory agreed to initiate all the disciples and reliable, worthy capable members into this new Order of St John in the Temple. Months passed as he instructed them in the techniques of hand-to-hand combat, teaching them sword skills and, when they became proficient, concluding by dubbing them Knights of the Temple. The head of the order would be St John, with Joseph of Arimathea second in charge. The third person was a big surprise to Rory when he met and initiated him. His identity was the biggest secret that was never to be revealed to anyone in the future, and it was never recorded. Knowing who it was easily explained how the Grail Box could be kept secret and hidden from the unfaithful. Needless to say, Pontius Pilate never went back on his vows or word or wavered in his resolve to protect the Grail Box.

The winter equinox was fast approaching following the 36th Christmas Day, and it was now three years since the resurrection. (* See Appendix.)

Rory felt the alarm bell of the equinox ringing within him and knew he had to move forward in time to see how this seed he had planted would turn out as he left Jerusalem to find a secluded spot to summon Ben, his giant Scottish eagle friend. Rory had only to think of him, and his giant eagle friend was above him, the full moon illuminating his silhouette in the sky. He was an impressive sight with his wings fully extended. Batman's illuminated bat light paled into insignificance compared to the sight of the eagle's black image framed in the full moonlight. The giant spread-eagled bird could easily be seen by anyone looking up, which included all the members of the secret Order of St John who were looking towards the sky expecting a sign of Rory's departure. As they watched, a smaller object travelled upwards from the ground like a fired rocket, joining the eagle, landing on Ben's neck.

Rory blew his Hagpipe, and they both glowed as white as the moon behind them and vanished!

* * *

During its long history, Jerusalem has been destroyed twice, besieged 23 times, attacked 52 times, and captured and recaptured 44 times. This secret order Rory had started would have to be totally that, a secret, and stay hidden and underground. Mammoth changes were about to take place as Rory and Ben moved forward in time over a thousand years into the future. The basic landscape remained the same, but the constructions on it were going up and down like

Lego pieces, similar to the graphics on a historic computer game showing buildings being destroyed, modernised, and rebuilt. Countless lives were being lost below in a religious war, with all parties believing that their God, who historically is the same God, would see them victorious. The aim of this Holy War was to hold a piece of land of major religious significance, but only a very few knew of the real reason why it was so important.

The next time Jerusalem would be under Christian control would be under the rule of the Roman Emperor Constantine in AD 324, to whom Rory had unknowingly given a sign and converted to Christianity. He would cease the persecution of Christians in the Roman Empire and would issue the Edict of Milan, decriminalizing Christian worship. A significant wave of Christian immigration was beginning as Constantine reunited the Roman Empire, banning Jews from entering the city, which was renamed and became known as Jerusalem. Two years later, his Christian mother, 'Helena', would visit Jerusalem and order the destruction of Hadrian's temple to Venus, which had been built on Calvary. The excavation reportedly discovered what they thought was the True Cross, the Holy Tunic and the Holy Nails from the Crucifixion of Christ. This cross would be used later and carried in front of the Christian armies as they marched into battle!

Rory watched time move forward in front of him; the Galilee earthquake of AD 363 hit the land below, followed by more building and Christian expansion until AD 610. A Jewish revolt was taking place, and the Temple Mount became the focal point for Muslim Salat (prayers) known as the first Qibla, following Muhammad's initial revelations. (Wahy Islamic Source.) AD 614 came, and Jerusalem was again under siege, falling to Khosrau, the second Sassanid Empire of the Byzantine–Sassanid War of AD 602–628. The Church of the Holy Sepulchre built by Constantine was burned, and the True Cross and other relics were taken. As Rory watched from his invisible vantage point in the sky, he slowed down time to watch important events occurring as most of the Christian population below were massacred and vast areas of the city destroyed. He felt the urge to intercede, but he did not have the power or the authority to change the events unfolding as Jerusalem lost its place as the focal point of Christianity to Muslim prayers to Mecca following its destruction.

Rory fast-forwarded through time, despairing at the nature of man as he watched more fighting, destruction and rebuilding. The Christians would not obtain this land again until the Siege of Jerusalem in AD 1099, when the first Crusaders would capture Jerusalem and slaughter most of the city's Muslim and Jewish inhabitants. The Dome of the Rock, where the First and Second Temples had stood and where, by this time, the now fully completed Grail Box was concealed and buried in its secret chamber under the first Temple of King Solomon. Jerusalem would again be converted by the Crusaders into a Christian Church under Godfrey of Bouillon, the head of the now open and powerful Knights Templar would become the protector of this Holy Sepulchre and begin his work to reclaim the greatest prize known to humanity!

After this First Crusade recaptured Jerusalem in AD 1099, many Christians made pilgrimages to various holy places in the Holy Land. However, though the city of Jerusalem was under relatively secure control, the rest of the Holy Land was not. Bandits and marauding highwaymen preyed upon pilgrims who were routinely slaughtered, sometimes by the hundreds, as they attempted to make the journey from the coastline at Jaffa into the interior of the Holy Land. It was at this time the Knights of St John, which had been founded by Rory, became an open military order and very powerful, protecting the travelers, many of whom joined their ranks. Safe houses and hospitals were constructed and manned, providing accommodation and places of healing on the route to Jerusalem.

They became known as Knight Hospitallers, supplying the first functioning hospitals which flourished under their protection, publicized by the sign they wore of the Red Cross of St John. In the future, this symbol would represent 'The Red Cross' a body for medical aid which we still know. In Great Britain, it would also be adopted and used by the St John Ambulance Service. A reincarnation of a famous fictional time traveler who was a doctor also uses the sign of the Red Cross of St John. You can see it on the right-hand door of his blue police box called the TARDIS.

More than one Christian-based religious order was present in this Crusade, each with their own distinct identities, but joined together to fight against their common enemies. They were all created from the same basic ritual that Rory had started, but like all words passed by mouth from one person to another, like Chinese whispers, the rituals changed over the centuries as they were translated into different languages from the original one taught by Rory to St John. This meant the several different orders had their own versions with only the secret handshake and identifying word remaining the same. One other common factor remained between them all, which was to protect and claim the Grail Box as their own!

CHAPTER 6

Crusade

Rory watched time progressing before his eyes as he visualized the preordained moment revealed to him in the picture shown to him by St Columba of his recovering the Grail Box. Time was slowing again, and the attempts by the Knights of the First Crusade to find the Grail Box had failed as Jerusalem was lost in AD 1187 to a new, very powerful military force under the Rule of Sultan Salah Ad-Din, known to the west as Saladin!

All the Muslim armies were united and unstoppable under his authority and clashed with the combined forces of the Second Crusaders at the site of an extinct volcano, which was exerting a magnetic force on Rory to watch this rout of the Crusaders. Rory saw the double hill (Known as the "Horns of Hattin") and the pass between them through the northern mountains between Tiberias and the Roman Darb al-Hawarnah Road from Acre. It travelled from the east Mediterranean coast on this main east-west passage between the Jordan fords and the Sea of Galilee.

The Crusaders could not compete with the organisation and vastness of Saladin's armies, which quickly re-conquered Jerusalem and several other Crusader-held cities, taking the relic of the True Cross which had previously been recovered by Constantine from them at the Siege of Tiberias and which was then fixed upside down on a lance and sent to Damascus. (The sight of an inverted cross and its significance is not lost even today, branding those using it as devil worshippers.)

The vast majority of the Crusader forces were captured or killed by the Muslim armies under the control of Saladin, removing their capability to wage war. The Holy Land was again under their eminent military power, with the Dome of the Rock again converted to an Islamic centre of worship. Almost immediately, the period of the Third Crusade began. This time it was led by King Richard I of England (Richard the Lionheart) and King Philip II of France. They regained a foothold in the fortified seaport of Acre, taking it from Muslim control in AD 1191 and making it the de facto capital of the remnant Kingdom of Jerusalem. This was a very strategic base from which to plan the retaking of Jerusalem again!

Rory felt the fast-forwarding of time slow to a stop and knew he would have to part company with Ben, his eagle friend, again. He was very concerned at witnessing so much loss of human life and tried to console himself that he was not, in some way, responsible for it. Forces were at work that he could not control, and they were far more powerful than he alone! He had Ben drop him some distance from the seaport of Acre in a remote area so as not to upset any locals seeing a giant bird swooping down on them. He telepathically thanked Ben for his help, instructing him to find a portal and return to his own time. He was sure he would not need him again once he joined the Crusaders and set off on foot towards Acre.

Hopefully, he was right?

Rory had lost all sense of his own personal time as he joined the road to Acre. In real time his own lifespan had completed another year, and he had already passed his 18th birthday on the 24th of June. He was currently in the month of August on the 24th in AD 1191. He could feel the additional potential of more power from the Hagpipe, concealed beneath his clothing and beating in unison with his heartbeat. He was not concerned about growing older as his personal age was extended by the Hagpipe, and he had reached the peak of his enhanced physical growth on his sixteenth birthday. He would not grow any taller than his powerful six-foot-four-inches. It would be a long time before he started to age, and that would require him to remove his contact with the Hagpipe.

Rory really missed his beloved Heather, but he planned to return at the same time he had left on his adventure from Castle Sween at the winter equinox. That way, he would ensure there would be only one of him in that time period. He would have grown in life experiences and was determined to appear as unaffected inside as he would look on the outside.

For Heather, practically no time would have passed before she saw Rory again!

War was afoot as Rory approached Acre to see the full force of the Crusaders army led by Richard the Lionheart leaving its fortified gates, marching south towards Jaffa to engage the Saracen Muslim Army of Saladin at the historically famous Battle of Arsuf. (* See Appendix.)

The vanguard of the Crusader army consisted of the Knights Templar under their current Grand Master, Robert de

Sablé. They were followed by three units composed of Richard's own subjects, the Angevins and Bretons, then the Poitevins, including Guy of Lusignan, the titular King of Jerusalem, and lastly the English and Normans, who had charge of the great standard of the cross, mounted on its wagon. The next seven corps were made up of the French, the barons of Outremer and small contingents of Crusaders from other lands. Forming the rear guard were the Knights Hospitallers led by their Master, Garnier de Nablus. The twelve corps were organised into five larger formations with a small troop, under the leadership of Henry II of Champagne, which was detached to scout towards the hills. A squadron of picked knights under King Richard and Hugh of Burgundy, the leader of the French contingent, was detailed to ride up and down the column checking on Saladin's movements and ensuring that their own ranks were kept in order.

Rory watched the army and followed it and saw his chance to join the infantry of the Knight Hospitallers at the rear, all of whom were dressed in a white tabard adorned with the Red Cross of St John on its front, identical to his own. Periodically, a soldier would fall out of line to relieve himself at the roadside. Rory saw his chance as the supply wagon passed and stripped off his grey cloak, throwing it in the rear of the wagon and joining the rest of the infantry. A quick secret handshake with the adjacent marching troops with the password HAGI saw Rory accepted into their ranks as one of their own. Rory knew far more than they did.

After all, he had started it!

The Crusader army's pace was dictated by the infantry and baggage train, while the Ayyubid army of Saladin was largely mounted and had the advantage of superior mobility. Efforts to burn crops and deny the countryside to the Frankish Army of the Crusaders were largely ineffective as it could be continuously provisioned from the fleet of ships which followed their line of march along the coast and moved south parallel with it.

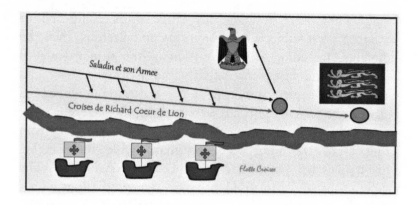

Richard the Lionheart was aware that he needed to capture the port of Jaffa before making an attempt on Jerusalem as he began to march down the coast from Acre towards Jaffa. Saladin, whose main objective was to prevent the recapture of Jerusalem, mobilised his army to attempt to stop the Crusaders' advance. Richard organised the advance with great attention to detail. A large part of the Egyptian fleet had been captured at the fall of Acre, and with no threat from this quarter, he could march south along the coast, with the sea always protecting his right flank. He was mindful of the lessons of the disaster at Hattin that Rory had witnessed. (* See Appendix.)

Richard knew that his army's greatest need was water and that heat exhaustion was its greatest danger. Although pressed for time, he proceeded at a relatively slow pace. He marched his army only in the morning before the heat of the day, making frequent rest stops, always beside sources of water. The fleet sailed down the coast in close support, a source of supplies and a refuge for the wounded.

Aware of the ever-present danger of enemy raiders and the possibility of hit-and-run attacks, he kept the column in tight formation with a core of 12 mounted regiments, each with a hundred knights. The infantry marched on the landward flank, covering the flanks of the horsemen and affording them some protection from missiles. The outermost ranks of the infantry were composed of crossbowmen. On the seaward side was the baggage train and also units of infantry being rested from the continuous harassment inflicted by Saladin's forces! Richard wisely rotated his infantry units to keep them relatively fresh.

As Rory camped with his new fellow knights that night, they all told tales of the battles they had been in. A Scottish voice caught his attention, and Rory looked at the speaking knight. He was a younger double of Mason Knight Templar, the St Columba senior priest from Kilmory Chapel near Castle Sween, who had taught Rory the secrets of the Knights Templar. He was his double, a well-built man of six foot in height, but instead of being in his seventies, they were the same age. Rory had no doubt now he was on the right path to recover the Grail Box and knew he must, at all costs, make sure no harm should come to this ancestor of Mason. If not, then he would never exist and not be able to tell Rory the secrets of the Templars. Time travel and its implications were very confusing, but Mason had to survive and return home to enable Rory to be here. Also, the moment was rapidly approaching when this young Mason would recover the symbol of St John and place it in a coffin, along with the clothing Rory was wearing, for him to recover in the future!

The knights all arose before daybreak to eat and break camp in the coolness of the day. It was now the 25th of August as the army continued south. As the Crusader rear-guard crossed a break in the terrain, it was almost cut off by a surprise attack from an ambushing group of Muslim soldiers. Rory had positioned himself at the rear of the knights and used his superior senses to listen for any attack. When it came, he was prepared and dropped back, leaving a gap between him and the rear-guard, using the excuse of going for a call of nature. Hans, his sword, was ready and very willing and keen for some action as it jumped into Rory's hands. The 30 ambushers had no chance as Rory moved with lightning speed, disarming them and leaving them with only minor injuries as he forced them to flee. As a smiling Rory re-joined his comrades, he was sure they didn't even realise he was missing!

From the 26th to the 29th of August, Richard's army had a respite from attack because, while they hugged the coast and had gone round the shoulder of Mount Carmel, Saladin's army had struck out across country (Note: See Diagram A) and arrived in the vicinity of Caesarea before the Crusaders, who were taking longer because of their route. From 30th August to the 7th September, Saladin was always within striking distance and waiting for an opportunity to attack if the Crusaders' ranks were vulnerable.

A forest was in front of the Crusaders, and they managed to traverse about half of it with little incident before they were attacked. They responded and gave as good, if not better, than they got. Rory was having great fun at the rear of the vanguard as he jumped up a tree, spotting the enemy trying to mount a surprise attack and attacking them first. Rory could understand their language, and he was causing an element of fear among those unlucky enough to be ordered to attack the Hospitallers. He was being called a "Red Devil" by them with his red hair framing his head and his sword flashing through the air, cutting their scimitars in half.

Rory and the Crusader army rested on the 6th of September with their camp protected by the marsh lying inland of the mouth of the river Nahr-el-Falaik (Rochetaillée). The truth was that the Saracen Army was being rotated, with those in it who were too superstitious and scared to attack the rear of the Crusader's army being replaced or killed by their own command for cowardice, thanks to Rory!

To the south of the camp, there was another 6 miles (9.7km) that the Crusaders needed to march before gaining the ruins of Arsuf. At this point, the forest receded inland to create a narrow plain of 1 to 2 miles (1.6 to 3.2km) wide between wooded hills and the sea.

This is where Saladin intended to make his decisive attack!

At dawn on 7 September 1191, as the Crusader forces began moving out of camp, enemy scouts of Saladin's army were visible in all directions, hinting to King Richard that Saladin's whole army lay hidden in the woodland, waiting to attack them. Rory was aware of this as well and knew the biggest battle and trial of his abilities was imminent as he positioned himself near Mason to protect him. King Richard was taking special pains over the disposition of his army. He was vastly experienced in warfare and knew the probable posts of greatest danger were at the front and especially the rear of the column where Rory was. He was totally unaware of the special abilities of Rory and delegated command of these positions to the military orders with the Knight Hospitallers, including Rory, protecting the rear.

The military orders had the most experience of fighting in the East and were arguably the most disciplined. They were the only formations which included the Crusader Turcopole Cavalry, who fought like the Turkish horse archers of Saladin's Ayyubid army.

The first Saracen attack did not come until all the Crusaders had left their camp and were moving towards Arsuf. The Ayyubid army then burst out of the woodland. The front of the army was composed of dense swarms of skirmishers on horseback and foot, Bedouin, Sudanese archers and the lighter types of Turkish horse archers. Behind these were the ordered squadrons of armoured, heavy cavalry: Saladin's Mamluks (also termed ghulams), Kurdish troops, and the contingents of the Emirs and Princes of Egypt, Syria and Mesopotamia.

The army was divided into three parts, left and right wings and centre. Saladin, surrounded by his bodyguards, directed his army from beneath his banners showing a half-crescent moon. Accompanied by his kettle-drummers banging loudly, he attempted to destroy the cohesion of the Crusader army and unsettle their resolve. The Ayyubid onslaught was accompanied by the clashing of cymbals and gongs, trumpets blowing, and his men screaming war cries.

History records imply that the Ayyubid army outnumbered the Crusaders three-to-one quoting numbers of 300,000 against 100,000. Whatever the exact number, the Crusaders, on paper, had no chance of victory. But like the bumble bee scientifically proven incapable of flight, no one told the bee or the Crusaders!

The repeated Ayyubid harrying attacks followed the same pattern: the Bedouin and Nubians on foot launched arrows and javelins into the enemy lines before parting to allow the mounted archers to advance, attack and wheel off, a well-practised technique. Crusader crossbowmen responded, when this was possible, although the chief task among the Crusaders was simply to preserve their ranks in the face of sustained provocation.

When the incessant attacks of skirmishers failed to have the desired effect, the weight of the attack was switched to the rear of the Crusader column, with the Hospitallers coming under the greatest pressure. Rory had a shield in his left hand and Hans, his sword, in his right as he moved with breathtaking speed, knocking arrows and javelins from the air, protecting himself and Mason from this aerial attack raining down on them.

Now, seeing the rear guard of the Crusaders buckling, the right wing of the Ayyubid army made a desperate attack on the squadron of Hospitallers Knights and the infantry corps, including Rory and Mason. The Hospitallers could be attacked from both their rear and flank. Rory and Mason, and many of the Hospitallers' infantry, had to walk backwards in order to keep their faces and shields towards the enemy.

Saladin, eager to urge his soldiers into closer combat, personally entered the fray, accompanied by two pages leading spare horses. Say-al-Din (Saphadin), Saladin's brother, was also engaged in actively encouraging the troops; both brothers were thus exposing themselves to considerable danger from crossbow fire being returned from the Crusaders. It was mayhem, with the Crusaders holding on with survival instincts and quick reflexes.

But they were vastly experienced and getting very angry!

All of Saladin's best efforts could not dislocate the Crusader column or halt its advance in the direction of the ruins of Arsuf and protection from this onslaught. King Richard was determined to hold his army together, forcing the enemy to exhaust themselves in repeated charges, with the intention of holding his knights for a concentrated counterattack at just the right moment. There were risks in this, because the army was not only marching under severe enemy provocation, but the troops were suffering from heat and thirst. Just as serious, the Saracens were killing so many horses that some of Richard's own knights began to wonder if a counterstrike would be possible. Many of the unhorsed had no option but to join the infantry to survive.

Just as the vanguard entered Arsuf in the middle of the afternoon, the Hospitallers crossbowmen to the rear were having to load and fire, walking backwards. Inevitably they lost cohesion, and the enemy was quick to take advantage of this opportunity, moving into any gap, wielding their swords and maces. Rory was trying hard not to lose all restraint by giving in to the urge from Hans, his sword, to have free rein to maim and kill as he moved to intercept them.

For the Crusaders, the Battle of Arsuf had now entered a critical stage. The Master of the Hospitallers, Garnier de Nablus, repeatedly pleaded with Richard to be allowed to attack. He was refused and ordered to maintain position and await the signal for a general assault; six clear trumpet blasts. King Richard knew that the charge of his knights needed to be reserved until the Ayyubid army was fully committed, closely engaged, and the Saracens' horses had begun to tire.

Goaded beyond endurance, the Master and another knight, Baldwin de Carron, thrust their way through their own infantry past Rory and Mason, charging into the Saracen ranks with a cry of "For St. George!"

The rest of the Hospitallers Knights, including Rory and Mason, had endured enough and charged forward into hand-to-hand battle. Moved by this example, the French knights of the corps immediately preceding the Hospitallers also charged!

This precipitate action of the Hospitallers could have caused King Richard's whole strategy to unravel. However, he recognised that the counterattack, once started, had to be supported by all his army and ordered the signal for a general charge to be sounded.

Unsupported, the Hospitallers, including Rory and Mason and the other rear units involved in the initial breakout, would have been overwhelmed by the superior numbers of the enemy.

The Frankish infantry opened gaps in their ranks for the mounted knights to pass through to join the counterattack on the Saracens. To the soldiers of Saladin's army, the sudden change from passivity to ferocious activity on the part of the Crusaders was disconcerting, and appeared to be the result of a preconceived plan, not just a group of men who had lost their temper and basically had, had enough!

Having already been engaged in close combat with the rear of the Crusader column, the right wing of the Ayyubid army was in compact formation and too close to their enemy to avoid the full impact of the charge. Indeed, some of the cavalry of this wing had dismounted in order to fire their bows more effectively.

They were the first to feel the full force of Rory, who had now surrendered to the same red mist as his fellow knights, removing all restraint on Hans to fulfil its lust for blood. As a result, the Saracens suffered a great number of casualties, with the knights taking a bloody revenge for all they had had to endure earlier in the battle.

Memory is a very selective thing with the rush of blood to the head when one is recording events and involved in the heat of battle and you can understand where this story evolved. One person was winning this battle practically single-handed with the Red Cross emblazoned across his chest.

Rory had lost sight of Mason as he had left him safely behind with no one to fight. He let his instincts take control, massacring all those who threatened him. The rout was complete as he reached the centre division of Saladin's army when it turned in flight. He looked down at his blood-soaked hands and sword. As he watched, the blood ran down his hands towards the black metal blade until they were clean. The blade was covered in blood, but it began to vanish as if being eaten by the sword until it too was clean, gleaming in the light, gorged full and satisfied.

Rory replaced the living sword, Hans, back in his scabbard on his back. He had remade it using a black meteor rock containing super-strong Cliftonite. (* See Appendix.) It was contaminated by an unearthly parasite that was alive and intelligent! It was this that gave the sword its magical properties, and he had just fed it!

The adrenaline-fuelled red mist that had encouraged Hans, the sword, to possess him receded now that he had no contact with it. Rory looked up and saw the trail he had made through Saladin's ground troop of Turkish infantry. For over half a mile, the blood-red ground was covered with the remains of dismembered and halved bodies.

Reality struck home! He had done all of this single-handed!

All of this blood and death was on his hands or not, in this case, as it was consumed by his sword. He was responsible in any case, letting go of his restraint over it, giving it free rein to murder!

Rory could not believe what he had done, but his body could as he doubled over in revulsion at his actions, and he was sick to the bottom of his stomach. As he retched, he knew he could never use Hans again. It had taken control of him now and been fed and would want to be fed again. It was pure evil, his opposite, and the opposite of the haggis tusk of the Hagpipe around his neck. It was made with the left carved haggis tusk of the first haggis built into its Nessie-like serpent grip that hissed when it was removed from its scabbard.

This made sense now. The sword was Rory's snake in the Garden of Eden. The control he had over it was gone; it would now possess anyone who lifted it to feed on blood!

He would have to keep it safe until it could be destroyed!

But how do you destroy something that is indestructible?

CHAPTER 7

The Grail Box

Rory pulled himself upright and resolved that, no matter his circumstances, he would not use the sword again as he feared it would possess him with a blood lust to kill. Looking to his left, he saw the mounted Ayyubid army of Saladin in rapid flight, under attack by the mounted knights. Despite the considerable casualties it was suffering, it was not destroyed, but it had been routed. This was considered shameful by the Saracens, who prided themselves on their bravery, but it was flee or die, and they decided to flee and fight again another day. This sight boosted the morale of the Crusaders, who, despite being drastically outnumbered, had achieved a momentous victory. The intervention of Rory under the evil influence of Hans had swung the battle but at what cost?

Turning from the fleeing Saracens, Rory walked back through the blood-covered ground, stepping over the multiple dead for whom he was responsible. He had never felt as low before and was very remorseful and guilty at his actions. Mason was kneeling over the dead body of his Hospitaller Grand Master, Garnier de Nablus, who had fallen in the battle. He was holding a shiny gold-coloured object that Rory recognised instantly!

It was the brass symbol of St John that Rory had made, the same one that he had given to St John to start the secret order to protect the Grail Box!

Mason saw Rory approaching, and before he could conceal the symbol, Rory asked him how it had been recovered. Mason knew by now not to underestimate the knowledge Rory possessed with regards to the order. He explained that the Hospitallers in Jerusalem had undertaken excavations in the area around the Temple Mount during the First Crusade in an attempt to find the Grail Box, and the only artefact they had recovered was this symbol concealed in a lead box. They took this as a good omen and began constructing their new base on the spot where it had been found. It was a prized possession and the closest the order had ever come to reclaiming the Grail Box. The brass triangle gave them great influence over the other orders who shared the secrets it symbolised.

Mason had totally immersed himself in the secret work of the order with his family basing their names around it. He tested Rory and found that he could explain what all the secret words and symbols on it meant. He had seen Rory attack the enemy, leaving him behind and cutting them all down as if he was a human scythe mowing grass. Mason knew Rory was no ordinary man, especially with his superior knowledge of his order's rituals, and he suspected that he was the mythical man mentioned in all of the rituals, called "The One"!

Rory's spirits lifted on being reunited with his brass symbol, which he noticed was weathered with a few scratches but otherwise in very good condition. It was a sign to him that his quest was drawing to a close. Mason was the most senior member of the Hospitaller office-bearers still alive after the battle, and he was now in charge of the symbol until the next meeting of the senior office-bearers who had to elect a new Grand Master. With the current campaign underway to take Jaffa, that could be some time away. Mason was in awe of Rory and trusted him, unquestionably promising to comply with his request to convey the symbol back to his home at Kilmory in Scotland. He would bury it in a coffin at the chapel marking it with a gravestone of Rory's image, along with a tabard and cloak. The past would become the future!

* * *

A major battle had been won for the Crusaders at Arsuf, but the war was not over. Saladin was able to regroup and attempted to resume his skirmishing method of warfare, but it had little effect on the Crusaders, confident of their invincibility. Saladin was shaken by their sudden and devastatingly effective counterattack at Arsuf, and he was no longer willing to risk a further full-scale attack. This battle had dented his reputation as an invincible warrior and proved King Richard's courage as a soldier as well as his skill as a commander. King Richard moved his forces towards Ascalon on the way to Jaffa. Anticipating Richard's next move, Saladin emptied the city and camped a few miles away. When Richard arrived at the city, he was stunned to see it abandoned and the towers demolished.

The next day when Richard was preparing to march on Jaffa, Saladin attacked.

Rory was prepared for this as he had been informed of this day by the descendant of this Mason Knight Templar, the priest at Kilmory Chapel. He was hampered in his ability by refusing to use his sword, Hans, taking a spare one from the supply wagon. Even then, he was superior to the rest of the troops with his enhanced abilities. However, he refused to kill and was reluctant to even cause permanent injury to the opposing force, making it more difficult for him to disable them. The leaders of the Crusaders were in conflict with Lionheart, wishing to pursue and wipe out Saladin's army. Richard knew that taking Jaffa was far more strategically important, and Saladin knew this too. Both leaders were very alike, with a very good understanding of military strategy. The hatred and blood lust the leaders had for each other overrun their logic, and a furious battle took place where both armies were decimated. Rory had to use all his abilities in aiding Mason and King Richard to ensure they escaped with their lives and in regrouping the Crusader army.

Richard was then able to take, defend and hold Jaffa, which was a strategically crucial move toward securing

Jerusalem. Saladin's Saracen forces suffered the most in this conflict, suffering heavy losses at the hands of the Templar Knights, and again they were forced to withdraw. This was the last major battle between the two forces.

In November of 1191, the Crusader army advanced inland towards Jerusalem. On the 12th of December, Saladin was forced, by pressure asserted from his emirs, to disband the greater part of his army. Learning this, Richard pushed his army forward, spending Christmas at Latrun. The army then marched to Beit Nuba, only 12 miles from Jerusalem. Muslim morale in Jerusalem was so low that, had Richard known, the arrival of his Crusader's army would probably have caused the city to fall quickly.

The winter equinox was fast approaching again, and Rory saw the opportunity was close for him to enter Jerusalem and recover the Grail Box.

Others' eyes were watching as the equinox arrived and a defeated Warlock Stan returned from Southend after his failed attempt to kill St Columba. (* See Appendix.) He was bitterly disappointed at being thwarted again, but a parcel was waiting for him on his return, sent from his son, Johnny, at Urquhart Castle. It was practically calling out to him as he opened the wrapping to see a red robe within. He could feel the power emanating from it as he joined the Grant Witch in the middle of the pentagram. The robe left his hand, floating in the air in front of him, opening for him to insert his arms into the sleeves. The power from the robe coursed through him as the witch looked into the inky black of their time mirror, searching for Rory. He was unbelievably easy to find. 'Hans the Sword' on his back drew their gaze straight to him like a transmitter mast on receive. They both laughed, feeling the evil power emanating from the sword. It flowed through time into their black crystals as they extended their wills to access its malevolent power.

Rory was camped with the rest of the Crusader army 12 miles from Jerusalem as King Richard deliberated over whether or not to attack Jerusalem when the storm struck. Giant hailstones rained down on the camp, ripping through the tents like tissue paper, catching those unlucky enough to be asleep on the head, thereby causing them a permanent sleep!

Panic ran through the camp as lightning forked across the sky with bolts striking the knights on the ground, with the unlucky who were still wearing their armour being cooked in it. The horses of the mounted division bolted from the camp as the sky grew black and the ground began to freeze! A great evil was at work, filling everyone, no matter how brave they were, with a soul-wrenching fear! Rory knew this evil; he had faced it before but not with this level of intensity. It felt close, very close, practically over his shoulder! He quickly removed the two-armed shoulder harness fixed to the scabbard and 'Hans the Sword' on his back. The normally white ivory carved grip of Nessie was black and pulsing with malevolence. The evil, unearthly bacteria, alive in the metal of the living sword, had multiplied after feeding on human blood and travelled to the grip. Rory could feel it directing the attack towards him as he jumped out of the way, zigzagging from side to side from several giant hailstones, the size of boulders and just as heavy. They impacted into the ground around him, throwing up dust and mud into the air, leaving craters where they landed. One strike of these would even kill Rory! He had to do something, but what? This was a new type of attack, one of concentrated pure evil. It was very focused and close, coming from his sword. It was multiplying the effects of the storm, which had travelled through time sent by the combined forces of Warlock Stan and the Grant Witch. The sword was in the same time as Rory, and very near, and connected to him. It had found a new master, a blood brother, evil just like it, and it was time to feed!

Only good can beat evil, and Rory did not feel good after killing so many people! He was alone. Everyone had run off looking for shelter as he stood in the epicentre of the storm. Guilt, remorse, shame and every negative thought filled him, emanating from the sword, willing him to give up and die! Another barrage of hailstones sparked Rory's self-preservation instincts as he thought of his loved ones back home: his mum, dad and beloved Heather.

That was it!

Taking out his Hagpipe, he clasped it with both hands, filling his thoughts with the love he felt for them! Rory burst from head to toe into the same white light in which he had been covered when he had cured his mum of cancer and saved her life. (* See Appendix.)

Rory screamed in agony; this was not what it had been like before, he burned with a pure white fire, and he could not have been in more pain if he had walked into the fire of the foundry in the blacksmiths. Every nerve in his body felt that this fire was real, cauterising him. It burned him to the very centre of his soul, removing and erasing all the negativity and the evil acts he had done. He had been infected with the evil parasite from 'Hans the Sword'. Black wisps came to the surface of the white fire and burnt off him, blowing away in a cloud of smoke until the pain stopped and he stood, glowing like the sun. He was innocent again and totally pure; the light from him expanded outwards into a globe, surrounding him in an impenetrable bubble. The meteor-like hailstones could not penetrate this globe of good and disintegrated into dust on contact with it.

Rory retained hold of his Hagpipe with his left hand as he took hold of the Ivory Nessie grip of Hans the Sword with his right. It resisted his grip, trying to slip from it; black sparks burst from it into the air, which then turned into white flames, purified in the bubble surrounding him. Rory expanded his now pure will, focusing all that was good in life and his rediscovered innocence and love down his right arm and hand and into the ivory grip. A multitude of black sparks shot into the air in this battle of good against evil, bursting into more white flames as the ivory handle of Nessie slowly turned from black to translucent white! Victory was not fully secured as

Rory exerted his will down the blade of 'Hans', which shuddered and shook in his grip, squirming like a snake grabbed by its tail. Rory forced home his advantage, sterilising the bacteria in the blade in his antiseptic white light, turning the blade from black to stainless white.

Goodness won!

The sword was still alive with the bacterial life force, totally alien to earth; it was deep-rooted and forged into the metal, but it had no control over Rory's will now. He was its master again and could safely use it as before. If anything, it was like a puppy that had been trained and eager to follow Rory's every command, wanting to please him and getting enjoyment from doing so.

Rory was changed as well, totally cauterised of all sin and pure again!

As with all evil, it had to go somewhere, and it recoiled back to John Grant (Warlock Stan) within the pentagram, pushing the Grant Witch out of it onto the stone floor of the cottage. All the evil focused on the red-robed John Grant, who convulsed and screamed in agony. The malevolence had come home!

The storm did not stop, but it became a normal one. King Richard accepted this as an omen and decided not to proceed to Jerusalem. Concerned that his forces, if they besieged Jerusalem, might be trapped there by a relieving force, he took the decision to retreat to the coast for the winter months. He occupied and refortified Ascalon, which had earlier been razed to the ground by Saladin. The spring of 1192 saw continued negotiations and further skirmishing between the opposing forces. The Crusader army made another advance on Jerusalem, coming within sight of the city, before being forced to retreat once again because of dissension among its leaders. During this period, Richard became seriously ill. He began to receive disturbing news of the activities of his brother John and the French king, Philip Augustus. (* See Appendix.)

As the spring gave way to summer, it became evident that Richard would soon have to return to his own lands to safeguard his interests. He had only 2,000 able-bodied soldiers and 50 fit knights left to use in battle. With such a small force, he could not expect or hope to take Jerusalem from the bolstered multiplying numbers joining Saladin's Saracen army. However, being a shrewd tactician, he negotiated the Treaty of Ramla in which Saladin agreed that western Christian pilgrims could once again worship freely in Jerusalem.

The war was over, for now!

The summer solstice was close again, and another birthday for Rory and his 19th year. He entered Jerusalem, stooping to hide his height. He was dressed in his grey cloak and looked like every other pilgrim but ensured his hood was up to cover his shock of ginger hair. There were no red-haired men in the Holy Land, and horror stories were still retold of the mythical Red Devil who could destroy vast armies single-handed with his flaming sword.

The city had been destroyed and rebuilt many times since his last visit, with the new streets inside the walled city going in different directions than he remembered. He decided just to follow the other pilgrims so as not to get lost. He hoped that at least one of them knew where he was going as he wound his way through the cobbled, narrow, winding streets, lined on each side by buildings. As Rory followed, he watched the front pilgrim subtly checking a chiselled mark on each corner building of every street. As he passed, he looked at the mark and saw a tiny square and compass indentation angled like an arrow pointing in the direction to travel.

Rory laughed at the ingenuity of his fellow brothers of HAGI leaving a clear path for those with the knowledge to follow.

After what seemed like an eternity of walking through this stone maze, the narrow street opened into a large open square revealing the Dome of the Rock and the Al-Aqsa Mosque, which were nearing completion again following Saladin's retaking of Jerusalem in 1187 and eradicating all traces of Christian worship from the Temple Mount.

Rory nearly burst out laughing!

He recognised this square and remembered it very well although nearly 1200 years had passed since he was last here. The Dome of the Rock and Mosque had been rebuilt in the wrong place and were nowhere near where the Holy of Holies had been, over the original site of King Solomon's Temple. St. John and the secret order had been very busy with misinformation, ensuring the site moved with every rebuild! Rory carried on walking past the Dome of the Rock and Mosque, following the pilgrims to a large stone building. A high stone wall surrounded it, with a large courtyard situated in its middle. It blended with the surrounding buildings, all of which appeared to have been built at the same time, at the far end of this ancient city. The pilgrims all lined up at the high, double, solid wooden front doors recessed in the exterior wall. Rory knew he had arrived when he recognised the noise made by the first pilgrim as he knocked on the door with same four distinctive knocks which Rory had taught to St John! The door opened, and the pilgrim entered quickly with the door closing even faster behind him. This continued until only Rory was left outside. He looked at the building for any identifying sign and saw it! In the middle of the arch above the door was an engraved, indented small cross of St John. This was the headquarters of the Hospitallers!

Rory gave the knock and entered a confined hallway to be confronted with two knights pointing drawn swords at him. The door closed behind him, and he felt a third sword tip pressed against his back. There was no way forward and no way back as a voice behind him demanded a word. Rory stifled his humour; he knew this word, he had taught it and uttered it for the first time to St John, and he gave it in full ancient form.

He expected to be ushered forward through the next door but was rapidly taken by both arms as a cry of 'impostor' went up, and more guards entered with drawn swords from the door in front of him. A purple-robed man with his hood drawn over his head stood behind them, demanding that Rory should repeat the word. With trepidation, Rory repeated the word, wondering what he was doing wrong. The purple-robed man said in heavily accented English, "And now say it in your tongue." Rory realised he had said it in Aramaic, the way he had taught St John and said 'HAGI' in English.

The purple-robed man said, "Remove his hood."

Rory felt his hood being pulled back, revealing his red hair and the protruding grip, showing the carved handle of Nessie on Hans the sword. The next instruction took Rory by surprise as the guards were told, "Remove his sword." Rory stood still and began to remember his last conversation with St John to figure out what was happening. He recalled showing him his sword and placing it into the stone ground in front of him after he had convinced him of who he was. The guards were having great trouble trying to remove Hans from the sheath on Rory's back. The sword was totally loyal again to Rory, and their hands slipped off it as if they were grabbing a block of butter. The purple-robed man pulled down his hood, revealing his grey hair and a battle-scarred clean-shaven face. He walked up to Rory and tried to remove the sword himself. The grip still proved a slip, and no matter how he tried, he could not take hold of the Nessie-shaped grip.

Taking a step back, he said to Rory, "Remove the sword and place it in the stone," pointing downwards at the stone floor. Rory sent a mental thought to 'Hans' who, with a hiss, flew out of the sheath into his right hand. In one fluid motion, he twisted it in the air with a flourish and embedded the sword into the stone floor in front of him up to its hilt.

All the guards, including the purple-robed man, exclaimed simultaneously, "He is risen," and pointed at the sky with their right index finger.

Rory was quickly released, and the purple-robed man spoke again, "I am Grand Master Fernando Afonso. Follow me." The guards all parted like the Red Sea in front of Rory as he passed through the next door to a large hallway. Behind him, he heard the guards swearing in frustration as they took turns in attempting to pull the sword from the stone.

We all know how that works out!

The building was huge, constructed of solid stone, and similar in style to a monastery. It had many individual cells off the long corridor with a large refectory at its end. Rory followed the Grand Master to his cell, which was poorly furnished with a bed, a wooden table and two chairs. Rory was ushered to a chair. The Grand Master sat on the other and removed an old book of ritual from the desk drawer. The Grand Master spoke, "This ritual describes your return, Pure One, to recover the Grail Box. St John was quite specific, detailing it in this, the original copy. We will assist you, knowing that only you can recover it and record a new ritual, describing how it has been made safe."

Rory was very impressed with St John. He had kept his word, making this easier than he had imagined. Rory said, "You can start your new ritual with the words. *In 100 years to the day of the recovery of the Grail Box and its disappearance, it will reappear!* Your order will assist in its safe passage to its final resting place." This was suitably cryptic for the leader of an order based on cryptic instructions to understand. His order would be superior to all of the other orders who were in search of the Grail Box.

This made Alfonso feel very important for his role in history, and his name would never be forgotten. The Grand Master said, "This instruction will be passed down in a new degree for the senior office-bearers of the Hospitallers and will be followed implicitly for 100 years until the Grail Box returns. All the pilgrims visiting the Holy Land, if found worthy, will be indoctrinated in the new degree." This was no small number; the pilgrims comprised builders, healers and fighters. A great many of them, at the moment, were employed as labourers, digging in the large walled courtyard, trying to find the concealed entrance to the secret vault of King Solomon.

Rory was shown to a cell for his use, where he removed his clothing for a good wash in the facilities provided; he then dressed in a clean white shirt, kilt and boots. He was hungry; it had been some time since he had consumed a decent meal, and he walked to the refectory. Word of the arrival of "The One" had travelled fast within the compound, and he caused quite a stir among the other knights, not just because he was a 6ft 4inch Scotsman with shoulder-length red hair. Everyone wanted a look at him, but he was far too important to be introduced to unless by the Grand Master himself; he had given implicit instructions that he was not to be disturbed.

Rory was desperate to view the work in progress in the football-park-sized courtyard. It was a hive of excitement with some holes in the ground 40-foot deep and going nowhere. As soon as he set foot on the dirt, Rory knew they were digging in the wrong place. He could feel the Grail Box calling out to him from below the ground. It was as if he was divining its location through the soles of his boots. (* See Appendix.) Rory could feel the location of the hidden chamber getting stronger or weaker, depending on where he walked. A crowd was gathering to watch the kilted giant Scotsman as he marched up and down the courtyard until he stopped in a previously unexcavated spot calling for a shovel. Rory began to dig at a furious pace and was soon 10 feet below the surface when the shovel hit stone with a clunk. He cleared the loose dirt from around the spot, revealing the top of the keystone of the Arch of the secret chamber of King Solomon. He knew this was it as St John had marked the top of the stone with the symbol of the equilateral triangle, enclosing an open All-Seeing Eye. It was the very same design as on the brass one Rory had given him so long ago! Tomorrow was the 24th of June and Rory's 19th Birthday, and that was when he decided he would enter the secret vault.

He remembered the picture in the *Book of St Columba* that he had been shown so long ago of him being lowered into the chamber. He jumped up out of the hole 10 foot into the air, landing on the ground next to a large group of pilgrims, startling them. All work had stopped in the courtyard, with everyone congregating around Rory with shovels and picks in hand. The Grand Master was nearby frantically recording the events as they unfolded for his new ritual as Rory instructed the keen pilgrims to clear the site for the next day! Rory knew that, according to his plan, he would not be returning to the surface from this vault until the time was right in 100 years. He went back to the hall at the entrance to the Hospitallers building and pulled Hans, his sword, from the stone floor, restoring it to the sheath strapped to his back. He rolled his tabard up in his grey cloak, ready for the next day and went to sleep in his cell.

The labourers worked through the night clearing the ground surrounding the arch until the top of it was exposed at the bottom of a 10-foot crater. They worked in shifts enthusiastically, proud to be involved and present at this momentous time. The refectory supplied food and drink to the workforce throughout the night, and the last shift was still being fed as Rory entered for breakfast to a hushed silence. The Grand Master joined him with a big smile on his face, knowing his order was about to become the most important of them all. He asked Rory if he needed anything for the task ahead of him. Rory answered that a long length of rope and some sturdy, strong backs to lower him into the vault was all he required. An exit from the vault in 100 years would also be appreciated! The Grand Master laughed at this, knowing he would not live long enough to see Rory again after today, but said he would arrange it.

Rory would just have to trust him!

It was approaching midday, with the sun at its zenith as Rory returned to the keystone, crowbar in his left hand, his bundle of clothes in the other. Hans was safely strapped to his back as he easily levered the wedge-shaped keystone up and out of the arch, putting it aside on the ground. As he removed it, a loud sigh was heard coming from the opening as centuries of old, stale, foul air escaped. The pilgrims all put a hand over their faces and noses to protect them from the smell as the Grand Master recorded this sign for his new degree. Rory removed two more stones on either side of the keystone to ventilate the chamber and to let in more light from the midday sun, which was overhead. The opening was now large enough for Rory to fit in. Tying the end of the rope over his left shoulder and back up in a loop, he dropped his clothing into the vault, listening to see how long it would take to hit the bottom.

Rory did not even have to ask for help as the biggest and strongest Hospitallers Knights lined up, all wearing their tabards emblazoned with the Red Cross of St John. They had changed from their working clothes of toil in respect for this momentous moment, desperate to be part of it. They all wanted the honour of holding the rope that would lower Rory through the hole into the domed arch. They would be recorded in the ritual as the artists sketched this scene. Rory instructed them that if he was in difficulty, he would tug on the rope twice to be pulled back up. He dropped over the edge, feet first, holding on to the top of the rope with his left hand.

Once clear of the opening, the sun directly above shone inside, illuminating the interior of the perfect circular cavern. It was filled with golden light reflecting off the surface of the treasure of King Solomon filling the vault. Rory had never seen so much gold and piles of precious gems and let out a sigh at the wealth of man. The Hospitallers were going to be wealthy beyond their dreams, thereby reinforcing their historic presence as the guardians of the treasure of King Solomon.

The most important piece of this treasure could not be seen. Rory gazed all around the chamber until he looked down directly below his feet. On a six-foot by six-foot white marble four-sided slab table below him was the six-foot by three-foot by three-foot-deep Grail Box, with the Red Cross of St John on its top. Rory's heart leapt on seeing it as he swung on the rope, descending the thirty-three-foot distance to the floor and moving to the right side of the box to avoid stepping on it. On either side of the Grail Box were two smooth rods or staffs. One was longer than the other, which, unknown to Rory, was the staff used by Moses to produce water from a rock. It was the same one that transformed into a snake in front of the Pharaoh of Egypt and which Moses had held when he parted the Red Sea. The other staff or stave was the rod of Aaron, Moses's brother, which was also endowed with miraculous power, dating back to the Plagues of Egypt. These were the only objects with enough power to make contact with the Grail Box as they fitted through the holes on either side of it near its top and into a hole at the bottom, allowing it to be carried. The holes had been created by the nails driven into the wrists and feet of Jesus when he was crucified on the cross that was subsequently used to make this Grail Box. The dark red cross of St John, where the bloodied head pierced by the crown of thorns was still visible on the top panel. The wooden box lay inert on the marble altar, showing no sign to Rory of the divine power it contained.

If only he had known more of the true nature of the Grail Box. He loosened the rope around him, shouting up to the knights to pull it up. He looked at the Grail Box and remembered being told by St Columba that only one person could make contact with it and survive.

The Pure One!

Rory hoped that he was that person after being burnt clean in the pure white cauterising light from his Hagpipe. He reached out with his left hand, placing it on the top of the wooden box and vanished!

CHAPTER 8

Bruce

Rory opened his eyes, or what he perceived to be his eyes. He was in a sparkling white landscape that stretched to infinity! The white light surrounding him was not coming from the sky; there was no sky. It emanated from floating white balls of energy that were surrounding him. They filled the entire landscape, above and below him. He was floating among the bright globes which gathered around his ethereal body. A reassuring peaceful, calm voice spoke into his head, though he had no head or body, arms or legs for that matter. It was like it was part of him, similar to the telepathy he had with his animal friends. However, this was totally inclusive, and it felt normal to him as if this was how it should be.

He wanted to stay here forever and felt totally at peace!

Rory realised now that he was not the Pure One and that he had failed. He was dead, and the only part of him still in existence was his soul floating here. He was just another part of the white lights, just like the rest of the innumerable souls surrounding him!

"No," came the voice which entered his consciousness talking to him. "Your journey is not complete. You must go back, or they cannot stay."

Rory's awareness was drawn to a whole area of lights that were flashing on and off. "You must save the ancestor of the man you know as Bruce and secure the Grail, or they and yours will not be."

A strong bright light was pushing closer and closer to him, along with two other lights which were flashing on and off. Rory's heart, if he had one, leapt; he recognised them. The closest light was his beloved Heather, who was desperate to join him. The calm voice pushed her back, saying, "This is not the time, soon."

Rory felt the great joy coming from her being replaced with a great sadness. He felt in his soul that he recognised the other two lights next to Heather; they were his daughters!

How could this be?

The voice returned, "Yes. You're right, but they won't exist unless you go back and save them!" Rory was filled with love for them, and he felt them receive his love and return it!

The disembodied voice continued, "There is no time here. It is what it is and what it should be! You must will yourself to leave and restore all things. If not, you will end up floating in the darkness of limbo, separated from all the souls you love."

This afterlife was intoxicating, Rory had no will to leave and no Hagpipe here to help him, but he must, for the sake of Heather and his children. He focused on his love for them and, with an almost breaking heart, pulled away; looking for his body, he felt himself tumbling downwards into an area of darkness.

As the lights went out, he heard the voice echo in his being, "Don't touch the Grail Box again. Use the rods!"

Rory continued to fall into the centre of the darkness; he realised it was the opposite of the happy place of the white globes. The blackness was full of spheres devoid of light. He could sense the deep despair emanating from them as they rushed towards him, looking for a way to escape this limbo by touching him. He saw one area of light in a small circle in the centre of the blackness. He willed himself forward towards it and saw that it circled an endless ladder stretching upwards towards the light that he had just left. On it was a constant stream of people frantically climbing, they were attracted to the brightness as if they were human moths. Rory recognised what he was seeing and recalled the stories he had been told as a child at Sunday School.

It was 'Jacobs Ladder', the stairway to heaven!

Rory willed his spirit forward and burst through into the circle of light, leaving the black globes chasing him stranded on the other side in limbo. He did not look up; he had been there and focused on looking for his body down below. He saw a golden cord coming up towards him and felt it tighten around where his chest should be. The cord of life rapidly began pulling him downwards, doubling in speed every millisecond as he prayed that he would have a soft landing or he would be revisiting the afterlife sooner than he wanted.

* * *

Bruce had used many names to keep himself safe. He was currently calling himself Lee Chan as he travelled the Silk Road from China to the west in his two-horse-drawn wagon, carrying his cargo of precious silkworms along with other rare goods with which to start a new life. He had a price on his head. He was not safe and would never be safe in China. If Kublai Khan, the leader of the Mongol Empire, knew of his survival, he would hunt him down. He thought he was dead, like his two brothers, killed when Khan had conquered the Song Capital in 1276. Bruce had been very lucky; the Shaolin monks had rescued him as a child. Kublai Khan would massacre even them if he found out they had saved him. He could never divulge his real name, "Zhao Bing", to anyone. (* See Appendix.) Zhao was the last of his dynasty, and he had been spirited away by the monks to Mount Song, one of the five sacred great mountains of China. Its summit was over 4,900ft (1,500 metres), and the perfect hiding place for their Shaolin Temple as the slopes rose steeply from the valley and were thickly clad with trees. This was the birthplace of Zen Buddhism, and they were famous for their Kung Fu Martial Arts. He trained harder than all the other novices as he would have to be better than everyone else to survive. He learned every skill, from fighting to healing and from science to sword making. He had the ultimate sword, which he had made with the ancient knowledge that he had been taught and possessed the skills of a true ninja warrior. It would take many determined men to defeat him in combat, but he was a pacifist and would not start a fight but definitely would not lose one.

He could not be trained any further or learn anything else as he had left the Shaolin Temple at 20 with the pocket full of precious gems that he had been found with when rescued. His only hope for a life without fear was to flee to a future in the west. He was being drawn there, knowing that he could not remain in China. It was now united under total Mongol control, and he would never be safe. Zhao looked like every other traveller of his day as he made his way to Beijing with his shaven head and pony tail, his 5ft 8inch muscular frame concealed below his loose-fitting clothing. He intended to join a caravan of traders travelling the Silk Road, named after the trade in silk, which was the main trading route from China to the West. He concealed himself among the traders who had banded together in a large caravan as it was unsafe to travel alone.

Kublai Khan, the Mongol leader, had thought Zhao had drowned as a child but had now heard rumours of his survival. The Shaolin monks had dragged the seven-year-old from the swollen river, still clinging to the body of his dead bodyguard. Only they knew his real identity as the true Emperor of China, and this meant they must all die.

All was going according to plan as Bruce travelled from Beijing to Lanzhou, taking the north route to Hotan (Khotan) and Kashgar, passing the huge Taklamakan Desert into the treacherous narrow rocky paths of the Pamirs and the Hindu Kush Mountains and south to Bukhara, into the land now known as Afghanistan. He then travelled west to Iran and south to Hormuz on the Arabian Sea to avoid more deserts. The journey continued north-west to Tabriz and the now Iranian Azerbaijan. He proceeded west again, through Persia, now known as Syria, to Antioch. He was almost there with a straight run to Acre in the Holy Land in a country now known as Israel.

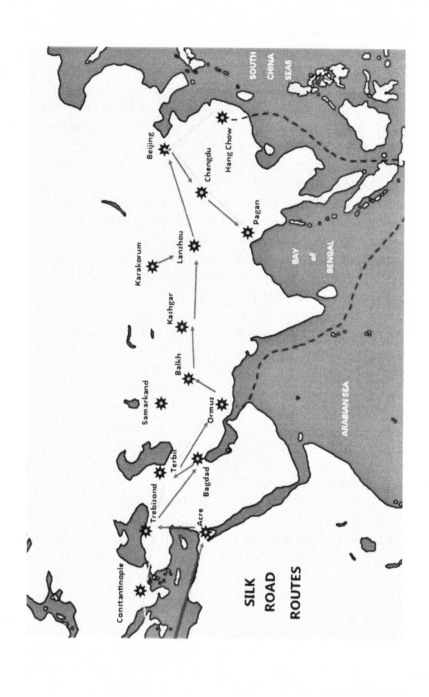

Bruce had traversed mountain passes, plains and deserts, fighting off raiding bandits while stocking up with rare spices on the way. He travelled over one of the most inhospitable and largest continents in the world, keeping one step away from the Mongols who were expanding rapidly behind him. If only he knew: a bigger problem even than Kublai Khan that of the Mamluks and Saracens were in front of him!

They were a new power in play led by Sultan al-Ashraf Khalil, the leader of the Mamluk Sultanate military, for control of the Holy Land, and he was amassing a huge, vicious, suicidal slave army of Mamluks warriors. He was working in unison with Melik de Serif, who was in charge of an overwhelming force of Saracens. Both were determined to finish the Crusaders' rule of the last 100 years and drive them from the Holy Land forever.

* * *

With a gasp drawing air into his body, Rory opened his eyes. He could see nothing; it was pitch black, he thought that he had gone blind. He reached out with his other senses and felt that he was lying on a cold stone floor. Reaching about with his hands, he found a bundle of clothing at his toes. He felt the other way and connected with a tall cold, smooth surface. It was the marble altar holding the Grail Box; he was back in the secret chamber still below the ground in Jerusalem. He reached for his Hagpipe, checking it was still there. It illuminated on his touch, emitting an ivory glow from his left hand. It was enough to see by, and Rory noticed things had changed in the vault. It was almost empty; the only items in the chamber except for himself were the Grail Box and the rods on the altar. It was cold in this cellar, and he put on his tabard and cloak to save carrying them. He checked and found that Hans, his sword, was still strapped to his back. He looked around the arched vault, using the Hagpipe as a torch. All the gold and treasure of King Solomon was gone, replaced by a new wide staircase built against the far wall, leading up to a wide landing. Time had changed since he entered the vault, and the Grail Box must have travelled with him when he touched it. But was he where he wanted to be, 100 years in the future from the time he entered the cavern?

Rory walked up the staircase and saw that the original stone of the arch had been altered; a secret door had been built into it, similar to the one he used in Urquhart Castle so long ago. He easily found the concealed lever and pulled it, causing the door to silently open outwards into a large tunnel; it spiralled around the outside of the arch of the chamber to the right and upwards. He could hear human voices echoing down the corridor towards him and mentally commanded Hans to come to his right hand. Light was shining through the cracks around a door at the end of the passage. His enhanced eyesight could see without aid, and he put the Hagpipe away below his shirt. A meeting which sounded very similar to his initiation in Urquhart Castle was taking place on the other side of the door.

Rory gave it three sharp knocks and another one for luck with his sword's hilt, laughing at the reaction this would cause inside. He was right; the room went deathly quiet. One brave man, who sounded as if he was near to the other side of the door, spoke, saying, "Master, there is an alarm from the chamber."

Rory was practically wetting himself with laughter as he heard the obviously shaken Master reply, "Guardian of the Vault, can you confirm it was empty?"

This was replied with a "Yes, Master" and more nervous silence until the Master, true to form, put the onus on the doorman.

Rory heard swords being drawn on the other side of the door as the Master said, "Find out who knocks at the door." The door swung open inwards.

Rory stood with his sword in front of him in a vertical position in the shape of a cross. He was an imposing sight with his red hair untied and falling to his shoulders on his six-foot-four muscular frame. His cloak was open, revealing the Red Cross of St John on his chest as he said in a loud voice, "The Pure One seeks admission!"

Never before at any meeting had an entire room been struck dumb!

Rory stepped into the room, which was a perfect copy of King Solomon's Temple, and embedded his sword into the middle of the stone, chequered floor to gasps from the crowded room of knights dressed in a similar fashion to Rory.

The Master, with great composure in the circumstances, recovered quickly. He had been studying the new ritual that Grand Master Fernando Afonso had written 100 years before as he banged on his dais, saying, "Salute the Pure One with the sign."

Every knight in the room stood and covered his nose and mouth with their right hand as Rory replied with the same sign, to stifle his laughter, not because there was a bad smell in the air!

Fernando Alfonso had a good sense of humour if nothing else!

Formalities over, Rory returned to the chamber, followed by a procession of knights carrying torches to illuminate the vault. They all wanted to see the Grail Box. The Master despatched two of the most junior knights to prepare a suitable wagon and horses in which to carry the Grail Box, much to their disappointment. Rory retraced his route back to the chamber, which was soon fully illuminated. He instructed no one to touch the Grail Box on pain of death. Walking up to it, he recovered the rods of Moses and Aaron from either side of it. He went to the bottom of the box and slid the smaller rod of Aaron smoothly into a perfect-sized hole in the middle of the bottom panel at its base. A quarter of its length was left protruding for two men or one Rory to grasp.

He then took the longer rod of Moses, and walked to the front of the box. A short distance in from the front panel where there were two holes, one on either side at its base. They aligned perfectly, and Rory slid the rod through the Grail Box like a magician cutting a woman in half with metal blades. Rory was relieved that no white light appeared this time as he instructed four of the biggest, strongest knights to take hold of the protruding rod, two on each side and to carry it on their shoulders when it was lifted. Rory went to the rear and took hold of the rod of Aaron. On his instruction, the four knights lifted the Grail Box, which was incredibly heavy, containing the stone tablets of the 10 commandments, books and artefacts within it, not to mention the weight of the box itself. With his enhanced strength, Rory lifted the rear easily as the procession wound its way back up the stairs and through the concealed doorway. It had been designed with ample room to accommodate the removal of the box, as had the corridor and the whole extension.

By the time they passed through the temple, the knights were puffing with their exertions carrying the box as they carried on out the double doors to the rear courtyard of the Hospitallers building. With a final grunt of effort, they lowered the Grail Box into the concealed false bottom of a large reinforced double wagon which had been kept in storage in the new stables building in the courtyard, waiting for this day. The wagon had been specially designed to allow the rods to be left fitted into the Grail Box, making it safe to handle. The hatch in the bottom of the wagon was closed and covered with a large piece of hessian cloth concealing it.

The Hospitallers had planned well in advance for this day and harnessed two large, fit and well-rested horses to the wagon as other knights went to a nearby wooden store room, returning with several obviously occupied coffins, going by the smell emanating from them. Now was a time to cover your nose with your hand. Not every pilgrim survived his trip to the Holy Land, but it was usually their assailant who lost his life, and it was these assailants who now occupied the coffins, dressed in the garb of a pilgrim wearing a grey cloak. Rory was impressed as six experienced, proud knights dressed as pilgrims mounted horses and insisted on accompanying him to protect the Grail Box on its journey to the seaport of Acre and to safety. Rory climbed into the wagon, taking charge of it, glad of the company as the party left the Hospitallers courtyard by its double gates into Jerusalem. The city was again under Muslim control, though the pilgrims were still allowed free passage through the narrow streets. They passed the Dome of the Rock and Al-Aqsa Mosque in the fortified city, under the gaze of the devout going to offer up evening prayers as the sun was setting.

They approached the main gates of the city, which was under heavy guard with every person visiting and leaving being interrogated as to his purpose. Rory had been informed by his companions of a graveyard outside the city and of the custom of burying the dead prior to sundown. They were quickly allowed to pass, as the dead in the coffins were rather pungent due to the heat of high summer and the guards examining the coffins all having weak stomachs.

A short journey later, the unknown dead were buried, and Rory was on his way to Acre with the most precious cargo known to mankind!

Acre was currently under the administration of the rich and powerful Knights Hospitallers Military Order. The city had continued to prosper under their control, and it was the major commercial hub of the eastern Mediterranean. The old part of the city, where the port and fortified city were located, protruded from the coastline, exposing both sides of the narrow piece of land to the sea. This could maximise its efficiency as a port, and the narrow entrance to this protrusion served as a natural and easy defence to the city. Acre was of strategic importance and a city through which it was crucial to pass, control, and, as evidenced by the massive walls, protect.

Sultan al-Ashraf Khalil, the ruler of the Mamluk Sultanate military, knew this and was envious of the city, which he desired to conquer and wipe the infidels from the face of the land. He had amassed a formidable army of Mamluks, the most feared and viciously heavily armed force of its time, which was now marching towards it!

CHAPTER 9

Mamluks

Mamluk is the term most commonly used to refer to Muslim slave soldiers and the Muslim rulers of slave origin. Under Saladin and the Ayyubids of Egypt, the power of the Mamluks increased until they claimed the sultanate in AD 1250, ruling as the Mamluk Sultanate military. Slavery continued to be employed throughout the Islamic world until the 19th century. The Ottoman Empire's gathering of young slaves lasted until the 17th century, while Mamluk-based regimes thrived in such Ottoman provinces as the Levant and Egypt until the 19th century. They were trained in the use of various weapons such as the sword, spear, lance, javelin, mace, bow and arrow, and tabarzin or "saddle axe". From a young age, they were indoctrinated in wrestling, and their martial skills were honed, first on foot and then perfected when mounted. They were popularly used as heavy knightly cavalry by a number of different Islamic kingdoms and empires, including the Ayyubid dynasty and the Ottoman Empire.

Rory, accompanied by his six knights, travelled north and east from Jerusalem, keeping to remote roads and tracks to join the main road from Antioch to the sea port of Acre while trying to avoid contact with anyone. He did not want the knowledge of his recovery of the Grail Box to be divulged, especially within the secret orders who had vowed to protect it. Neither did he want them to become aware of his intention to remove it from the Holy Land. An internal battle within the order would ensue with each one wanting control of the Grail Box, and a whole new type of Holy War could begin.

The knights accompanying Rory were loyal and enthusiastic to be involved in this great adventure which was, after all, the reason they had come to the Holy Land in the first place. Each took it in turn to scout the road ahead. They were not the only lookouts in the area as an advance party of 100 mounted Mamluk warriors were coming from the north, preparing the route to Acre for the main Mamluk Sultanate military 10,000-strong army.

Unfortunately for Bruce, they had already reached the main road in front of him as he approached in his wagon, filled with his precious silkworms and exotic goods bound for the west. He turned and tried to outrun the armoured, vicious-looking horsemen in full armour. They made ground quickly as the laden wagon hit a pothole and broke a wheel, tipping on its side. The best Bruce could do was to release his two horses to run for their lives and defend himself from the circling Mamluk horsemen. He had travelled so far and endured so much already, escaping the Mongols, now to face an even more uncaring and unforgiving enemy who took obvious pleasure in terrorising this strange little pigtailed man. The first 10 Mamluks who dismounted and approached him on foot were taken by surprise at his speed and by his rapier-like sword, which easily penetrated their heavy leather armour and detached their heads from their bodies as if they were flowers being deadheaded from a stem. The rest of the advance party of 90 were more cautious after seeing their comrades being so easily defeated. They circled Zhao and the overturned wagon; it was like a scene from a Wild West movie as they planned to charge him from all sides at once!

Rory and the knights saw the circling Mamluk scouting party on the main road in front of them. This was the only route available to them, and turning and running was against their code, especially when Rory saw the image double of Bruce Lee Chan, who was an old friend, standing on the top of his wagon, sword extended and fighting for his life. He urged the horses pulling the cart into a run, right into the middle of the Mamluks. He had three knights on each side as he joined the overturned cart to assist Bruce.

An Egyptian Mamluk warrior, in full armour and pointed helmet with a spike at the top, is a very imposing figure. But 90 of them would put fear into the bravest of men. Common sense said it was suicidal that eight could defeat ninety. All the Mamluks were very heavily armed with a lance, shield, Mamluk curved sword and a pistol worn on an accessory belt on the side of the body. But surprise was on their side, and the Templars were itching for a fight, believing they were invincible on their holy mission as they cut a path through the circling Mamluks. The Templar Knights had not taken a vow not to kill, unlike Rory, but had taken one to give their own lives for the success of their mission; they gave no quarter to their enemy who lay in quarters as a result of the wrath of the knights. The initial surprise attack wiped out a quarter of the Mamluks as the knights engaged the nearest Mamluk in horse-to-horse combat. Rory leapt onto the overturned wagon, calling out to the image of his friend Bruce, in Mandarin, that he was an ally. They began fighting back-to-back as Lee began scything down the Mamluks, attempting to climb atop of it. Rory was determined not to kill anymore but had no issue, in the circumstances, with giving Hans, his sword, permission to disable the attackers. Rory continued to speak to Bruce, warning him of any danger as they fought.

The Mamluks had not expected this extreme resistance, so changed tactics from engaging in open attack to standing back and drawing their single-shot pistols. Rory held Hans in front of him, making use of all of his advanced abilities, as he easily deflected the bullets with his sword back towards the Mamluks. They were beginning to realise they were not fighting an ordinary enemy as this giant man with red hair billowing at his shoulders stood smiling at them, on top of the wagon, with the small pigtailed man guarding his back.

The Mamluks were very superstitious and thought they were facing demons. Stories from their history told of a red-haired demon, and they were convinced they were facing it now. The Mamluk leader looked around at the devastation of his scouting party. Over half were dead and a quarter seriously wounded, with not one of their enemies bearing as much as a scratch. He sounded his horn, ordering his men to withdraw and uplift their wounded. He justified this to himself that it was better to withdraw and warn his advancing army. He needed reinforcements to defeat these demons. If they died, who would be able to report back? The fact that he was scared and had met a foe he could not easily defeat had nothing to do with it!

The six knights harried them as they left, returning after a short time with big smiles on their faces at this momentous victory. They heard Rory and Bruce in deep conversation as they buried the dead Mamluks. The small man was speaking very fast in a language that sounded like bells ringing, asking Rory, "Who is this Bruce that you were calling me?"

It was then Rory realised that he was talking in Mandarin and explained that it was the name of a friend who had taught him his language, which was sort of true.

"I like that name; I will keep it as I am going to the west and need a strong, friendly name," said the now 'Bruce Lee'.

If only he knew!

The knights helped finish burying the dead and filled their empty-looking wagon that concealed the Grail Box with all of the possessions from Bruce's wrecked cart. All watched with great interest at the care Bruce took with the silkworms that had survived the attack. He was treating them like children, being very careful with them. If they knew how valuable they were to make silk and that they would be the first ones to be bred in the west, they would understand the attention he was giving them. Bruce joined Rory in the front seat of the wagon as they resumed the journey to Acre, glad to have someone with whom he could talk. Rory wanted to help him, as his descendants would return the favour to him in the future and began teaching Bruce to speak English, which he knew he was going to need! The conversation between Rory and Bruce became more personal during the journey as Rory gained Bruce's confidence and trust. Bruce told him he had been rescued as a seven-year-old child by the mysterious Shaolin monks as he was clinging unconscious to his guardian in a river, and they had educated him. He had been incredibly lucky to be rescued, and Rory wondered if this was just luck or if he should go and make sure this happened after he had saved the Grail Box?

Bruce explained that he was the last descendant of the Song Dynasty, which was wiped out by the Mongol Empire that had taken control of China. He kept secret the fact that he was the Song Emperor! This resonated with Rory, who had lost his father at that age, but he still had his mother's love. Bruce had grown up without any family or relatives and been educated by strangers with the only motivation in his life to strive to work hard and please them. He had no compassion for anyone wishing to do him harm, albeit he had very good self-control. His survival instinct was very strong, and this explained the clinical way he had despatched the Mamluks who were attacking him. He was the last of his kind and was driven to survive to continue his bloodline. Rory understood Bruce: he took no pleasure in killing, unlike his sword, Hans, but he would not hesitate to kill to save himself and would feel no remorse for killing. If it was the decision of his assailants to attack him, they would soon discover that they had picked on the wrong person if they thought he was a weak, easy target.

It was their own fault if they were bullies with a death wish!

Only 10 fit, surviving Mamluk warriors led by the scout leader limped into the main camp of the 10,000-strong Mamluk Sultanate military camp with 20 injured soldiers draped across their horses. They did not know that they were seen by Sultan al-Ashraf Khalil, who was standing at his command tent watching their return from his elevated position on a small hill. They were very brave or foolish to return to the camp, as defeat was not an option unless one died in an attempt to win. Either way, death was inescapable. It was known as a suicide army!

The walking members of the scouting party were quickly summoned to the Sultan and related the story of the red-haired demon and his pet ponytailed man. Sultan al-Ashraf Khalil had also heard stories of this red-haired demon before, who had appeared at all of the famous battles in the past when the Muslim armies suffered their biggest defeats. The other man was a new adversary, and his description was very strange: with his yellow skin, strange narrow eyes, bald head and a long ponytail. These were the main targets of his army. He would make sure his generals made them the focus of any attack. He ordered the camp to break. Two persons, even if they were demons, would not survive an attack by his entire army. He would have them dead before they reached the safety of Acre. He would be generous to the returning soldiers and let them live to fight again, at the very front of his army and against the Red Devil!

CHAPTER 10

Acre 1291

Following the failure of the Crusade by Richard the Lionheart to retake Jerusalem and regain total control of the Holy Land, the Templars were forced to relocate their headquarters to other cities in the north, such as the seaport of Acre, which they held for the next century despite many attempts to dislodge them.

German merchants from Lübeck and Bremen had founded a field hospital in Acre, which became the nucleus of the chivalric Teutonic Order where they resided, along with the closely-connected Templars and Hospitallers. It was the home to many Christian and minor orders, with many languages spoken within the fortified walls.

This was now the time of the Sixth Crusade, and the city was placed under the administration of the very rich and powerful Hospitallers Military Order. It was known to some that it had a secret order hidden within it, called the Knights of St John. It was rumoured among the other orders that this sub-order had beaten all of its adversaries and discovered the site of King Solomon's Temple in Jerusalem. It was whispered that this was where the Hospitallers had obtained their unbelievable wealth, which they had been known to possess for the last 100 years. They had a powerful presence in the city, and it was suspected by the other orders that this wealth had come from the hidden treasure of King Solomon, and they wanted a part of it.

Many from the other orders wanted to enter this secret order but had to prove their worth first. Only by strict examination and by being vouched for by two existing members of the Knights of the Temple and following an additional degree and oath of allegiance to this high order and conclave of knights was a new initiate admitted to find out the truth!

Acre continued to prosper as a major commercial hub of the eastern Mediterranean, but also underwent turbulent times due to the bitter infighting among the less enlightened Crusader factions, desperate to find out the location of the Grail Box. This occasionally resulted in civil wars between them. It was true that the Hospitallers knew what had happened to it and, unless you were one of them, you would never find out. Most knights respected their own secrets, which had to be earned; convincing proofs were required before a stranger was admitted to their individual meetings. Usually, the highest-ranking members could progress to the next level of understanding, but not always, and ignorance could cause a great deal of trouble.

The old part of the city, where the large seaport and fortified city were located, protruded from the coastline, exposing both sides of the narrow piece of land to the sea. This could maximise its efficiency as a port, and the narrow entrance to this protrusion served as a natural and easy defence to the city. Separate gates had been built into the high fortified stone city walls, guarded by the Crusader order or nationality in charge of that part of the city, with the Hospitallers, Templars and Teutonic orders all having their own private access. Several warning towers were situated along the length of the wall, which were constantly manned, giving extra protection to the city and early warning of any approaching enemy. (See Image 3.) Both the archaeological record and historic Crusader texts emphasised Acre's strategic importance. This was a city through which it was crucial to pass, control, and, as evidenced by the massive walls reaching to the sky in front of Rory, to protect!

Rory and Bruce sat in the wagon, flanked on each side by three Hospitallers Knights, now proudly attired, displaying the Red Cross tabard of St John, their cloaks discarded in the rear of the cart. Rory, too, discarded his grey cloak, displaying his tabard, below which his powerful frame was accentuated by his red shoulder-length hair, which billowed in the sea breeze coming from the nearby coast at Acre. Good time had been made on the road, travelling from early in the morning to avoid the heat of the day, and all were glad of this cool coastal breeze as noon approached. They were about half a mile from Acre and could see the high fortified walls and protective towers in front of them. It was then that the alarm sounded from the nearest tower of King Hugh, which overlooked the road. Rory gave Bruce the reins and stood and turned, looking behind the wagon. A dust cloud was rapidly advancing on them. Rory used his enhanced eyesight to look through the heat haze towards it.

This was no storm!

The dust was thrown up by a line of 1,000 Mamluks driving their horses on in the heat with no consideration for their health, as some fell from their exertions. They were determined to stop the Red Devil before he reached the safety of Acre, and at the current speed they were advancing, they would!

Rory took charge of the reins, urging the two horses onto a full gallop, picking the straightest, smoothest route to Acre and avoiding any potholes to ensure the safety of the cargo he was carrying. Several alarm bells were ringing in Acre now as knights manned the walls, armed with longbows to protect the rear of the approaching wagon and knights under attack. The gate to the Hospitallers section of the city in front of them was open as Rory skirted the edge of the Tower of King Hugh the 1st of Jerusalem, the Tower of the English and the Tower of the Countess of Blois. (* See Appendix.)

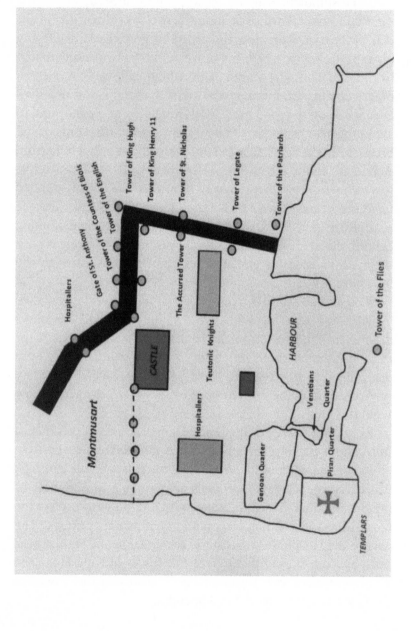

Montmusart

Hospitallers

Gate of St. Anthony
Tower of the Countess of Blois
Tower of the English
Tower of King Hugh
Tower of King Henry 11
Tower of St. Nicholas
Tower of Legate
Tower of the Patriarch

CASTLE

The Accursed Tower

Teutonic Knights

Hospitallers

HARBOUR

Genoan Quarter

Venetians
Quarter

Pisan Quarter

TEMPLARS

Tower of the Flies

The Mamluks were upon them as arrows rained down from the towers, manned by Crusader Knights, including a large troop of Hospitallers who had recognised the cross on their brothers' tabards. Rory passed the nearest entrance to the city at the Gate of St Anthony, the patron saint of the lost and found. It closed in front of him, preventing a safe and quick entrance to the city. This gate was not under the Crusader's control. When the dust settled, those who shut it would feel the wrath of the Hospitallers. They cried out from the battlements above at the lack of aid given by the order of St Anthony to their comrades. This gate would be lost to the cowards of the Latin quarter who refused to fight. It would be a long time before they would be found trustworthy again! The front line of the Mamluk horsemen was level with the rear of the wagon now as Rory urged the horses on towards the nearest gate under the control of the Hospitallers. Bruce jumped from his seat next to Rory, positioning himself in the middle of the wagon to protect Rory's back and also his precious silkworms.

The six knights continued to protect the wagon, three on each side, with swords extended, fending off strikes from the nearest Mamluks who reached them. Bruce was doing a fantastic job in the rear and was incredibly light and agile on his feet. As the cart bounced and rattled over the rough terrain, a Mamluk jumped from his horse into the wagon and promptly fell off again, dead. The huge double gates remained open in front of them as Rory raced at full speed into the city, surrounded by 50 Mamluk horsemen, including the 10 survivors from his first encounter when he had rescued Bruce. The gates closed behind him as the full force of waiting knights within ended the Mamluks' time on earth!

The rest of the vanguard of Mamluks outside the walls were being slowly slaughtered by the longbow archers firing on them from the battlements. They turned their exhausted horses and retreated to a safe distance, out of reach of the arrows. After a brief rest, they separated into groups, securing all the roads leading to Acre. This cut off all the supply lines to the city, and, by the time their leader Sultan al-Ashraf Khalil arrived with his full force, he found Acre under siege. He was pleased, but disappointed that the Red Devil, with his unholy power, had escaped. However, the sultan was satisfied that the Red Devil was going nowhere but the grave. He instructed his engineers to start the construction of the siege engines. He was not going to wait until they ran out of food and water. The walls protecting them were going to be pulled down! He would have the glory of destroying them all before the Saracens under Melik de Serif arrived, thus denying him this prize!

The six Hospitallers Knights guarding Rory and the wagon had fought bravely, sustaining only minor flesh wounds (Refer to *Monty Python and the Holy Grail*) and were warmly greeted by their brothers, some of whom they obviously knew. Secret handshakes and cool ale were being exchanged as they were vouched for to all in the vicinity.

The presence of Rory and Bruce was causing some excitement. This continued to increase as the whispering spread among the guards accompanying Rory and the surrounding brothers, who stared and pointed at Rory. The fighting skills of the little man with his strange hair and sword were also a talking point. Gossip had been slow lately after a long period of peace and inaction for the knights who had become bored. But all of that had changed. The crowd around the wagon parted as a senior knight approached Rory stating, "The Maréchal wants to see you."

Rory could tell by the tone of his voice that this was not a request as he was surrounded on all sides by knights who ushered him towards the high stone fortress of a building in front of him. It was very similar to the one he had visited in Jerusalem but with narrower and more easily defendable corridors that doubled back on themselves. It was a maze of a building and not one that anyone would be able to leave in a hurry.

He instructed Bruce, in Mandarin, to stay with the wagon, much to the surprise of the surrounding knights on hearing this strange language, except for his own six, who laughed and said they would stay as well. They had been paying attention on the journey!

Rory passed through the labyrinth until he came to a heavy wooden closed door which the guide opened, ushering Rory into the sparse functional stone room while shutting it behind him.

The Maréchal Matthieu de Clermont, the head of the Hospitallers, was standing inside with his right side facing towards the door.

He was of average height, about 5ft 10inch, medium build, dressed in breeches and the normal red cross tabard of the order. He had the short greying black hair of a mid-fifties man and turning to face Rory, his appearance took him by surprise. His left eye was missing and covered by an eye patch; he also sported a large scar from his temple down his left cheek. It was then that Rory noticed that his left hand was also missing, replaced with a large shiny metal hook. (Visualise Long John Silver without the peg leg, and you would not be far off!) He gave a crooked smile, obviously accustomed to this reaction, using his appearance to put strangers off-guard as he asked Rory to show him the sign.

Rory remembered this one and stifled a smile as he put his right hand over his nose and mouth. He spoke in French to the Maréchal, saying, "I hope this is what you want, but I have other proof," as he mentally compelled Hans, his sword, to his hands. In a blink of the eye, it flew out of the holder strapped to his back, into his hands and, in a fluid motion, Rory embedded his sword up to its hilt in the stone floor in front of the Maréchal.

It was the Maréchal's turn to look surprised as he exclaimed, "It's true!"

A long discussion then took place, and fortunately for Rory, the Maréchal was also the current Grand Master of the

Knights Templar Order in the city. They were renowned as an order of seafarers and explorers as well as famed warriors. Since the disappearance of the Grail Box, they had travelled the seven seas, sailing in search of it under their black flag, showing the emblems of eternal life, the skull and crossed bones. It is strange how stories get distorted, and everyone mistakes them for pirates led by Long John Silver!

They had made great discoveries and obtained great wealth but had not found the treasure they were seeking until now. If only they had possessed a map with a cross on it!

The pride of the fleet of Templar ships, Maréchal's ship, the flagship *Eternity*, the largest three-masted galley ever constructed, was berthed at the main pier at the sea gate. It was well-armed with catapults on its decks to disable the masts of attacking ships with large rocks, and if the hulls were hit, they were more than capable of sinking them. It had just been re-supplied and was ready for the sea.

Rory was encouraged and accepted the hospitality of his host on behalf of himself and his companions as he withdrew Hans with a hiss from the floor. He could see the Maréchal's questioning look and slid his sword back into the groove on the floor. Everyone wanted to try and pull it from the ground, and the Maréchal was no exception. Rory stood back and, with a nod of his head and a wave of his hand, gave permission for him to have a go. Maréchal pulled on the hilt with his right hand until he was red in the face and even tried pulling on it with his hook, all to no effect.

He conceded defeat as Rory put his right hand above his sword without touching it. Similar to a piece of metal being pulled by a magnet, it rose out of the ground into his hand. Rory laughed to himself as he saw the look on the Maréchal's face at this magic; he had easily won this game of who could most surprise the other!

CHAPTER 11

Flee

Mamluk Sultan al-Ashraf Khalil's wish for glory was not fulfilled even as his huge siege engines were completed and readied for action. The massive catapults were an early version of a trebuchet, capable of throwing car-sized boulders over hundreds of metres through 270 degrees from a net at the end of a long wooden arm with the use of a heavy counterweight.

The Saracens, under Melik de Serif, were arriving and obscured the horizon behind him, making the Mamluks force of 10,000 appear like just one of the regiments of the Saracens' 100,000-strong army. Their sheer numbers could, with body pressure alone (if it could be applied), be capable of toppling the walls of Acre. But the bigger the force, the bigger the problems. They all had to be fed and watered, and that meant a massive amount of supplies, making the advance very slow. Mamluk Sultan al-Ashraf Khalil still had time to attack before the Saracens arrived!

Rory joined Maréchal on the Tower of King Hugh. Even without Rory's augmented eyesight, the Maréchal could see that it was a hopeless cause to stay in Acre. No matter how bravely the forces within fought, they would eventually be swamped by the sheer numbers of foes. He ordered the discreet removal of all valuables from the city to the seven Templar ships in port with specific instructions that the wagon and possessions of Bruce, which included the concealed Grail Box, were to be stored on his flagship *Eternity*.

Maréchal knew the mindset of the population, many of whom would fight until they were killed and would never accept defeat; they preferred death to dishonour. In this respect, both forces were very similar. Those sensible enough to leave and loyal to the order had to be identified; they had to escape to rebuild and start again.

Maréchal knew they would be called cowards by the remainers, who would die rather than leave, but the Grail Box must be saved!

The Mamluks pulled several catapults into striking distance and well out of arrow range from the longbows situated on the city battlements, unleashing a shower of boulders which rained down on the city walls. No construction could withstand this destructive force as the walls crumbled under the onslaught as if hit by a modern steel demolisher's ball. The walls fell like wooden sticks piled high in a children's game after the bottom one was removed.

The city organised its defences to repel the ground troops that soon would be pouring through the holes in the fortifications.

Time was running out as Rory, Bruce and the Templars, along with the Hospitallers loyal to the Maréchal, hurriedly evacuated the city, escaping to the flagship *Eternity* and the six smaller galleys in the dock moored at the sea gate; there were plenty willing to leave but not enough room for all. Only the crying women and children were taken, pulled apart from their husbands and elderly relatives who were left behind to die. Space was limited on board the ships, and soon they were all squeezed below deck like sardines in a tin.

The city walls were reduced to rubble as the full force of Saracens arrived in time to see the ground troops of the Mamluks launch a full-frontal assault on Acre. The Saracens did not want to be excluded from the spoils of war. Wishing to rid their land of these Crusaders infesting it, they joined the attack.

The combined forces of Mamluk and Saracens poured over the walls like water, and it looked like an ant hill had been poked with a stick as they swarmed into the city. The defenders fought bravely, fighting from street to street, but the opposition's numbers were just too great as they were surrounded and slaughtered where they stood. Their dead bodies were trampled on as the marauders pushed onwards towards the closed water gate leading to the docks.

Rory felt sick to the bottom of his stomach, but he was helpless and unable to assist or change the course of events unfolding around him. His enhanced senses shrieked in revulsion as he listened to the screams from the city, witnessing this atrocity; the population were being mutilated, abused and eventually killed before his closed eyes. It seemed to Rory to take an eternity for the ship to cast off from the pier to the relative safety of the sea. His soul was being tortured as his mind visualised each act of violence that matched every scream he heard as he was driven to despair with his incapability to help the innocent. Mamluk Sultan al-Ashraf Khalil and Saracen Melik de Serif showed no mercy to the occupants of the city; they massacred all 60,000 inhabitants, including all the women and children.

The days of the Crusaders in the Holy Land were over.

Evil had won!

* * *

Following his attack on Rory with the giant hailstones at Jerusalem, red-robed Evil Stan stood in the middle of the pentagram in the cottage of the Grant Witch. The full force of the living bacterial alien evil within Hans the Sword recoiled into him as the Grant Witch was flown out of the pentagram. It was as if she had been pushed by an invisible hand, as the evil emanating from the sword focused all its malevolence solely on John Grant. When he adorned himself with the red robe, the ancient evil within it had instantly consumed him. It greeted the additional evil transferred from Hans the Sword like an old lost friend, merging with it like a long-lost lover.

It was one, reunited at last after centuries apart. Stan stood with his head bent backwards, his arms outstretched as his body convulsed; every molecule of him was possessed. Black tattoo-like marks, in the shape of pentagrams, appeared on the palms of his hands and on the soles of his feet. John Grant was eradicated from existence, and the human-shaped husk known as Evil Stan stood in the pentagram in his place.

Unlimited power soared through his body, transforming him into an inhuman being. The magic the Grant Witch had trained him to use was like that of a children's entertainer compared to the power he now had. He had access to the eyes of the world's most evil creatures and could connect to them at will. They were his to command as he watched Rory through those of a great white shark circling the bay of Acre's harbour.

He could see what the shark saw as Rory fled Acre on the galleon *Eternity*, and he took great joy from all the evil occurring in the city. He fed on it like a vampire feeding on blood. He gorged himself, growing stronger with every single futile death of the 60,000 lives being lost, taking extra pleasure from and absorbing the souls of the innocent children. His senses went into overload, experiencing an out-of-body transference, leaving the body of the shark as his power grew. He could feel and see outside of this physical link which was just a connection to this point in time and place.

He invisibly looked down on the flagship *Eternity* and could see the power of the great enemy pulsing in the hold of the ship. Evil Stan instinctively knew that he no longer needed to wait for the power of the solstice to travel and attack. He had an enhanced chilling intelligence and ancient knowledge within him now, having the patience and willingness to wait for the right moment to cause the most despair to his prey and the most enjoyment to himself. He was like a cat tormenting a mouse, and his mouse was Rory!

He was comprised now of pure evil; he was not 'Stan the Man' anymore.

All humanity within him was gone. His true nature was revealed, and back to full power.

It had a name: 'Satan'!

* * *

The seven Templar war galleys sailed away from Acre, their main decks and holds full of the refugees from the city and every valuable that could be carried. Bruce had seen barbarity, but even he was shocked at the lack of humanity shown by this enemy to the innocent and vulnerable. He resolved to help the Knights Templar with his knowledge of gunpowder and cannon construction to replace the inaccurate catapults on their ships.

Unknown to him, this would create a new era for them, creating the most powerful naval power in the Mediterranean, which would be used to attack Muslim ships. History records no Christian ship was ever attacked by the Templars as they sailed under their black flag displaying the white skull and crossed bones, their symbol of eternity!

In a short time, in AD 1307, the Knights Templar Order would be falsely accused of crimes by Pope Clement V and King Philip IV of France and be officially disbanded by them in AD 1312, and their wealth would be split between them and the Order of the Knights of St John. If only they knew how involved they were with each other, the Templars would survive. They would soon be known as pirates but would live on through the Order of St John, and it is reported that they continue to survive, in secret, even to this present day!

* * *

Rory still felt sad as he stood with Maréchal Matthieu de Clermont on the bridge of the *Eternity* as the fleet sailed towards Cyprus, into the fortified harbour and the Knights Templar-controlled Castle Kyrenia, which towered over the port. (* See Appendix.) The bedraggled refugees from Acre disembarked to the relative safety of Cyprus as Rory discussed his future plans with Maréchal and Bruce.

After much debate, it was decided that Bruce would remain with the Knights Templar in Cyprus to upgrade their weapons on the promise of free transport on the first ship returning to the British Isles. Rory had a very detailed conversation with Bruce in Mandarin, explaining his destiny in Scotland and, more importantly, with the MacDonald Clan in Dunscaith Castle on the Isle of Skye. Bruce promised to go to Scotland, taking his silkworms and knowledge with him, as a payment for his life to help Rory's people. He was totally unaware that his future wife would be waiting for him, and a whole new dynasty would start that would cause ripples through time, connecting again with Rory. Bruce left to unload his possessions, including his precious silkworms, from the ship as Rory asked Maréchal for a very big favour. He wanted his ship *Eternity*, which he promised he would return to the Knights of St John and Hospitallers in 274 years. The Maréchal was confused, but he knew what was at stake: the safety of the Grail Box.

As with all the Grand Masters Rory had met, Maréchal promised to aid the Pure One and safeguard the Grail Box, which was the purpose of his order.

Rory explained to Maréchal that he knew from his history what the future was for the Templars, but this must be kept secret to guide their path. This revelation confirmed to him how special Rory was, and he listened intently, memorising Rory's every word as he spoke.

Rory stated that the occupation of Cyprus by the knights would be short-lived, and they must relocate in a few years in AD 1310 to Rhodes, where they would rule until AD 1522 and then be forced again to move before settling in the Island of Malta in AD 1530. The island would be given to them by the Holy Roman Emperor Charles V of Spain on condition that they protect it from the Moorish Rovers for the payment of a single Falcon each year. And so, the story of the Maltese Falcon was born.

Rory explained that a great enemy was after the Grail Box, and he had memorised a special book called the *Book of St Columba* that told him what to do, and he was creating a false trail to hide its location.

Maréchal looked at Rory in awe at this revelation as he began to comprehend the reality of the situation he was dealing with and the position and responsibility the Order of St John had to protect the holy treasure. He agreed to Rory's request and asked if there was anything else that he could do. A big smile spread across Rory's face as he whispered a message to him to be passed down to his successors in 274 years to assist him!

CHAPTER 12

The Ghost Ship

The *Eternity* was the newest, fastest, sleekest galley of its day that was owned by the Templars. It had two masts, one at the front for the forward triangular sail and a large central one to hold the main triangular sail. Flags identifying the ship were flown from the top of both masts, at the front of the ship and at the rear on top of the beam holding the mainsail. A large central deck was located behind the main mast, stretching back to a raised viewing platform from which the rudder was controlled. From the central mast forward was the enclosed living quarters and galley where the food was prepared, and the stores were kept below deck.

Double doors gave access to a large storeroom on the same level as the main deck. This was where Rory went to check on the safety of the Grail Box, which was still concealed within the hidden compartment in the reinforced wagon. It looked empty now since Bruce had removed his possessions, with a ground sheet the only obvious thing on it, covering the wooden boards. The ship was quiet and empty now as it creaked, moving gently in the harbour. All the crew and passengers had left on shore leave and, in the case of the refugees, to start a new life.

Rory pulled back the covering sacking and opened the concealed rear hatch and doors in the floor, causing it to fold down the hinged sides, revealing the Grail Box within. The staff of Moses and the shorter rod of Aaron were still inserted in the oblong box, creating points to carry it at the front and rear and making it safe to touch. Rory carefully removed them, laying them next to the box and reassembled the wagon, making it look like an empty one again. Rory did not want the box to be safe to touch in case he failed in his task as he left the storeroom and secured the double doors.

It was a still spring night with a clear moonless sky lit by a myriad of bright stars not affected by modern light pollution as Rory carried out a final check of the *Eternity*, making sure he was the only one aboard. He checked that the forward rope that should have held the anchor was long enough and tied it in a large loop. He needed a friend's help to achieve his plan as he cast off from the pier, letting the ship drift out on the outward tide away from the harbour.

The city was asleep, and those guards on duty had been hand-picked by the Maréchal to turn a blind eye to his ship's departure. Rory stood at the front of the *Eternity*, above the place where its name was written in gold on either side of the hull and blew his Hagpipe. The air shimmered in front of him as it vibrated to a primordial squeal, as it travelled through time and place as Rory mentally called out, searching for Nessie.

She had been enjoying her holiday and grown to become the largest sea creature in history, even bigger than the blue whale, as she soaked up the sun and warm waters of the Mediterranean. Nessie had been snacking on a variety of fish that were new to her and very tasty. The Hagpipe transmitted through every point in time and to every natural portal on the ley lines created on the dawn of creation and connected by the living magma of the planet. The nearest portal in her current time was at the Azure Window (see image 5) on the Island of Gozo near Malta. It illuminated with a transparent shimmer as the call she had been waiting on emitted from it.

Nessie heard the summons and responded immediately. She turned, swimming at full speed with a huge sharp-toothed smile on her face, pleased to be at last reunited with her master and friend, hurrying with expectation towards the location of the call.

The window continued to shimmer as she swam through it and out the other end into the same Mediterranean water and time period as Rory. The call ceased on being answered, and all the portals switched off. Time is a strange thing and the call self-adjusted to allow for the journey from the portal to Rory's location. The happy face of Nessie popped out of the water next to him practically instantaneously.

Rory was as pleased to see Nessie as she was to see him. He mentally communicated with her and reached down to tickle her behind her antenna, on her rubbery grey/blue head. It was a joyful reunion as they exchanged stories of the events that had happened since they had last met.

Rory communicated to Nessie that he wanted to go to Melita, the ancient name for Malta, and Nessie replied that she knew the way as Rory dropped the rope into the sea. This was an old trick; Nessie had been doing this since she was a baby in the cavern below Urquhart Castle when she towed Rory in a rowing boat. She slipped her head through the large rope loop to pull the *Eternity*. The ship was a great deal larger than a rowing boat and more than twice the size of the *Stag*, the birlinn, that he had previously towed to rescue Rory's father. (* See Appendix.)

Nessie was fully grown now, in her prime and as large as the ship she was pulling. She was confident she could do this without Rory's help as he spread his feet on the deck and took hold of the Hagpipe in his left hand. His feet seemed to take root into the wooden boards of the deck as he willed the power of the Hagpipe to life, passing through his body and legs to his feet and into the *Eternity*. It continued to travel along the anchor rope to Nessie's neck and into her body, imbuing her with its power. Nessie telepathically spoke to Rory, thanking him as she felt the increase in power surging through her with its intoxicating effect. She smoothly took control of the *Eternity*, pulling it as easily as a child pulled a toy on a piece of string.

Rory was aware of the whole ship as his enhanced abilities sparked to their full potential, feeling that he was part of the ship, totally aware of his surroundings in every detail, even feeling the location and the exact number of rats on board. There was something else feeding off the Hagpipe, and it was alive, wakening up as it drew on the power from it. The Grail Box was beginning to glow like a beacon, extending its own power to join with the Hagpipe. Rory did not know what would happen when the greatest power known to mankind connected with his pagan power, and he mentally pulled his power away from the hold, isolating this area from the Hagpipe's influence until he felt the Grail Box subdue and go back to sleep. *That was close*, Rory thought, *Who knows what would happen? The rods of Aaron and Moses have been removed; they made it safe. If the Grail Box was touched, I know from personal experience that whoever touched it would be transported to the next life!*

The activation of the Grail Box had not gone unnoticed as Satanic Stan felt a shiver run down his back as if his grave, if he could ever have one now, had been disturbed. The Grail Box was the road to the only power that could challenge him, and action was needed. Rory was on the move, and it was now the time to finish him off once and for all!

Satanic Stan had friends in the warm waters of the Mediterranean Sea, and he called to them. The greatest danger to humankind responded, and man was just a quick snack to them. Twenty responded to his call, and although normally solitary hunters, they were in a frenzy now. Great white sharks (see *Jaws*) with the blackest soulless eyes that drew one into their abyss. He directed them to intercept the *Eternity* on its route and when the time was right. Attack!

The weather was kind as the *Eternity* was pulled along at a fast pace by Nessie, creating a wave behind it like that produced by a modern jet ski or speedboat as Rory left Cyprus. He sped towards the shallow waters around the Island of Rhodes and past the northern coast of the Isle of

Crete. The Greek mainland passed on his left as he entered the deep waters and the largest open stretch of the Mediterranean Sea, on a straight line towards the Italian mainland and the islands of Sicily, Gozo and Malta.

It was then disaster struck!

Nessie slowed to a stop, mentally calling out to Rory as she sensed a great danger ahead. Rory used his enhanced eyesight, looking at the sea in front of the ship, which appeared to be boiling. The frenzy of 20 great white sharks feeding on a pod of dolphins which had crossed their path. The sea was red as the sharks, sated in a blood lust, easily massacred the dolphins and suddenly stopped. The water went still and calm as the huge sharks, each about half the size of Nessie, spotted the prey that they were waiting for and began swimming at full speed towards it.

Rory was powerless to help and mentally instructed Nessie to flee. There was no way she would survive an attack by 20 of these killing machines of muscle, fin and teeth!

Nessie slipped out of the rope noose and dived deep down into the black water to depths that even these predators could not reach. The sharks were furious at the escape of their prey and took their frustrations and anger out on the *Eternity*, biting at the hull and ramming it, causing the ship to shudder.

Rory was unable to do anything to repel this attack as the sharks circled the *Eternity* repeatedly, ripping wooden panels from it like twigs pulled from a tree and battering it, cracking and denting the wooden hull, pushing it inwards, causing water to leak into the ship. The *Eternity* was not designed to withstand an attack of this kind, and it was just a matter of time until the ship would sink, leaving Rory to be torn to pieces by the sharks and the Grail Box lost at the bottom of the sea!

He rushed below deck to the inside of the hull which was filling with water by the breaks in the wood, which were multiplied after every new impact; it gushed into the hold in spurts like those seen in a modern strong shower jet. Rory quickly found the ship's carpenter's tools and spare boards and moved in a blur of super-speed, running around reinforcing and repairing each newly damaged area on the ship. The banging noises from the shark blows echoed around the hull. Rory was rapidly running out of boards and nails as he kept pace with each new break to the hull, but he knew he could not keep this up forever and could not continue repairs for much longer!

Nessie could feel the frustration Rory was experiencing and knew she had to help. The sharks had lost interest in her and were totally focused on sinking the *Eternity*. She understood sharks and their weaknesses but had only encountered one of this size before when it was alone. There is only one way to kill a shark. She would have to be careful and not face them head-on as she surfaced behind the outermost of the circling sharks.

The boards were finished, as was any furniture in the hold, which was now nailed to the hull. Rory could do no more as he made his way back up to the deck and drew Hans his sword, determined to die fighting the sharks. His thoughts were drifting to his beloved Heather back home and his loved ones as he realised he had failed in his task. He barely noticed that the banging on the hull had stopped!

Do you know how to drown a shark no matter how big it is? Nessie did as she grabbed the first one by its tail and pulled it backwards through the water. Sharks can only breathe if they keep swimming forwards, and they never sleep or stop moving. The two sides of its brain constantly swap control of the body as one side rests. They do not have a swim bladder like fish and cannot float. But they do drown very easily if you are big enough and brave enough to pull them backwards. The first 10 sharks were totally unaware of Nessie behind them as they sunk dead to the bottom of the sea. The next 10 were still focused on sinking the ship driven on by the evil force directing them. Satanic Stan could only see the imminent destruction of the ship and success over Rory at last. By the time the last shark felt Nessie take hold of its tail, it was too late as Satanic Stan became aware that his shark army had failed.

The *Eternity* was in poor condition but still afloat as Rory dumped anything heavy and nonessential overboard to raise the ship up out of water that was flowing in from some very large holes in its sides.

The heavy catapults and rocks were the first to go as he rushed around the deck, easily throwing them into the sea. Soon the *Eternity* had a new lease of life and was once again stable in the water. Nessie popped her head up out of the sea next to Rory with her big toothy smile to receive his congratulations, but they were short-lived. Rory felt it before he saw it; the Hagpipe vibrated like an alarm next to his chest.

The sky behind him was growing black, building up into the storm of all storms, beginning to twist first into a waterspout, pulling water up from the sea to the sky and then transforming into a tornado. Even if the *Eternity* had been undamaged, it could not survive a strike from this tornado. Like Dorothy's house in *The Wizard of Oz*, it would be lifted but smashed into the sea. In its current state, even a large wave would sink the ship.

Both Nessie and Rory saw the danger at the same time, and the only chance they had was to try and outrun it. Nessie put her neck through the noose as Rory took hold of the Hagpipe, transferring all of its power into Nessie. She took off like a rocket, lifting the front of the *Eternity* so far up out of the sea that water ran out of it from the gaps in the sides. They were moving fast but so was the unearthly tornado, willed into existence by the satanic evil power of Stan. Two white lightning eyes lit its top with a jagged forked-lightning mouth, shaped in a snarl at the bottom as it pursued the *Eternity*.

Two bolts of lightning spewed from the tornado's mouth, striking and shattering first the middle mast, and then the front mast as Rory dodged out of its way and it fell into the sea. Missing the weight of the masts, the ship sped up, putting a short distance between it and the tornado. The next strike would sink them. Rory looked forward to where Nessie was frantically towing the remaining wreck of a ship. He saw it, raised the Hagpipe to his mouth and blew!

It was the Azure Window!

The huge half-circular hole was situated in a jutting stone outcrop stretching out from the Island of Gozo into the sea and one of the oldest portals on the planet. It illuminated in white light as the air shimmered with primaeval power unleashed by the Hagpipe.

Nessie raced into it, pulling the *Eternity* with her, and they vanished to safety as the light of the portal went out.

The tornado hit the window with its full force of evil, dissipating itself through random timelines, finishing its journey in 2017. The portal's entrance went black, and the rock shelf so enjoyed by tourists to walk over and widely photographed exploded, collapsing into the sea. History would record this event and the destruction of the Azure Window, which would never be seen again!

Rory and Nessie emerged through the window and into their own time zone in March of 1565, and a very foggy morning sea. Nessie towed the ghost ship *Eternity* with its black flag and skull and crossbones still flying on its rear deck into the Grand Harbour of Valletta in Malta, where Nessie released it to drift.

Rory thanked her for her help and instructed her to return home, knowing somehow he would not be needing her aid again. As she departed, the alarm bells began to ring from the surrounding harbour watchtowers to the loud cries of 'Plague'!

CHAPTER 13

Melita

Rory took hold of his Hagpipe; he knew that he could not be found on the ship. He was unsure if the message that he had left with the Maréchal in the past would have made its journey 274 years forwards in time to aid him here. He knew now how to control time, just as he had controlled it in his personal past when he hid the haggis graveyard in Urquhart Castle, he used the power of the Hagpipe to hide himself. Rory willed himself out of synchronisation with real time and put himself three seconds into the future.

As the well-armed flotilla of small boats approached the *Eternity*, he vanished from sight, watching them like a ghost from the rear deck as the city guardians boarded the ship; they moved to Rory's eyes as if played back in slow motion on a film.

The Grand Harbour was huge with very deep water and many side channels giving it multiple natural harbours. It was the main reason the Knights of St John, the ultimate order incorporating the Knights Templar and Hospitallers created by St John and Rory, had taken possession of Malta due to its strategic location in the Mediterranean. The Knights of St John adopted another name at this time, being known locally as the Knights of Malta, where all of the sub-orders were united under the control of the most powerful and greatest Grand Master in their history, 'Jean Parisot De Valette'. He was so famous that the fortified city being built on this very spot would be named after him and called 'Valletta'.

A brisk north-easterly breeze began to blow as the Hospitallers Knights, who were in charge of quarantine enforcement of the port and island, boarded the *Eternity*. No ship was allowed to disembark passengers, crew or goods before being granted permission by the port sanitary authorities following various recent outbreaks of influenza, smallpox, cholera and the Black Death. Any ship showing any sign of infection was to be isolated and set fire to at sea and sunk. The *Eternity* was deserted and it was flying the black flag with the skull and crossbones which the Hospitallers had been warned to watch for. They had been ordered by the Grand Master to isolate any ship displaying it.

The sky was clearing rapidly as the sun burnt off the fog, which was being blown away and dispersed. Rory noticed the *Eternity* was sitting in the middle of the entrance to the Grand Harbour with the huge yellow limestone fort of St Elmo guarding it. Rory's enhanced eyesight noticed its cannons were trained on the *Eternity*, ready to blow it out of the water. Further along the harbour was the equally impressive Fort St. Angelo, which was protecting the bustling town of Birgu with its fine buildings and thriving shipyard, which the knights had picked as their main residence. The whole harbour was a hive of excitement as fortifications were being erected at a frantic pace. It did not take a genius like Rory to comprehend that they were preparing for war!

The harbour had three main peninsulas jutting into it with their own shipyards and ports which were full to overflowing with warships. The largest of these dwarfed the other ships with one of the same designs in each of the three ports. They were the Great Carracks: The *San Giovanni*, the *Santa Anna* and the *Santa Maria*. They were all three-masted floored ships about 60 metres long which could carry 2,500 tons of grain besides other cargo, with a crew of 300 sailors and 500 soldiers. However, in a time of war, they could carry up to 1,000. Included in the crew were a live-in carpenter, a caulker, a cooper and three blacksmiths. The carracks were self-sufficient with their own flour mills capable of producing 476kg of flour daily, baking their own bread in the ships' ovens, and could stay at sea for six months at a time. They were well-armed with lethal, accurate cannons, and it was obvious to Rory that Bruce had kept his promise to the knights to assist them! He would be dead now, and Rory hoped that he had made it to Scotland to start his family. Once he had the Grail Box safe, he would find out if his history was fulfilled.

The *Santa Maria* was the nearest carrack to Rory, berthed opposite Fort St Elmo. Rory did not hear the explosion that erupted in front of him in slow motion as sound did not travel forward in time, but he did see the main deck of the *Santa Maria* disintegrate, blown into the air, showering the smaller ships nearby in debris, and severely damaging them. It was a miracle so few were killed as slaves escaped from the ship jumping overboard to evade the fire taking hold.

Rory did not like slave labour, and he was determined to stop this practice, remembering how his own father had been treated when enslaved by the Vikings. The slaves of the knights were very well treated in comparison to his dad. Some were even living as family units. A majority of them were previously free men who had fallen into debt and, with no way of paying it back, were sold into slavery.

It was unclear if the *Santa Maria* was the subject of sabotage or the missing slave boy who went down to the powder room just liked playing with matches, but the whole port was in danger from the fire from the *Santa Maria*. The cannons from Fort Elmo were quickly repositioned from being trained on the *Eternity* to the *Santa Maria*, berthed in the first peninsula. It was blasted into oblivion to the deep waters of the harbour.

What was clear to Rory was the organisation and quick thinking of the knights in charge of the harbour. They quickly divided into groups, taking charge of damage control and the rescue of all those in the water and conveying the injured by boat to the new Hospitallers Hospital. It was being constructed on the mainland of Mount Sciberras (now the location of the city of Valletta), where Fort St Elmo overlooked the sea and harbour mouth. This location was where it was considered most needed to cope with the number of injuries that occurred building the new fortifications and its accessibility to the ports.

The Grand Master, Jean Parisot De Valette, was a striking figure with his curly grey-black hair and trimmed beard. He was not the tallest of men at 5ft 8 inches and medium-built frame, but he was very noticeable dressed in his black Benedictine monk habit, emblazoned with a white Maltese cross of St John on its front. He was visiting the new hospital to see if it could cope with the influx of casualties he was expecting. He had received word from his spies in Constantinople of an imminent invasion of Malta by the Ottoman Turks, who had amassed a large invasion fleet and wanted the ports of Malta to expand their empire.

It was at this time he heard the explosion and received word of the arrival of a suspected plague ship in the harbour. There was so much to do to be ready for the invasion, and now one of his most formidable warships had been destroyed. He made his way to the harbour to see the carnage in front of him and saw the *Eternity* drifting in the bay. He recognised it immediately, even with the damage it had endured. He had received the description of this ship, which had been passed down from one Grand Master to the next at their installation. He had dreaded this day as he looked at the skull and crossbones flag fluttering in the breeze at its stern. At every major time of crisis in the history of the knights, the Pure One had come, and at this time, he felt that he was not ready to assist him. If the prize that was foretold was on that ship, he did not know how he was going to protect it!

Rory watched the boarding party move about the *Eternity*, searching it from top to bottom, finding the locked storeroom off the main deck and forcing it open. Fortunately, they only performed a cursory search, looking for people and totally ignoring his seemingly empty wagon. A message reached them from a rowing boat from the mainland. Lines were attached to the *Eternity*, which was then towed by several large row boats to a secluded berth on the opposite coast to the main ports on the mainland of Mount Sciberras.

As the *Eternity* was tied up, Rory saw a very concerned-looking Grand Master Valette walking towards his ship, shouting orders to all on board to leave the ship. This was, without doubt, the man Rory wanted to talk to as he spied the white cross of St John emblazoned across his chest.

A perimeter of guards formed at the pier behind him, allowing no one to pass as the Grand Master, in slow motion, boarded the battered ship and walked to the open storeroom. Rory passed him with his three-second advantage and was standing next to the wagon as he entered. Rory could see the concern etched on his face emphasised by the time delay as Valette approached the wagon, located the concealed compartment and began opening it!

Rory took hold of his Hagpipe, willing himself back into normal time and appeared instantaneously in front of the Grand Master, saying in French, "I would not touch that if I were you."

The look of concern on the Grand Master's face changed to that of terror and surprised shock as he swore and said, "It's true!"

Rory was fluent in French, which was one of the key languages he had learned as a child and had a long conversation with Grand Master Valette, who explained about the impending invasion. Suleiman the Magnificent had vowed to wipe the Knights of Malta off the face of the earth and was ready to launch his attack.

Rory had experienced this before, and it did not surprise him. Everywhere he went, it was the same story the Muslims and Christians at war, and he would have to find a permanent solution to this problem, but how?

The safety of the Grail Box was his first concern, and then he had to assist the Grand Master. They discussed their options, and it was decided the Grail Box must go to a safe location until the invasion was dealt with. The Grand Master said he had a hunting lodge at Buskett, which in the future would be known as Verdala Palace. It was situated in the interior north-west of the island, which was secluded and away from any danger. Jean Parisot said he would leave the final defence of the ports to his subordinates and accompany Rory to it. He had planned on leaving anyway to supervise a surprise for the invaders by harvesting all the crops, including the unripe grain, to deprive the enemy of any local food supplies. He also had to poison all wells in their path with bitter herbs and dead animals so they would have no water to drink.

Malta was not a large island and slightly smaller than the Island of Arran on the west coast of Scotland, which was owned by Rory's father and the Clan MacSween. At 27km long by 14km at its widest, anywhere on the island was reachable within a day with transport. The Grand Master left to arrange a team of horses to be brought to the pier with a group of his most trusted knights.

Rory checked on the security of the Grail Box in the wagon, filling the back of it with what ship supplies were still good so as not to have the wagon look empty and suspicious.

The Grand Master returned after a short time accompanied by four knights to assist Rory, now clothed in his grey robe, to remove the wagon from the store and wheel it carefully over the double gangplanks to the pier. Rory had been vouched for by the Grand Master, and the knights accepted his presence without question. Rory helped push the wagon, using his super strength, and the knights were totally unaware of the weight it contained. It was a pity about the horses when they were hooked up with Rory in the wagon.

Rory knew they would tire quickly in the heat and hilly terrain of Malta, and he took hold of his Hagpipe through his clothing, activating additional power which passed along his arms and through the reins to the two horses. This had an immediate effect as they pulled the wagon as if it were empty.

A knight passed him, walking towards the *Eternity*, carrying a small barrel, and Rory watched as he poured the black liquid contents onto its deck. It was then towed back out into the harbour. The Grand Master saw the quizzical look on Rory's face and said, "All plague ships are dealt with this way; it is expected. It's naphtha, watch."

A flaming arrow sailed through the air, striking the deck of the *Eternity*, which burst into flames on contact with the burning oil and 'Eternity' for this ship was no more!

No one blinked an eye at the passage of the wagon, loaded with supplies, accompanied by a legion of well-armed knights led by the Grand Master as they left the populated coast. He was indeed very popular, receiving nods of respect from all those they passed. He had a very good reputation, having gained the trust of everyone he met with his easy approachable manner and appeared to be a man of the people.

They travelled at a brisk pace along the hilly, rocky and lush terrain, which would stay that way until the full heat of summer came when all vegetation would be scorched brown and turn to dust. There would not even be enough water on the island to support a large invading army in the hot months, which was why food and water in their path had to be destroyed. The island had no mountains and no reservoirs to contain water, with the only natural water coming from the underground water table. It was the most precious resource and was collected at every opportunity.

As Rory travelled, he saw the other two resources. One was staring him in the face as every building was constructed of it. Stone! More specifically, limestone! It sparkled like yellow gold. It was very strong, easily cut and quarried, abundant and turned a building from a furnace outside in summer to a cool haven inside.

The road was very busy with reinforced carts, very similar to the one Rory was driving piled high with limestone blocks from the quarry on their way back to the ports for the major construction work underway.

None of this would have been possible except for the most important resource of all: the Maltese people! They were the toughest humans that Rory had seen. All were small built, not one being over 5ft 10 inches tall with muscular frames and olive skin. They had fully adapted to their location. Everyone knew each other, and all were related to each other, either distantly or closely. The island was small, as was the gene pool. As a consequence, they had learned to adapt and deal with any situation. The history of Malta was one of constant conflict with both the elements and the numerous invaders conquering the island, but they had never been defeated as people.

As a result, their language comprised the best of each of the conqueror's tongues, including everything from Arabic to Italian, French and English. Rory thought that even he would struggle to be fluent in Maltese! The invaders had washed over them for centuries, but they could never wash them away. Rory admired their resilience and made a note to himself that he would have to get to know these people better. They had a spirit that could not be broken and only bent slightly in the breeze.

It was mid-afternoon when they reached the very hilly area outside Buskett and moved off the main gravel roadway onto a narrow winding pathway (Maltese name Ic-Cangar which was made up of large flat-surfaced hard stones individually mortised into the ground, used to lessen the hill's gradient. It was predominately used by farmers leading their loaded, horse-drawn, sturdy carts. It was just as well as no one would voluntarily climb the hill otherwise, and all were glad when they reached the stone lodge and stables for refreshments supplied by Rory, which included some very old rum and preserves that were still surprisingly very good despite being nearly 300 years old!

CHAPTER 14

St Elmo's Fire

The hunting lodge was a perfect temporary hiding place for the Grail Box, situated at the top of a very defensible hill overlooking the surrounding area. The Maltese caretaker, his wife and three children lived in their own modest stone house behind the stone stables, maintaining the large limestone lodge and attending to it and the vegetable gardens. There were no horses in the stables, as they had long since been used to feed the family following a severe winter. As a result, there was plenty of room for the cart and the company's horses within it.

Rory spoke to Grand Master Valette the next morning, arranging to give the supplies in his wagon to the caretaker to trade and use to help his poor family, to which Jean Parisot willingly agreed. Rory did not want the caretaker to be aware that he was leaving the wagon in the stables. This gesture was a good distraction as they unloaded it into their house, preoccupied with this bounty. Rory took the seemingly empty cart around the back of their house toward the road, passing the empty stables.

Along with the Grand Master, Rory detached the horses from the wagon, pushing it into the stables while keeping a saddled horse for himself and sending the spare one away with the Grand Master, asking him to wait for him at the bottom of the hill.

Rory shut the stable door behind him to prevent being seen and approached the seemingly empty wagon, taking hold of the Hagpipe with his left hand. He was getting good at manipulating time now. The maximum time he could go forwards or back without using a portal he had discovered by practising was 33 seconds. He put his right hand onto the wagon, which shimmered and vanished as he put it 33 seconds into the future. He made a mental note to remember its exact location and bring it back to the present, or it would be lost forever!

Rory rode down the hill to meet Grand Master Valette. They were unaware of the side effects of the Grail Box being placed out of real time and connected to the Maltese earth. An invisible circle of power 33 miles wide spread out from its location, creating an oasis of plenty as all the crops growing within it received a new lease of life, growing profusely within a perfect, mild climate within the zone.

It was a Garden of Eden on Earth.

There would be no hunger here!

The Grand Master and Rory joined the rest of the knights making their way north and to the south coast to supervise the preparations for the arrival of the invading army.

The fall-back plan, should the Turks succeed, appeared in front of Rory and dominated the skyline. It was the Rabat Plateau, the highest point on the island; it overlooked all four points of the compass. The Maltese people had been busy. Impenetrable-looking high walls were built into the rock surrounding the plateau, with a deep, water-filled moat at its foot. A single high bridge gave access to the city within, and it was the only entrance/exit. It was originally named Melita, the principal city of the Romans when they had control of Malta, and the fortress city is now known as Mdina, the Silent City!

It was well named with next to no noise within the city walls. Every street was constructed to the length of a discharged flown arrow, and they all doubled back on each other. Noise could not carry more than the length of the street. There were no ground floor windows in the smooth limestone walls of the streets, nor were there rear doors to create a shortcut from one street to another. The only ground floor access points were secure barricaded doors and metal barred, narrow windows at ankle level. Spears were thrust from them to stab at invaders who did gain access to the city. If the city defences were overcome after the enemy had been bombarded by cannon fire and the invaders did gain entry, they would not get out. The amount of force required to take the city was not cost-effective, the only tactic that would be effective in war was to blockade the city until the occupant supplies ran out. However, they had stockpiled a lot of supplies and had access to the only underground water table.

Grand Master Valette was the newest overlord of many to control this city, and he was a lot happier after inspecting it. He looked upon the Maltese with a newfound respect for their achievement in improving and maintaining this masterpiece of construction.

This area was the agricultural belt of Malta, the most fertile and well-watered, fed by a Roman viaduct supplying water to the areas that had none. It was very safe due to its location in the middle of the island, away from any sudden attack from the sea. The warning fires on the coast would be seen in time for those nearest the city to flee to it.

The city was surrounded by small hamlets producing all the fresh food needed by the population, who only went into the city for trade or refuge in times of war. The knights were dispersed as messengers to instruct all residents in the area to lift their crops and poison their wells. They were all told to take refuge in the city until the invading Turks were repelled.

Unknown to the Grand Master and Rory, no matter how they tried, they could not poison the water wells, which cleared shortly thereafter, and new crops began to grow after being harvested. The plan to poison the water and starve the enemy could not compete with the higher divine forces now at work.

Satisfied with the positive response from the residents and the organisation of the city defences, the Grand Master, knights and Rory carried on their journey and arrived at the north coast and St Paul's (Pawls) Bay, which Rory recognised. He remembered Paul; this was where he had been shipwrecked.

He was a long time dead now, but it seemed like yesterday when he had spoken with him in Jerusalem, along with John. Warning fires had been placed all around the coast at vantage points to watch for the invaders. In the near future, they would not be wooden pyres but be atop permanent stone towers built by a future Grand Master Alof De Wignacourt, along with a new stone chapel on the site of the bonfire that warmed St Paul.

St Paul's Bay was one of the earliest known tourist resorts first used by the converted Christian Romans on pilgrimage to the site where St Paul had set foot on Malta and is still a vibrant one today.

The party stopped for the night in the fishing village with its Il-Menqa (boat shelter) built into the shore. It was like a small harbour with a high wall and a single entrance/exit on its left, allowing the brightly-painted Venetian-looking fishing boats a safe place to berth. The fishing boats were a work of art in yellow, green, red and blue, all marked with the Eye of Horus (wadjet) on their prows.

Rory took the opportunity to bathe with his companions in the natural warm sea water spas carved into the shoreline by the Romans. These overlooked the point of St Paul's shipwreck and the small islands protecting the bay from the north-westerly winds. He asked a fellow Maltese knight next to him about the designs on the fishing boats. He replied, telling Rory that the eye referred to the Egyptian Goddess Wadjet and was a symbol of protection to ensure safe sea travel. The Grand Master told him another meaning of it that caught Rory's interest.

The Grand Master stated, "It also means Risen One!"

The largest island in the middle of the bay had been marked with a cross, as respect to St Paul, and a white statue erected, depicting him holding his bible to his chest with his left hand and with his right hand raised to the sky as if in salute or fending off a foe. Rory laughed at this as he had seen St Columba adopt a similar pose as he fended off Nessie so long ago. (* See Appendix.) Rory sat drying in the warm afternoon sunshine in his white shift, letting his long red hair dry in the breeze as he and his companions enjoyed a barbeque of grilled fresh fish and excellent local wine.

He enjoyed the company and felt homesick. He had, in his own time, been gone from his family and friends and fiancée Heather for four years come the summer equinox in June, and he still had so much to do. This was the calm before the storm as he dressed in his white tabard, displaying the Red Cross of St John or Maltese Cross as they called it here, emblazoned on its front. He looked now just like the other novice Knights of Malta who were sitting next to him and was probably, despite his young years, far more battle-hardened than them as they braced themselves for their return to the Grand Harbour and war!

The knights had a total force of 6,100, comprising 500 Hospitallers, 400 Spanish soldiers, 800 Italian soldiers, 500 from the galleys of the Spanish Empire, 200 Greek and Sicilian soldiers, 100 soldiers in Fort St Elmo, 100 knight servants, 500 galley slaves and 3,000 Maltese soldiers. The Ottomans had amassed a vast force of 40,000 ground troops from across their empire to fill the fleet of ships. This consisted of 193 vessels, including 131 galleys, 7 galliots (small galleys) and four galleasses (large galleys) the same size as the two remaining Great Carracks; the *San Giovanni* and the *Santa Anna* of the knights. The rest of invading fleet consisted of transport vessels. On paper, the knights had no chance as Suleiman the Magnificent gave the order for the largest Turkish armada ever assembled to set sail from Constantinople on 22 March 1565 to wipe the Knights of Malta off the face of the earth!

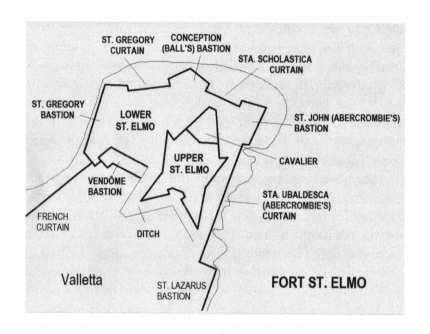

The fort of St Elmo protecting the Grand Harbour was named after Saint Erasmus of Formia in Italy, who was also known as Saint Elmo. He was a Christian saint and martyr who died in AD 303 and was venerated as the patron saint of sailors and abdominal pain. (This may coincide with the quantity of rum sailors drank.) He was more famously known for an incident when he was persecuted, beaten and, after suffering terrible injuries, was forced to go to a pagan temple where he refused to renounce his faith. But as he was dragged along the route lined with idols, they all fell and were destroyed. At this time, fire spouted from the temple, which began falling upon many of the pagans.

This was the first historic reference to St Elmo's fire. The second was still to come!

The Turkish armada arrived at dawn on Friday, 18 May, but did not make landfall at once. The first fighting broke out on 19 May. A day later, the Ottoman fleet sailed up the southern coast of the island, turned around and finally anchored at Marsaxlokk (Marsa Sirocco) Bay, nearly

10 kilometres (6.2 miles) from the Grand Harbour region. Fortunately for the Knights of Malta, the fleet was not led by Suliman the Magnificent but by two of his most senior underlings, the 4th Vizier Mustafa Pasha and the supreme naval commander, Piyale Pasha. A dispute arose between the leader of the land force and the naval commander about where to anchor the fleet. Piyale wished to shelter it at Marsamxett Harbour, just north of the Grand Harbour, in order to avoid the sirocco (similar to the Spanish calima, a cloud of dust or sand blown in the wind causing extreme heat) and to be nearer the action.

Mustafa disagreed because to anchor the fleet there would require first destroying Fort St. Elmo since it guarded the entrance to the harbour. Nevertheless, Mustafa relented, apparently believing only a few days would be necessary to destroy St. Elmo. Mustafa did not have a clue, and his name would be remembered from the phrase used today, "must have a", as used in 'a good reason to do something'. Both could not have been more wrong as they landed on the Sciberras Peninsula, placing their guns on Santa Margherita Hill. It was not until the end of May that the bombardment of Fort St Elmo began, and with it the start of the Great Siege of Malta!

Fort Saint Elmo (Maltese: Forti Sant'Iermu) was the key to retaining Malta from the invaders. Its star-shaped fortifications stood on the seaward shore of the Sciberras Peninsula that divides Marsamxett Harbour from Grand Harbour, and it commanded the entrances to both harbours. (See Image 6.) It was divided into two levels, Upper and Lower St Elmo, with very high reinforced triangular ravelin fortifications. (* See Appendix.) They faced outwards onto the sea and were heavily armed with cannons. The fort's only weakness was its vulnerability to an attack on its landward flank, and this was the very tactic employed by the Turks.

Grand Master Valette saw the attack coming and evacuated the peninsula inhabitants to his stronghold across the Grand

Harbour, leaving those fit and strong enough to enter the fort to defend it. It was as good as committing suicide for these unlucky volunteers, but the fort had to hold until the relief promised by Don Garcia, Viceroy of Sicily, arrived.

Aid was coming, and the west was very concerned should Malta fall into the hands of the Turks. Queen Elizabeth I of England wrote: "If the Turks should prevail against the Isle of Malta, it is uncertain what further peril might follow to the rest of Christendom."

The unremitting bombardment of the fort from three dozen guns on the higher ground of Mt. Sciberras began on 27th May, reducing the fort to rubble within a week. However, the Grand Master Valette evacuated the wounded nightly and re-supplied the fort from across the harbour. Rory was glad to help, rowing supplies across the bay and supporting where he could. This was another fixed point in time. He couldn't fight this war for the knights, but he could try to minimise how many were killed.

On the third of June, a party of Turkish infantry managed to seize the fort's ravelin and ditch. A fierce battle ensued, and by the eighth of June, the knights in Fort Elmo sent a message to the Grand Master that they could no longer hold it. The Grand Master rebuffed the messages, instructing that St Elmo must hold until the reinforcements arrived. The fighting was frantic, with the knights taking it in rotation to eat and sleep until that was no longer possible.

They were literally fighting for their lives! It was then they were inspired by St Elmo. They had a large supply of naphtha stored in the fort, and the Turks were all attired in silk robes.

This was the turning point!

This transcript of the battle by Francisco Balbi, a Spanish relief soldier, sums up the events. "The darkness of the night then became as bright as day, due to the vast quantity of artificial fires. So bright was it indeed that we could see St Elmo quite clearly. The gunners of Fort St Angelo across the bay were able to lay and train their superior cannons upon the advancing Turks, who were picked out in the light of the fires."

St Elmo's fire rained down on the invading Turks, turning them to flame and burning them to death. The fort survived for another 28 days due to the bravery of the defenders, many of whom were Maltese, until it was finally overrun on the 23rd of June by the Turks, who seized what little was left of it. The sacrifice of all 1,500 men defending the fort had cost the Turks at least 6,000 men and, more importantly, bought valuable time for the Spanish and Italian reinforcements to arrive.

This Ottoman victory would be very short-lived!

CHAPTER 15

Homeward Bound

Rory was distraught at so much death and destruction around him, but he was limited as to how much he could interfere in the events intertwined with his life. The *Book of St Columba* had shown him where and when he had to take action, but the battle for Fort St Elmo was a fixed point in time that would define the character of the people of Malta, and these events could not be changed. He had memorised an image from the book that he recalled now, and he looked forward to playing his part in this history before recovering the Grail Box and heading home. He was another year older, following another birthday alone and away from all that he loved. The Hagpipe now multiplied his power by 20x33, and as long as he wore it, he did not physically look any different than when he was 16. He felt the extra power flowing through him and was unsure what more he could do.

The cannons that had been previously trained on Fort St Elmo were now targeting the strongholds of Birgu and Senglea, levelling them. The Great Siege had been well named, as the population took refuge in underground tunnels and catacombs for safety. This was resistance fighting, but the Grand Harbour made it an equal fight. As long as the knights had sufficient cannon and weapons to repel boats attempting to cross the Grand Harbour, they survived.

At night, naphtha was the friend of the knights and a quick death for the Turks. Rory did his part, and no one could believe the distance and accuracy he could fire a flaming arrow. He did not like to kill, and the occupants of the boats he set on fire all preferred to leave it as it burned, swimming back to the safety of their own shore.

The knights survived, and on 7 September Don Garcia, the Viceroy of Sicily, arrived, landing 8,000 men at St Paul's Bay on the north end of the island. The Turks were caught in a pincer manoeuvre with nowhere to go, abandoning their attempt to eradicate the knights, turning their efforts into defeating the Italians.

Don Garcia was an experienced tactician, and the Grande Soccorso (Great Relief) positioned themselves on the ridge of Pawl tat-Tarġa, waiting for the retreating Turks who were burning all the remaining villages in their wake and slaughtering those in their path.

This was Rory's time as he left Grand Master Valette to rebuild and reorganise the remains of his soon-to-be city.

Rory joined the relief force of knights to attack the Turks from the rear. This did not interfere with history, and innocents being attacked and killed was too much for him to ignore. Rory led from the front and soon out-distanced his fellow knights, saving them from harm as he attacked the Turks with unbelievable speed. Hans his sword hissed through the air as he disarmed them, shattering their weapons and knocking those who refused to run into unconsciousness.

Stories had been passed down from the days of the Saracens of a flaming red-haired demon who could destroy whole armies. Children's tales of a red-maned monster in the shape of a man became a reality for the Turks who saw it moving, in a blur, behind them. It was their time to fear. Those that could fled to their ships, with the rest running all the way to St Paul's Bay, where a general charge from the Italian army and a massacre awaited them.

The Turks fled the islands on 11 September. Malta had survived the Turkish assault, and throughout Europe people celebrated what would turn out to be the last epic battle involving the Crusader Knights.

The Ottoman casualties were estimated at 30,000, with the 9,000 *defenders* managing to withstand a siege of more than four months in the hot summer, despite enduring a bombardment of some 130,000 cannonballs. The knights lost a third of their number, and Malta had lost a third of its inhabitants. The Ottomans never attempted to besiege Malta again, although the failure of the siege did nothing to reverse the increasing dominance of Ottoman naval power in the Mediterranean.

Jean de Valette, the Grand Master of the Knights of Malta, had a key influence in the victory against the Ottomans, with his example and ability to encourage and unite people. This had a major impact because the kings of Europe realised that the only way to win against the Ottomans was to stop wars between themselves and form alliances. The result was the vast union of forces against Ottomans at the Battle of Lepanto seven years later. Such was the gratitude of Europe for the knights' heroic defence of Malta that money soon began pouring into the island. This allowed de Valette to construct a fortified city that was named Valletta after him on Mt. Sciberras, where he finished his Hospitallers Hospital. He retained the underground catacombs and tunnels in the building of this new city, which would save the Maltese people again in the future when being bombed in the Second World War. His intent was to deny the strategic position of Malta to any future enemies, which almost worked, except for a future act of betrayal that would hand Malta to Napoleon.

De Valette died in 1568 after suffering a stroke while praying in his chapel, but his legacy survives to this day in one of the most beautiful and practical cities in the world.

For now, peace was restored.

Rory made his way back to the hunting lodge of Grand Master De Valette at Buskett, or Verdala Palace as it's now known. He recovered two of the strongest surviving horses, running wild in the countryside away from the battle as he travelled. He did not say any personal goodbyes to the knights or Grand Master Valette, whom he had grown close to, preferring instead to mysteriously disappear. Rory covered himself in his grey cloak and hood, thereby disguising his red hair. He had time to think on past events as he travelled and questioned the role of man on the planet. Why this desire to go to war and fight for possessions and territory when, ultimately, death came, and none of it could do any good?

Even with his enhanced intelligence, he could not understand!

The Grail Box was the answer, but what was the question?

Rory rode into the courtyard of the hunting lodge, which was deserted, the caretaker and his family having taken refuge in Mdina until the war was over. He opened the stable doors to see it was empty as he expected. Walking forward, holding the Hagpipe in his left hand with his right outstretched in front of him, he touched the distortion in the air. Rory focused his abilities and manipulated time, pulling the wagon back 33 seconds from the future until it popped into existence before him.

All was well as he checked the Grail Box was intact, safely hidden in the concealed false bottom of the wagon. He felt like some exercise and pulled the wagon out of the stables. He noticed new crops were fully grown in the garden, which he thought was very strange after the heat of the summer. On checking the well, he saw that it was full of fresh water.

Rory released the horses to eat the plentiful vegetation and decided to have an early night sleeping in the back of the wagon. It occurred to him, as he fell asleep, that the Grail Box must have been affecting the surrounding area. He made a mental note to pay attention to what else it could do as he drifted into dreams of home and of his beloved Heather and twin girls.

He was awakened by the bright sunshine early the next morning and loaded a supply of fruit and vegetables into the back of the wagon along with containers of water for himself and, more importantly, the horses. The frisky, refreshed horses were no match for his speed and agility as he ran after them just for a laugh instead of calling them mentally to him. He easily caught them, to their great confusion, and reattached them to the wagon.

Rory knew that, after the war, using a ship to transport the Grail Box to Scotland was out of the question. He dared not use the Azure Window (Also Known as Zerka Mirror) again, as after the last time it would be watched. As he thought this, he felt movement below his shirt like a mouse squirming at his chest.

It was the Hagpipe!

He pulled it out from below his clothes, letting it dangle on its thong around his neck. It rose up in the air, pulling the thong tight. Rory turned to his left, and it almost choked him, pulling in the opposite direction. He turned to his right, and it pointed straight ahead. It was behaving like a compass, pointing him in the direction he had to go. (It was like the first sat nav, only more accurate.) Well, that was that sorted. He had come to trust the Hagpipe implicitly and set off in the direction it pointed.

The main roads were busy with the Maltese people returning to their homes from Mdina, and he covered his head as he travelled past them to hide his identity. It was just as well, as he passed the caretaker, his wife and three children, returning to the hunting lodge. His timing was perfect in recovering the Grail Box, and they were totally unaware that it had ever been there.

The road the Hagpipe took him became narrower and into hilly terrain. Rory knew he was getting close to his destination as he felt his body begin to tingle. He was following a very powerful ley line and, as he topped a hill, he saw it.

In front of him was the Copper Age temple of Hagar Qim, built in 2,700 BC with its monoliths of standing stones, secret chambers and central altar. Rory did not have to use his enhanced intelligence to recognise who had built it. He had seen the very same constructions back home in Scotland, and he had met them.

It was the Druids!

They could move between points on the ley line network and obviously over vast distances. As he studied the temple from his vantage point, he felt his skin crawl with the activation of power. He zoomed his super eyesight in on the temple and saw two small four-year-old girls, one with jet-black hair, no wait; that was strange! As he looked, the girl's hair kept changing from jet-black to blonde. The other girl was her double, but her hair stayed blonde all the time.

What was going on?

Both girls were laughing and playing hide and seek among the ruins of the temple. As he watched, he saw they were chasing a large leathery lopsided animal that ran with an uneven gait, but for all its awkwardness, it was giving them a good run around with its speed. Rory recognised the animal straight away: it was Hag, his pet haggis and if that was Hag, then the two girls were his daughters!

The main portal to the temple, a large doorway of two monoliths topped with another, illuminated in a shimmering light as Rory heard the two girls giggle and run into it. Hag stopped as she was about to run after them as if in two frames of mind. She looked straight at Rory. He heard her sweet voice in his head, "I will protect," as she ran into the portal and vanished!

Rory was shaken. He had been told in the afterlife when he had touched the Grail Box that he had to save his daughters but had not realised how it was possible or how he would feel when he saw them. He knew now, and his heart was full of love. But how could they travel, apparently at will, through the portals? The whole world was their play park, and there was no way he could track them as they ran from one portal to another!

He had just been lucky to see them, and he still had to get the Grail Box safely home! He needed answers and, hopefully, Heather could answer them.

The Hagpipe pulled him forward, tugging at his neck as he urged the horses forward. The portal in front of him in the ruins of the temple was far too narrow to take the Grail Box. No sooner than he had considered this, the Hagpipe changed direction, pointing out a path down a steep slope towards the westerly sea dominating the skyline. Another larger circle of standing stones came into view at the bottom of the hill that was in perfect alignment with the summer and winter equinox. Rory considered them but really wanted a one-stop portal back to Urquhart Castle as he was desperate to speak to Heather. That meant he needed a sea portal to enter the cavern below the castle.

The direction of the Hagpipe changed again, taking him on a rugged high cliff road around the coast and down a steep incline down to a fishing village the Maltese called Weid iz-Zurrieq. It consisted of three small houses down a steep natural stone slope in a secluded bay. Several fishing boats were berthed, all painted brightly in gold, red and green with the Eye of Horus painted at the front. *"Perfect: the symbol of the "Risen One,"* thought Rory.

He dismounted from the wagon, approached a group of four fishermen attending to a catch at the pier and began speaking to them in Maltese. He haggled with them to buy the smallest fishing boat that was still large enough to hold the Grail Box. He tried to trade the horses and wagon and its contents of fresh vegetables and fruit for the boat. The fishermen laughed at this poor exchange as the boats were their livelihood. The smallest boat belonged to the oldest fisherman, and although he was getting too old to fish, this was his only asset, and he could not afford to retire. Rory smiled as he reached inside his clothing to his sporran, removing the small bag of gems from within it. He asked the old man to hold out his hand as he began placing gem after gem into it to ever-increasing looks of surprise on the old man's face. He agreed to the deal; he could buy a fleet of fishing boats with this fortune, and he did!

The other fishermen thought Rory was mad, but he was a rich madman, so they assisted him to unload his wagon and release his horses in the hope of receiving a gem. They were intrigued as Rory opened the concealed false bottom of his wagon, unfolding its sides, revealing the coffin-shaped wooden Grail Box. They did not know what it was and took it at face value: a coffin. Rory said he needed the boat to take his father home, which they accepted without question.

He placed the rods of Aaron and Moses into the holes at the bottom and top of the Grail Box, which took on the appearance of a cross when they were inserted. The red cross on its lid caused no surprise to the fishermen.

Why would it?

It was the Maltese cross.

The stranger's father must be Maltese!

Rory asked the fishermen to take hold of the rod of Moses, two of them on either side at the front, as he took on almost the full weight of the Grail Box by the rod of Aaron at the base. They were only there to keep the box stable as they carried it to the fishing boat, placing it in its centre.

Rory thanked the fishermen as he raised the sail and left the bay. The three younger fishermen were far more interested in the old man, now the richest and most important man in the village. He was cleverer than his age might suggest; soon he would own all the fishing boats and businesses in the village, and in the future his family would own all the pleasure boats visiting the Blue Grotto.

Out of sight, Rory released the Hagpipe from below his cloak. It then pulled him to the left into a turquoise, secluded, calm sea. In front of him was a large rocky cliff face with the most volcanic sea caves Rory had ever seen. It was portal central, and to the future western tourists to Malta, it would be known as the Blue Grotto, a 'must-visit' location. It was perfect and a great place to throw Satanic Stan off his scent as he sailed in and out of the caves, with the sunlight illuminating the pool water and tropical fish. It was as if he was sailing through a natural aquarium, which gave him a great sense of peace as he travelled through this natural wonder.

As he left every cave, he ignited the portals in a random sequence to various time zones and places that even he could not track back to their sources.

Satanic Stan would spend an eternity trying to find the Grail Box!

After visiting the last cave, Rory saw a stone arch in front of him through which the sea passed. The arch was a smaller version of the 'Azure Window' and more than large enough for the smaller boat to pass through. Rory thought of home, and six months after he had left Urquhart Castle to free Castle Sween in order to return it to MacSween control. The portal illuminated a yellow glow as he sailed through the shimmering curtain of power and into the waters of Loch Ness and the hidden cavern below Urquhart Castle.

He was home in Scotland and three years back in his own past, just in time to celebrate his 17th birthday on the summer equinox. He had a lot of questions for Heather and was eager to check that his journeys in time had not altered his history. Six months had passed for Heather and four years for Rory. He was a changed person from all his experiences, now very wise and mature beyond his years, though he had not physically aged a day since he had left due to the longevity effect of the Hagpipe.

The great evil pursuing him was still lurking to destroy mankind's only hope for peace and an everlasting future. He still had to make the Grail Box safe from it, and he could not get the vision of his giggling twin girls out of his head.

He must save them!

CHAPTER 16

Daughters

Rory coasted towards the sandy beach in the cavern below Urquhart Castle on the banks of Loch Ness in his small Maltese fishing boat, painted brightly in gold, red and green, with the Eye of Horus painted at the front. The symbol of the eye meant, in some translations, "Risen One", which was very symbolic as the boat contained artefacts from that very person.

He tied the boat up on the small sandy beach next to the rowing boat in which he had so much fun years before, remembering how he had been speedily towed in it by a young Nessie. He knew now where his pet haggis was. Hag was guarding his young twin daughters, and he considered how powerful they were at such a young age, without the possession of the Hagpipe. They were even able to travel through the portals, apparently at will.

He remembered the circumstances of his one and only union with his fiancée Heather, as he lost control of the emotions which had overwhelmed him after he had cured his mother from imminent death from an illness we now know as leukaemia. His emotions were high and out of control at that time, dominated by the feral and instinctive side of the haggis which had been released by the Hagpipe, the right tusk of the first haggis. He had left to regain Castle Sween shortly after that, regaining it from Sir John De Menteith the Younger, whose ancestors had stolen it from the family of Clan MacSween. Heather had seemed fine when he had left her, but he remembered the scream he had heard, travelling to Castle Sween at the winter equinox. He had gone back to check on her. She looked well, and she was definitely not pregnant when he had last seen her. He remembered being out of control under the primordial animal instincts of the Hagpipe when he had made love to Heather, and both of them had been engulfed in a red, fiery uncontrollable passion. That was it: the twins had been conceived under the influence and full power of the Hagpipe and must have inherited some of its power.

But she must have delivered the babies early, and what had happened to them?

Only Heather could tell him, but first he had things to do.

There was no one to help him as he unloaded the extremely heavy Grail Box from the boat, but he was unbelievably strong. He engaged the rod of Moses through the wrist holes in the top side of the acacia wood box made from the crucifixion cross of Christ. He then placed the rod of Moses' brother, Aaron, into the bottom hole where Christ's feet had been nailed, subduing the unfathomable power of the Grail Box and its contents, thus making the box safe enough to be touched. Rory easily lifted it from the boat and carried it on his shoulders into the cave of the haggis graveyard. Without any prompting, the entrance to the portal shimmered into existence in white pure light, and Rory passed through it into the sparkling cave, illuminated by the white crystals in the roof.

In front of him, the haggis graveyard contained a mound of white ivory haggis tusks in its centre. As he watched, they moved and flowed together into a rectangular shape, creating an altar for him on which to place the Grail Box. Even Rory, who had seen many strange sights, was surprised at this, and it confirmed to him that this was the place where the Grail Box should be. For extra safety, he removed the long rod of Moses from the top of the box from the holes left by the large coarse nails that had pinned Christ to the cross and the smaller rod of Aaron from its base. He started to push the rods into the altar of haggis tusks which before his surprised eyes moved slowly by itself out of their way, making a path for them until they had been totally concealed. Anyone touching the Grail Box now would be visiting the next life before their time, as he knew from his own experience when he had recovered it from Jerusalem. His soul had been guided back to his body by a quiet voice talking to him, and he could only guess and be awestruck at who or what was responsible for this great power.

Unknown to Rory, the supernatural power contained within the Grail Box, now released, was creating the life force of the haggis. The unrestricted contact of the box with the tusks was empowering the creation of the first haggis egg. Rory had already hatched this egg in his past, which contained Hag, his pet, which he had reared. All was connected; events were turning full circle; it was the ultimate question, what came first, the chicken or the egg or in this case, the haggis. The actions of Rory at present were creating his own past, and subsequently the Hagpipe, the source of his power. It came from the first haggis and was currently being created by the contact between the unfettered God power in the Grail Box touching the haggis tusks. Rory left the cave and took hold of the Hagpipe with his left hand as he inserted his right into the shimmering portal curtain at the entrance.

He had learned now how to modify and displace time. Without contact with a portal, he could only move time by seconds. With contact, he could vary it to any multiplication of 33, from 33 seconds to 33 minutes to hours, days and years.

He did not know that the Grail Box, when displaced in time, extended its life-giving protective force to a distance of each 33 multiplied by 10. So, for 33 seconds, it extended its power to a distance of 330 miles. For 33 minutes, it extended in a circle of 3300 miles and so on. Rory chose to move the Grail Box 33 minutes into the future. The majority of Scotland was now going to be even lusher green and more prosperous than ever before with the most stable climate in the world. The portal connected with the ley lines as the power from the Grail Box discharged into the earth. As Rory watched, the Grail Box and the altar of haggis tusks vanished, displaced in time 33 minutes into the future where no man on the planet could find it, leaving the cave, to all human eyes, empty!

Rory made his way to the spiral stone staircase connecting the cavern to the secret door situated in the east wall of the Temple of the Monks of St Columba, located in the grounds of Urquhart Castle above him. Nothing appeared to have changed as he pulled the concealed leaver, opening the door and stepping into rainbow-coloured light streaming in from the two large stained-glass windows. The left window depicted St Columba in his purple monk's habit, looking up and to his left, towards the right window. He was clasping a book to his breast with his left hand while pointing to a clump of heather with his right forefinger towards a rearing haggis. The right window depicted the Loch Ness Monster, looking down on St Columba from its backdrop of Loch Ness and surrounding mountains towards a small figure standing on the bank of the River Ness.

Rory remembered the events in the windows well. He had been there when they had happened. He was not surprised in the slightest and was expecting to see Abbot MacCallum, the head of the St Columba monks, sitting in the wooden pews in the west of the temple waiting for him. He possessed the *Book of St Columba* that Rory had memorised. It depicted Rory's life history recorded from the premonitions and visions of St Columba.

Rory remembered that he had seen this very scene with his silhouette bathed in the multicoloured light from the windows while facing the abbot who was smiling at him.

The abbot knew from this revelation coming true that Rory had succeeded in his mission to recover the Grail Box, and he rushed forward to embrace him. He loved and cared for him like a son following his orchestration in removing him from his abusive stepfather, John Grant.

The abbot had been like the father Rory had never had when he was growing up, and he had trained Rory, preparing him for all the events that had now transpired. He knew, just by Rory's presence, that he had been successful, and he had recovered the Grail Box, which was now here. He would have loved to have seen it but now was not the time.

He had a surprise for Rory waiting in his chambers!

It was Heather!

She ran, jumping up and into Rory's arms as he entered the room. The abbot closed the door, leaving them together and in peace. After what seemed like an eternity of tears, kisses and cuddles, they sat down together on two sturdy wooden chairs in front of the abbot's desk. Heather pushed back her tears as she said, "I have something very important to tell you."

Rory replied, "Is it about our daughters?" Heather was speechless. How could he know? Rory continued, "They are beautiful, one with jet-black hair, the other strawberry blonde like the sun."

Heather excitedly exclaimed, "You've seen them. Are they well?"

Rory continued, "They were running about laughing, playing hide and seek," which, by the look on Heather's face, drove her into total confusion!

Rory tried to explain how he had seen both of them four years into the future, but Heather was having difficulty understanding how he and her children could travel in time and from place to place. He changed the subject and asked her to explain what had happened to them after they had been born, bringing another fresh influx of tears. She told him of their early birth, of how they had grown inside her so quickly and how Granny Grant had helped her. She had taken her to a cave below the castle, where she had screamed as they were born. Rory knew it was Heather he had heard screaming, and told her he had returned to see if she was safe and well.

Heather said, "I know. I was pretending to sleep when you came in." She explained that she wanted to tell him then, but

Granny Grant had told her he had something important to do, and she had to keep quiet. She further explained how Granny Grant was flashing on and off, appearing and disappearing, and of the crystals falling from the cave ceiling onto the twins, who then vanished. It was then Granny Grant appeared again, but since then, she had grown very old and frail.

Rory knew he would have to speak to Granny Grant as she was the key to solving what was happening but not before he cheered up Heather.

He told her he would sort everything and bring the twins home to her. He did not know how yet, but he was determined that he would, as he changed the subject again. First, they would have to be married before everyone saw they had children. This took Heather by surprise again as she cuddled and kissed him, her face breaking into a huge smile. She believed Rory could do anything. His promise was good enough for her, and she had a wedding to plan!

Full of excitement, she rushed off to arrange a welcome home and birthday party for Rory. Everyone loved a party, and she wanted to be the first to tell everyone that Rory was back!

Rory realised he was not going to be alone in a strange land for this birthday, but what age was he? So much time had passed for him that he had lost count. He did not look any older, and he fitted into this time in the past with Heather, but chronologically he was celebrating his 21st birthday, not his 17th. The Hagpipe was counting the number of his birthdays, and at 21 he felt another boost to his abilities and more power surging through him. He was older than Heather now. She had been a year and three months older than him before his travels. She would be 18 on her birthday on the 26th of September, an old woman compared to some who became mothers at 16.

The 26th and Heather's birthday would be a good date for the wedding, Rory thought!

CHAPTER 17

Bella and Isa

The abbot had been very busy anticipating Rory's return and had instructed Father Doogan, also known as Pooie Doo, to contact Rory's parents at Castle Sween and his friend Angus MacDonald and wife, Esther, of his imminent return. They had all responded and already travelled to Urquhart Castle, where they were in hiding until the party in the great hall that night. Angus and Esther had brought baby Eoin, who was now approaching the terrible twos and causing havoc everywhere he went. They had decided to make a holiday of the trip and had travelled on the *Stag*, the birlinn ship of Esther's father, Captain Roddy MacLeod, and her mother, Lee Chan, the doting grandparents of Eoin.

Ruaidri and Mary, Rory's parents, had travelled by carriage from Castle Sween with a surprise for him, bringing his jet-black stallion, aptly named Jet, with them. Unsurprisingly, when Rory had left the monastery to go and visit Granny Grant, the castle seemed deserted as everyone wanted to be in on the surprise. The only person who could not wait to see Rory was wee Charlie Campbell, his best pal, who ran up to him and, like Heather, threw his slight frame into his arms for a cuddle. He had really missed Rory, as the tears of joy running down his face confirmed. Rory knew how much Charlie liked him and embraced him, lowering him to the ground from his height advantage over Charlie's five-foot-four inches.

They had a quick catch-up. Charlie explained that he was fully qualified as a saddler now, his work being much sought after following the gossip that had spread about him making the scabbard for Hans, Rory's magic sword. Unfortunately, he had not found a love for himself, but he was pleased for Rory, although a bit sad for himself. Charlie had always loved Rory and doubted that he would ever find anyone to replace him, but he really liked Heather, who was also his best pal. He was pleased that they both had found happiness together. Rory considered his friend's plight and vowed to himself that he would ask Charlie to be the godfather to his girls when he got them home. That would give him plenty to think about!

Rory walked to the wooden cabin of Granny Grant and was shocked to see the grey-haired, wizened, old woman hunched over her fire outside, even on this warm summer's day wrapped in her plaid. She was skin and bones with translucent paper-thin skin that almost cracked as she tried to smile at Rory.

As he sat next to her, he could see the life force draining out of her and that she did not have long to live. Rory asked if he could transfer some of the Hagpipe life force to her as he had done for his mother when he had cured her of leukaemia. Granny refused, stating that she had already received its power and could not receive any more. This confused Rory as he did not remember ever giving her any of its power.

Granny said, "Call me Bella. I have a story to tell you, Dad!"

Rory was floored. He had not been expecting this. Granny Grant was one of his twin daughters, but that meant the witch who had been trying to kill him was his other twin daughter!

This was the reason she had been flashing in and out of existence when she had helped deliver her new- born self. She was a hybrid human haggis, with its power flowing through her being. She could not take any more power from the Hagpipe, and meeting herself had drained her to the point of no return. She was going to die. Rory now realised this was how she had been able to lift Hans, his magic sword! (* See Appendix.) She was of his blood and was filled with the haggis power that flowed through him and Heather when she had been conceived. The sword was connected to her through the first haggis tusk making up its grip.

Tears filled Rory's eyes as Bella showed him the white crystal on the silver chain around her neck. It was flashing in and out of time in front of him, "My sister Isa will soon be gone as well," she said. "We took very different paths; I followed the road of good, learning the lore to help people with the aid of the white crystal, while Isa followed the route of power and force with the black crystal. I saw you that day on the hill but could not come back through the portal to you, we all had to go together at that time, and Isa did not want to return; she was having too much fun."

Rory reached over and gave her a very gentle cuddle as Bella continued, "It was at this time that she began to change and started taking lessons in the dark arts from the red-robed Druid with the pentagrams on his hands. I know who he is now. He is not even human anymore; he was your stepfather, John Grant!"

Rory was reeling at these revelations; everything was beginning to make sense. Bella's voice was becoming very weak now as she continued, "He is more powerful than you now. You can't stop him. Your only chance is to change our future."

He felt Bella beginning to disappear in his arms and looked deeply into her eyes as she vanished from existence with her last words ringing in the air, "I came to help you. Now you must save us!"

* * *

Isa, the Grant Witch, was lying in her basic cot bed in her cottage all alone. She was of no use to Satanic Stan now. He had left to pursue his plans to destroy Rory and the Grail Box.

She had lost her power, and just like her twin, she flashed in and out of existence with her.

There was no one there to give her a comforting cuddle; no one cared for her. She thought no one ever had. She felt her dad comforting Bella and wanted some of it. She felt a glimpse of love from her father in unison with the love he felt for her sister.

She liked it; it was something she did not know. Isa had not experienced unconditional love before. If only she had experienced this before, her whole life would have been so different!

The last thought she had, as she ceased to be, was of regret. What had she done? Her parents did care, and she had destroyed everything, including them!

Had it been worth it?

Rory was devastated. His daughters were dead, and the only person that had been wise enough to advise him how to save them was his daughter Bella. He could think of no one to turn to for help.

What was he to do now?

For the second time in his life, he was facing a happy time mixed with a very sad time, remembering how sad he had been when he had lost the Hagpipe after the joy of discovering his dad was alive.

Bella had mentioned a red-robed Druid. The twins must have grown up in the time of the Druids, so that was a good place to start. *I will go back and speak to the ones who gave me the broken sword; they may know of the twins and where to find them*, he thought.

At this time, the giant frame of the 6ft 8inch Constable John Gregg, now steward of the castle, blocked out the sunlight shining on Rory, who was still sitting, holding the non-existent shape of Granny Grant, his daughter. The constable was a very practical man, not used to the strange or supernatural, but Rory was a brother and he looked in need. Rory told him of the demise of Granny Grant but decided not to tell him that the old woman was his daughter, this was far too farfetched for him to understand.

The constable recommended Rory visit the brewery and distillery behind the smithy for something medicinal. He stated that he would attend to the cabin and whatever possessions that belonged to Granny Grant. Rory accepted the help; he could not face doing this himself and walked to the smithy.

Hamish Cooper, Jimmy Black, Gordon Grant and Allister Mac Allister, nickname Pally Ally, were all still there having a laugh as they worked. Rory's fellow apprentice, Pally Ally, had grown into a fine young man and was now in his twenties, full of muscles and almost as tall as Rory. He was being allowed to do most of the work and train some new apprentices as the three older blacksmiths sampled the latest batch of the water of life from the distillery. (Whisky/Gaelic Uisge-Beatha.)

Hamish had married Heather's mother and would soon be Rory's father-in-law, and he saw the look on Rory's face as he approached and had a full glass in his hand for a nip before he even allowed him to speak.

Granny Grant had helped every single person in the castle and Castletoun and surrounding area at one time or another and would be sorely missed. A glass or several was raised to her memory, and Rory was soon feeling a lot happier, especially as he had not had a proper drink for so long.

CHAPTER 18

Party

Rory woke up a few hours later. *What was in that whisky?* he thought. All he had added to it was some spring water, drawn from the smithy pump and supplied from the mountain above the castle. He looked inwards and studied how he felt; he had no sore head or hangover and he felt good, better than good, rejuvenated in fact and cheerful. He remembered the Grail Box effect on the Island of Malta. In the summer heat, the island had been transformed into a land of plenty after the box had been advanced in time by 33 seconds. This time he had advanced it 33 minutes; already the water was having a healing effect! If he advanced the Grail Box by weeks or years, it would turn the nearest water supply into a fountain of youth and keep illness, maybe even death, at bay.

Stopping hangovers was fine, but he did not want to meddle or use that kind of power; it was not his to play with. The rest of his drinking partners had gone off to lie down themselves. He decided to get ready for the party Heather was throwing for him that night. On checking his own clothing, he discovered that no matter what layer he was wearing, it was badly worn, dirty and smelly. He stripped to his kilt, which he kept on to cover his modesty and began scrubbing himself under the hand pump with the multi- purposed red rough carbolic soap.

Once clean, he started on his clothing, including the grey cloak, the knight's tabard and his white shirt, removing all the blood and stains that had accumulated over the years. The combination of the soap and pure, invigorating water cleaned away all traces of their bloody past. He hung the clothes up to dry on a string between the rafters in the smithy, pleased with his efforts.

His back was turned to the open double doors to the courtyard when he heard an excited quiet moan from behind him. He turned to see who was there as his shoulder-length red hair billowed in the breeze like the flames of a fire. The late summer sunshine illuminated his six-foot-four-inch frame, glistening off his muscle-ripped torso where the white ivory Hagpipe hung on its thong, sparkling in the light.

Heather let out another moan and seemed to Rory's enhanced eyes to be weak at her knees as she held out wrapped presents for Rory's birthday. Rory wondered if she was ill. She was stuttering, trying to speak, she seemed unsteady on her feet, and he took hold of her and sat her down. She had a funny look in her eyes as he asked if she was feeling OK.

She mumbled something like, "Great," as she handed him the presents of a new white dress shirt and a new, short, summer Clan MacSween tartan kilt and socks (hose).

Rory had been in the company of men for so long that he did not think about his modesty as he slipped the new long shirt over his head. It dangled below his waist as he removed his well-worn old kilt. For all his life experiences, he was still very ignorant about women. By the time he had dressed in the new kilt and hose, Heather was practically shaking and flushed red in the face, desperate for her wedding day to come as soon as possible.

Rory thanked Heather for the new clothes and let her take his muscular left arm to support her as they walked towards the great hall for his party. The castle was unusually quiet. In fact, it was practically deserted as they walked through its grounds. Rory took the opportunity of the peace to suggest a wedding date of the 26th of September to Heather. She stopped him in his tracks and jumped into his arms, kissing him. It was perfect, not that long away and her birthday. What a present!

Rory had some difficulty prising Heather off him, but he was happy that she was happy and took time to look at her slim frame, dressed in a pretty blue party dress with her jet-black hair framing her heart-shaped face. He smiled at her, and her face lit up as she smiled back at him. He could feel that stirring that had caused so much trouble before and willed it down. The Hagpipe would be removed the next time, and they would be married first! They walked up the stairs, past the great kitchens and cellars, to the great hall which ran parallel with Loch Ness, its large oblong windows facing onto it. It was very quiet, but the apparent silence could not fool Rory's enhanced hearing as he heard sniggering and hushing noises from within. He knew there were a great many people within the great hall from the background noise of the sound of them breathing but decided to play along with this surprise party!

Word of the death of Granny Grant had reached all within, and a silent toast or two had been made to her memory. There could be no funeral as she had disappeared to the next life. Everyone felt blessed to have known this mystical woman and expected nothing else from her than something unusual. It confirmed to them that death was not the end of life. They were all strangely happy that she was at peace and had moved on to the next phase in her existence, thanks to the comforting words spoken by Abbot MacCallum. Rory opened the large double doors to the packed hall already full of half-drunk people. They were sitting at the long feasting tables as the band on the raised stage at the far end began playing. Shouts rang out of 'surprise' and 'happy birthday'.

Everyone was dressed in their finest clothes, and he was glad he had taken the time to wash and change into his new presentable clothes. Heather was beaming at his side as he noticed his drinking buddies from earlier in front of him, along with the unmistakable frame of the constable. The noise was interrupted by the squeal of a child shouting, *"I want Unkie!"* The crowd parted slightly in front of him as a small boy rushed forward and grabbed his leg. He bent down and lifted him up to eye level, receiving a slobbery cuddle around his neck. It was Eoin, his godson, and that meant Angus and Esther were here!

He saw them emerge from the throng in front of him. They had been busy as Esther was obviously about to extend her family and looked to be about six months pregnant. He warmly greeted them as the crowd parted again to allow the laird, young Johnny, his half-brother, to approach him with a big smile on his face. Rory was glad to see Johnny and lifted him up into the air, much to his dismay and enjoyment, for a cuddle with his spare arm enfolded around Eoin. Johnny had settled down under the guidance of the abbot and the constable and was turning out to be a very nice, sensible young man, much to the relief of everyone.

Rory's senses were in overdrive as he scanned the room, spotting Captain Roddy and his wife, Lee Chan, who had literary wiped the floor with him not so long ago. (* See Appendix.)

The room was full of his friends, monks and acquaintances, with wee beaming Charlie at the front of the queue wanting to talk and congratulate him. If only his mum and dad were here, he thought, it would be the perfect party as he felt a tap on his shoulder and put Eoin and Johnny down and turned. The tall red-haired man in front of him with the small dark-haired woman at his side was the mirror image of Rory. A surge of emotion caught Rory in the throat at the sight of them.

They were here!

It was their turn to be swept into his arms as the best party in his life started!

Rory took time to speak to everyone present, and all were enjoying the new whisky and its special mixer of Grail water which, literally, was the water of life! (Uisge Baugh, pronounced "ish'ka'ba'ha".)

Everyone was well, and just as he remembered them. Captain Roddy was enjoying himself to his usual high standards and well on the way to receiving the silent treatment the next day from Lee Chan. Rory had a deep conversation with her in Mandarin, causing a few funny looks from the non-speakers. However, he was soon joined by Angus, Esther and baby Eoin, who also knew a few words. Rory wanted them to tell him the story of Bruce again; he had to know if there were any changes to it after his involvement with him in the past.

The story was the same with the inclusion of the silkworms he had brought to Scotland, which he had successfully bred, starting a silk industry and making them very rich. Should he have helped him save the worms? Rory wondered. What difference could this make? It was just a matter of time until they came anyway?

Bruce had brought the knowledge of gunpowder and cannons from China to Scotland, and this was just as it had been before. There were no new consequences of his trip into the past.

Well, not yet?

The party was in full swing as Rory was dragged up onto the crowded dance floor by Heather, along with her mum, Moira, and stepdad, Hamish, to join Rory's parents and Roddy and Lee Chan, who was standing in front of the windows overlooking Loch Ness. Lee Chan let out a scream of alarm as the band stopped, wondering what had happened! A huge shadow filled the window, and Rory looked out and laughed.

Ben the eagle filled the sky with his huge wingspan shutting out the sunlight, and Nessie rode high on the waters of the loch. Both were looking in the window at Rory.

They wanted to come to the party too!

CHAPTER 19

Unholy Alliances

Satanic Stan was not fooled for a second by Rory muddying the water with his false time trails from the portals at the Blue Grotto. He knew he would return home to where he felt safe, to his place of power, where he had developed his gifts and was surrounded by his allies. That's what Stan would do. He still had ears in Urquhart Castle, knew of his return and of his celebration party. So, Rory thought he had defeated him!

Stan was more powerful than ever before, and it was now his time to amass an army and destroy Castle Urquhart and the Grail Box. He would end Rory; he was nothing more than the puppet of his ultimate adversary to control Earth. He would eradicate any chance for mankind to embrace each other and live in peace. He wanted the Earth to be a place of chaos, hate, fear, and blood, all of which he would feed on until he ruled supreme!

Not everyone in Scotland loved the MacSween's, and he would unify them all together with the lure of greed, power, wealth and jealousy, starting with Sir John Menteith the Younger, who had reason to hate them more than most.

Next, he would unify the enemies of their allies, which were many. The Campbells, MacGregors and the poor relatives of the MacLeod's and MacDonalds, led by Red James. All were fed up with leftovers from the tables of the rich and of living in ruined castles. With these promises, they would be easy to convince and willingly fight with the English lords to regain control of Scotland.

Satanic Stan's glee-filled laugh vibrated in the air, sending shivers down the spines of those with ears to hear him as he spoke, "No one will recognise me in the shadows, worming my way into their thoughts, convincing all to do my bidding, thinking they are helping their people. Just like that foolish old woman, driven by hate, they will do my bidding and won't know it until it's too late!"

* * *

Rory had gone out to his friends, mentally speaking to them. The only one missing was his pet, Hag his haggis, which in a way encouraged him. If she was still looking after his twin daughters, then they were still alive in the past, and he must be able to go back and save them from the future that lay in front of them. But this would change the whole life of Granny Grant and the influence she had on his life. But what had she done that had altered his actions? She had avoided any direct involvement, leaving that up to the monks of St Columba and the book! If he changed things, the twins would grow up in a loving family, and he would stop Isa's trip on the dark path. *That can only be good, and for the best,* he thought. *But first I must find them!*

Rory was too late!

Satanic Stan knew where they were, and an old oak tree stump would not stop him this time. They would not even recognise him. He placed his pentagram-marked hand face-down on the ground, feeling through the soil until he found the location of an active ley line of power. He willed himself into it, travelled far back into the past to the time of the first Druids at Urquhart Castle. They were still constructing the stone circle on the site of the current castle chapel and had not yet planted an oak tree to grow over the altar to protect it from evil.

He appeared in front of the working Druids as they used a lever system to raise a large stone into place.

His sudden materialisation alarmed those nearby, seeing him dressed head to toe in a red habit with its large red hood over his head, and standing at the site of the altar. The Druids let go of the rope that was pulling the stone, causing it to fall towards those below. Certain death under the weight of the life-crushing rock awaited the group propping up the pulley. Satanic Stan gestured his cloaked hand in their direction. The stone hovered in mid-air, raised itself perpendicularly and slid into the prepared hole for its base.

The next gesture put a shade over their eyes, disguising his appearance to look just like them as his robe shone white.

They were under his power!

His every word was obeyed as he instructed them to introduce him to the head Druid, who was with his wife in the underground cavern below the site of Urquhart Castle playing with his twin daughters, celebrating their fourth birthdays.

The head Druid was having trouble controlling them as their abilities were far beyond his own, being able to pass through the portal at the entrance to the cave at apparent will. The stranger was brought to the head Druid. The guardian haggis of the twins sprung to its feet from the resting place next to them, baring its teeth and sharp tusks to the stranger, stepping between him and the twins.

The actions of the protector of the twins were always heeded, and all the Druids in the cave, along with the head Druid, reached for weapons to defend themselves.

Satanic Stan stared at Hag, laughed inwardly and telepathically communicated in the head of the haggis. "You are no match for me, you puny beast. Be silent."

The light in Hag went out as she was lobotomised and fell to the ground, a pathetic shell of herself with no will of her own!

The head Druid and all the others were just as easily controlled, accepting Stan as their new leader. Only Bella, the fair-haired twin protected by the white crystal, saw the red-robed Druid in front of her, not the one in white that even her sister Isa, who possessed the black crystal, saw!

The whole history of the Druids changed at this point. No longer were they philosophers, star-gazing and working with the life force of the planet for the betterment of the human race and for good.

In one fell swoop, they became power-hungry, looking for the blood of virgins to sacrifice, in their now-blinkered eyes, to open the ley line portals. They travelled the planet, building their temples on the sites of power in tribute to their new master. The temples were still all aligned with the winter and summer equinox to channel the power of the sun, activating the magnetic lines, but they ignored this free means of travel.

Instead, they built sacrificial altars in the centre of the temples of stone, with channels to carry their victim's blood away along the ground to connect with the outer circle of the edifices. This was not necessary, as they were ritualised into performing these evil ceremonies at the time of the equinox when they would have activated without the need of blood. The Druids were controlled by the great evil for its own pleasure, bloodlust and joy in controlling man, thus causing misery. It made this evil stronger, and as it gained more power, it craved even more power.

Satanic Stan had a plan and patiently waited, training and teaching Isa in the dark arts, encouraging her lust and desire for it.

He left Bella alone as she was pure of spirit. He was waiting until she turned 16 when he would have her sacrificed in front of her father, Rory, whom he would call to witness her death.

Rory would not be able to resist the call, as Stan would broadcast his daughter's cry for help to him through the portal. He would then force him to watch as he spilled Bella's blood and enslaved Rory's tortured shell!

* * *

The day after the party, Rory made his way back to the cavern below Urquhart Castle, dressed in his shirt and kilt with his sword, Hans, strapped to his back in its Nessie scabbard with his skein dubh in his right sock. He planned on revisiting the Druids who had returned the broken sword to him and questioning them regarding his daughters. He did not want to risk using the portal situated in the entrance to the resting place of the Grail Box in case he alerted Satanic Stan to its presence and opted to travel by the one in the baby Nessie cave.

He entered the pool cave and positioned himself on the rocky shelf next to the pool, ready to walk back out to the cavern after activating the portal.

Rory took hold of the Hagpipe which warmed in his left hand, visualising his previous trip to the Druids. He no longer needed to blow it to activate its power, which appeared to be part of him now, flowing in his blood. He reached forward with his right hand, activating the portal, which shimmered blood-red, feeling and testing it was at the right point in time in the ancient past. He stepped through the curtain of power and into the far past, long before Urquhart Castle had existed.

He made his way to the spiral stone staircase and up towards the surface above the cavern. He could hear chanting from above as the Druids performed some ritual. It had been like this before when they had summoned him to recover the broken sword that he then remade into Hans.

It was night-time, and he could see flickering torchlight and smell smoke as he reached the surface behind the stone altar. He looked up, adjusting his eyes to the bright moonlight shining on the altar where a fair-haired white-gowned sixteen-year-old girl lay. The same white-bearded head Druid was standing over her with a long dagger held in both hands, poised to stab her in the heart.

The eyes of the Druid were blank, and he did not even see Rory in front of him, so strong was his intent in plunging the knife into the virginal child's breast. Something was wrong, very wrong, as Rory looked past the Druid to a large bonfire where a red-hooded figure floated in its middle unconsumed by the flames. Rory could feel the evil in the air around him. Everything was wrong. The Druids had never been evil before!

The dagger came down!

Rory moved with lightning speed, disarming the head Druid, taking the knife from him and throwing it at the apparition in the bonfire. It passed straight through the Red Druid as if it were a cloud of red dust. The Red Druid regained its shape and began emitting an eerie, spine-tingling laugh!

Rory grabbed the girl from the altar. She came out of the trance she was under with a scream as he touched her. He looked her in the eyes as he placed her on the ground, shouting at her to run. The stone circle was full of white-hooded Druids who moved strangely, almost robotically, turning towards Rory while drawing the same evil-looking daggers from inside their heavy-weaved gowns.

In front of him stood the head Druid like a statue now that he was unarmed. Rory recognised him: it was the same man who had helped him and talked with all those years before, but he was now totally devoid of any will of his own. Rory wondered what was going on.

The Druids began walking towards him like zombies, daggers outstretched, ready to stab downwards; the red-robed figure in the fire continued to laugh. It was not actually there, Rory decided. It was just watching from some other location. The young girl's path was blocked from reaching her parents by several Druids on the outer circle who had their daggers raised to kill her.

Rory had wanted to try something for quite some time as he withdrew his skean dubh from his right sock. It possessed part of the right tusk of the first haggis in its grip, and Rory wondered if it would obey his commands like Hans his sword.

He turned it so that its grip was facing away from him and threw it at the Druids. The skean dubh obeyed his will, flew like a remote-controlled drone and moved as quickly as Rory could run. It sped through the air, striking each Druid with the haggis-tusk grip on the back of their heads; each one was knocked unconscious and fell to the ground possession-free.

Once all the Druids had been neutralised, the skean dubh flew back into Rory's outstretched hand. The un-possessed and unconscious Druids were no threat to the girl, who ran past them into the arms of her parents, who had been watching from a safe distance.

The rest of the Druids were almost upon Rory as he threw his skein dubh again. It flew around them, knocking them all out cold and free of the hold the Red Druid had on them. The apparition was not laughing now and was becoming more solid each second in the fire as the skein dubh returned to Rory's hand.

Rory knew he was not going to find any answers here and decided discretion was better than valour. This was not the time to pick a fight with this powerful enemy. He ran back down the staircase to the portal and the relative safety of his own time.

He had a lot to think about.

If that was the Red Druid his daughter Bella had spoken of, then his twins were in far greater danger than he thought!

CHAPTER 20

Wedding

Rory spent every spare moment travelling the portals, looking for his daughters. Something fundamental had changed in the time lines with the corruption of the Druids. He moved from point to point, travelling to all the countries that the Druids had influenced, despairing at what he found. From Stonehenge to the ancient temples situated in the volcanic islands of the Mediterranean, he found the same story.

The Druids had become symbols of fear and suspicion and were given a wide berth by the local population, who considered them to be devil worshippers. In the circumstances with their heritage having been hijacked by Satanic Stan, the red-robed Druid, this was correct. History was being rewritten as they kidnapped and sacrificed young girls for their own evil purposes, causing despair and fear solely to feed their leader. Rory took it upon himself to rescue as many as he could, but he would have had more success if he had tried to stop the incoming tide. He was becoming quite depressed at his inability to change things back to the time when the world was dominated by good.

Evil had gripped mankind, and it was winning!

If it hadn't been for the support of his beloved Heather, who was overflowing with excitement at their imminent wedding, he would have slipped into despair at his inability to fight the evil taking over the will of everyone it touched. He could not think straight, and each minor victory saving a life did not change the fact that he could not lift the possession of the evil that was afflicting the Druids.

The invitations to the wedding had been sent out by carrier pigeon and by couriers to all the Lords of the Isles and all the friends, allies and family members on both sides. The number of guests on Rory's side far outnumbered Heather's; everyone wanted to be at the wedding of the Pure One who controlled the beasts of land, sea and sky. Extra accommodation was required to cope with the influx of guests, and giant marquees were erected in the castle courtyards to give the less important visitors a place to sleep. The remainder were given quarters depending on their status or family connexions within the castle, monastery or Grant Tower. Both the main kitchen in the castle and the refectory were commandeered for the sole purpose of preparing food for the wedding.

This was the biggest and most expensive wedding that Scotland had known, and the resources of the MacSween's, although healthy, could not cover the cost. Fortunately, Rory and Heather had asked Abbot Malcolm MacCallum to conduct the service. He was the chief banker of the monks of St Columba, and the credit of the MacSween's was good. A great deal of important business was going to be conducted with so many influential leaders all in one place. He was therefore convinced a huge profit would be made by the monks, and the wedding costs would be wiped out as his present to the happy couple.

Rory was returning the favour of being best man to his friend Angus by asking him to be his. Angus was over the moon, as was his son, Eoin, who was desperate to see 'Unkie' again as he spoiled him by giving him a lot of sweets. Wee Charlie was upset at not getting the honour, being Rory's oldest friend, but Rory promised him a position as usher and organiser of the stag party, which cheered him up and positively filled him with enthusiasm for the role. Every time Rory saw Charlie, he was in a conspiracy, whispering in small groups with all the castle and Castletoun boys from the rugby and footie (football) clubs Rory had played with when he was growing up.

Things were more subdued but no less frantic in the preparations of the bride who had asked Esther, the wife of Angus, to be her head bridesmaid. No matter how beautiful she was, being late in pregnancy, she was not going to detract from Heather's big day and had great ideas for the design of Heather's wedding dress and those of the bridesmaids. The mistakes she experienced at her own wedding were not going to be made again! (Refer to Book 2, *The Rescue*.)

It was like a rerun of the surprise birthday party for Rory as the big day approached and the wedding guests from the islands arrived along with Rory's parents. A meeting was arranged in the temple, with Rory conducting a special lecture on his trip with his unique insight into the origins of the secrets. All the brothers of HAGI knew the secrets that they had been initiated with. But to find out how they originated proved to be an eye-opener for them. (Especially the sign showing the covering your nose, as if from a bad smell.) The abbot furiously took notes at the meeting to compile a new ritual of this conclave of knights, which would be passed on to their future generations.

The meeting was followed by a special harmony in the refectory with a buffet and, more importantly, a bountiful supply of ale and whisky. After several drinks, Rory was hijacked by a group of thugs led by wee Charlie, Angus, Ally, Captain Roddy, his own father and everyone in the hall, including all the blacksmiths and assorted monks. He had no chance of escape without using his powers and submitted to being overcome, especially when the 6ft 8inch frame of the constable lifted him into the air and onto the shoulders of the group, surrounded by all his laughing schoolboy and team friends.

He was carried through the castle grounds with much hilarity and noise to the smithy, where he was quickly stripped naked and chained to a wooden beam, leaving only the

Hagpipe dangling around his neck. Charlie had planned this exercise well with buckets of axle grease lined up, waiting for the victim to arrive. Rory was soon covered from head to toe in the sticky, slimy grease and then covered in grit, which made him look like one of the Halloween special candies: a macaroon bar. Buckets of freezing cold water followed until the stag party, content with their work, retired to the brewery for more whisky and beer. Fortunately for Rory, the camera or CCTV had not yet been invented, and the only record of his humiliation was in the memories of those present.

Rory flexed his muscles, snapping the heavy chains restraining him like thin, soft wool. Cold water had no effect in removing the grease and stones covering his body, and he was getting married the next day!

It was a much longer than estimated time later that a red-raw scraped Rory, who looked very much like a lobster, re-joined the stag party, much to their hilarity. The whole party, including Captain Roddy, were well inebriated. Even his hollow sea legs were full as he staggered outside from the brewery past Rory to the privy.

Everyone was pleased to see Rory, and each had a cup in his hand from which he had to drink. It was a concerted effort as they tried to get Rory so drunk that he would miss his wedding the next day or at least make him feel terrible with a massive hangover.

It was a balancing act for the best man, Angus, who had to be seen to encourage Rory to get drunk but, on the other hand, keep him sober enough to make the wedding. He had been warned within an inch of his life by his wife, Esther, to look after Rory, who had looked after him.

Discretion won; Angus was more scared of his wife than the stag party. Every second cup passed to Rory was whisky-flavoured water, not the pure whisky ones, filled to the top that he was encouraged to drink in one swallow.

Rory found time for a quiet talk with his dad, who was now in the prime of health. He told Rory he had restored all the MacSween estates, including those on the Island of Arran and in Kilwinning in the lowlands. He stated he had gifted the ancient Druid site there to the monks of St Columba for the construction of their new abbey in gratitude for all their help and support.

Rory wanted to discuss the Hagpipe with him and the effect it would have on him when he was with Heather on their wedding night and honeymoon. His dad was surprisingly unflustered by this conversation and was glad Rory had brought this subject up as he did not know how he was going to. He explained this was why he kept the Hagpipe in its box when he was with Rory's mum and only put it on when he required its power. Unfortunately, this was why when he was ambushed, he could not protect Rory when he was a little boy because he could not get to it in time, a fact he still regretted. He told Rory he wanted to age at the same pace as his wife, growing old together, as this would not happen if he were to wear it all the time. He had found he could not wear it in the heat of passion and was scared of the effect it would have on any children conceived under its influence.

Rory blushed as he knew now exactly what the effects would be and told his shocked father about the twins. Ruaidri was both elated and deflated at being a grandfather and at the plight of the girls. He promised to assist Rory in any way he could and encouraged him, saying, "I know you will save them, son; I believe in you!"

The tears welled in Rory's eyes. If only he had the same faith in himself as everyone else did.

Heather, too, was receiving her own pep talk from Moira, her mother. Heather was taken aside a short time later by Mary and had a very similar conversation in private with her. This caused much blushing on Heather's part. She was warned about the influence the Hagpipe had regarding intimate relations. Mary knew all about its power after it had cured her bone cancer and saw Heather's reaction when she was giving her advice. Heather had grown close to Mary and confided to her, in tears, about the twins conceived under the power of the Hagpipe. Mary cuddled her and said that, when married, Heather would be moving to Castle Sween with Rory. She was sure he would save them, and Heather would live happily ever after with her family.

If only this were true.

Satanic Stan was preparing plans of his own. He still had many Clan Grant spies within Urquhart Castle and knew of everything that was happening. He had sought out Sir John De Menteith the Younger, who had taken refuge with Clan Campbell, and recruited him to carry out a task in return for his help in regaining the estates of the MacSween's. The happy couple were in for a big surprise!

The next day was the wedding, and Castle Urquhart and Scotland were experiencing an Indian summer due to the effects of the Grail Box on the climate. The late September weather could be easily confused with a hot summer's day. The castle was a buzz of excitement and activity. Heather and the bridal party had taken over Grant Tower, which was a female-only zone except for baby Eoin. Rory, his father and Angus and all the boys, including his half-brother, Johnny, had been expelled to the rooms above the foundry. Wedding chambers had been prepared for Rory and Heather in a secluded room above the great hall, with special plans for the honeymoon arranged by Rory for the day after. All their dress kilts had been prepared and were hanging, waiting for the sleeping dead to rouse themselves.

The only alert one was Johnny, who had been too young to get drunk the night before but had listened carefully to all the conversations while sitting invisibly in the corner of the brewery. Thankfully, the rejuvenating effects of the Grail-induced spring water aided the recovery of the groom's party, getting them into a near-normal state dressed in their different clan tartans.

They paraded to the chapel through the castle grounds to much oohing and aahing noises from the maids and female servants as they passed. Their heads were held high as they gave a swoosh of their kilts to the passing women, knowing how fine they looked and enjoying the attention.

With his red hair plaited and dangling behind his head, Rory planted Hans, his sword, vertically into the stone floor of the smithy for safety. He was not going to be wearing it with his dress kilt, black waistcoat and silver-buttoned jacket. The young bucks at the stag do had heard of the sword and could not resist having a go at pulling it from the ground. This had caused much hilarity to the older members of the party, especially Captain Roddy, who remembered his own pathetic attempt trying to remove it years before at Dunscaith Castle.

Rory had his possessions packed, including the box for the Hagpipe, which he had found below his mother's bed when he was eight years old. His dad had recovered the box and had given it to him the previous night. It was his now, but the Hagpipe was staying around his neck until he and Heather were alone. He had lost it once and was determined not to lose it again.

Rory knew now why Angus's knees had knocked when he had married Esther as he walked down the centre of the chapel, over the chequered floor, noticing that the chapel was full to overflowing with many faces he knew and even more he didn't.

Rory stood in front of the beaming face of Abbot Malcolm MacCallum, dressed in his ceremonial purple robe. He looked very much like the vision of St Columba portrayed in the stained-glass window above him as the sun shone through it, bathing him in multicoloured light.

The images of his friends looked down on Rory from the coloured windows; he knew that Nessie and Ben were safe. He was unsure of Hag's location and hoped that she was still protecting the twins. Even with the power of the Hagpipe coursing through his blood, Rory could feel his legs trembling as he waited at the altar for what seemed like a lifetime for Heather to arrive. Angus saw his plight and smiled at him, remembering his own discomfort. It was certainly easier to be the best man, he thought, until a panicked notion crossed his mind as to the location of the rings. He patted all the pockets in his jacket and checked his sporran until he found his wedding present to Rory of the two pure gold matching rings. They were identical to his own, made of the MacDonald gold they had discovered together on Rory's quest to remake his sword. It was Rory's turn to smile, seeing the panic on Angus's face until he again was gripped with trepidation, hearing the crowd's gasps behind him.

It was the arrival of the bride!

Heather was wearing the purest white wedding dress of the finest silk, which clung to her petite frame, showing off her curves. She sported a veil of fine transparent silk over her head while towing a long silk train held by her bridesmaids, Esther and Rory's mum, Mary. They appeared like sisters dressed in ivory white silk dresses the same colour as the Hagpipe. Words could not do their beauty justice, and even heavily-pregnant Esther exuded a glow that attracted the eyes of the congregation to her, similar to that of the pull of a magnet. Heather glided up to Rory's left side. He turned to look at her; his knees buckled on seeing her beautiful face looking up at him from below her veil; it radiated a smile of pure joy and love causing his heart to almost leap from his chest.

Abbot MacCallum took charge, conducting the ceremony before a hushed crowd until he raised Heather's veil, saying, "I now pronounce you husband and wife. You may kiss the bride."

The chapel exploded in noise as Rory lifted Heather up into his muscular arms and did just that!

CHAPTER 21

Trouble in Paradise

The happy couple, wearing their matching rings, only had eyes for each other. All other concerns and worries were forgotten, lost in this moment of pure joy. They walked to the door of the chapel to the sound of cheering from the waiting crowd outside and were immediately covered in rice and flower petals thrown by them. Rory caught the eye of his mother waiting outside. He thought that had he never seen his mum look more radiant and beautiful, and going by the grip his dad had around her waist and the look in his eyes, neither had he.

As they left, they saw the constable, dressed in his best uniform and accompanied by his junior officers, line up at the exit from the chapel as a guard of honour, batons crossed above their heads. A corridor of people formed in front of Rory and Heather as they walked through its middle, to slaps on the back and congratulations from all the people on either side as they made their way to the great hall. The constable and his officers followed on behind them. There were going to be no upsets to this day, and any excessive drunkenness and unruly behaviour would be resolved with a night in the cells, no matter who was involved. Rory thought he had met all the guests, thanked them for all the expensive gifts he had received and trusted his enhanced senses to keep him totally aware of all around him.

No person could catch him off-guard, so it was a complete surprise when he felt a tap on his shoulder, which almost made him jump. He spun around to see the smiling olive-skinned, ponytailed head and face of Bruce, dressed in his red silk pyjamas and obviously taking great pleasure in doing exactly that. Only he, with his advanced martial art skills, was capable of silently approaching and surprising Rory. He was very pleased to see him and told him so in Mandarin. The last time Rory had seen that face was when he had left his ancestor in the past in Cyprus with his silkworms, the descendants of those same creatures were currently responsible for the wedding dress being worn by his beloved Heather. At least that part of his trip into the past had produced a positive outcome.

Bruce joined his wife, Martha MacDonald, standing next to her brother Eoin MacDonald the Lord of the Isle of Skye and father of Angus, who was standing with his wife, Esther, and baby Eoin. The family was complete when the sister of Bruce, Lee Chan and husband, Captain Roddy, joined them for the biggest wedding feast Urquhart Castle had ever hosted.

The drink flowed like water, and the speeches were humorous and all at Rory's expense, including the tales from his best man, Angus, about Rory in Stornoway Castle being thrown about like a ragdoll by Lee Chan and Esther. He further recalled how bad a singer Rory was, describing when he was 16 and unable to hold his drink. He was very drunk after consuming just one pint of Old Shipwreck (a rather strong real ale) and began singing sea shanties. The crowd loved it, the great hero being beaten up by two wee wummin (women) and drunk after one pint. Rory remembered a slightly different version of events, but Angus was correct in one respect. His singing was terrible!

It was soon time for the first dance, which again filled Rory with dread. For all his skills, he had never embraced or truly learned how to dance, moving as if he had two left feet while wobbling from side to side. From the beaming smile on Heather's face, this did not concern her, and he soon relaxed, enjoying the moment. Time appeared to stop as he looked into her eyes. No one else noticed, but time, in fact, with the subconscious influence of Rory on the Hagpipe had not stopped, but it had slowed down to such an extent one could not tell the difference. This was their moment, and nothing could interfere with it. Love is the strongest power in the world, and they both were so much in love.

This bond between them would never be broken!

The wedding was a great success with only a few minor scuffles between drunken rival clansmen, which were quickly resolved when the shovel-like, iron hands of Constable John Gregg grabbed them by the scruff of the neck. The abbot was pleased as he walked around the room; he had already secured several appointments for the next day with the clan leaders to draw up valuable trade contracts. The wedding costs had been well and truly covered, inclusive of a healthy commission rate for the monks.

The happy couple were the centre of attention until a cry of alarm resounded around the great hall. A circular space formed around Esther and a puddle on the dance floor as the constable rushed forward, thinking there had been a murder. Esther had enjoyed the dancing a bit too much, and child number two had decided to join the party. A beautiful little girl, just like her mother, and a young sister for Eoin, arrived in the world.

Esther had stolen the limelight from Heather or, to be more precise, baby Jackie had. This resulted in another event to celebrate as everyone had to wet the baby's head. (Not literally; a Scottish custom with a toast to the health of the baby with a glass of something strong.) The new grandparents, Lee Chan and Captain Roddy MacLeod and Eoin MacDonald were overjoyed to meet the latest addition to their joint families. Jackie Chan Lee MacLeod MacDonald had been born into a dynasty of great heritage and power. Time would tell what she could achieve under the scholarship of her uncle Bruce Lee.

This was the perfect opportunity for the newlyweds to sneak off to their wedding chambers as the party would continue long into the night. Rory kept up with the tradition of carrying his bride over the threshold into the room dominated by a large king-sized feather bed. He threw the giggling bride onto it and watched with a look of horror on his face as she screamed, and with a loud thud, all four legs of the bed gave way, collapsing to the floor!

His friends had been busy. How many more surprises were in store? he wondered.

The honeymoon couple did not get much sleep their first night together. By the time Rory had reattached the bed's legs and they had climbed below the sheets with the background noise from the party below being a constant irritation, the giggling drunken party guests began banging on the door to the suite and running away. Just as Rory took Heather in his arms in a lull between disturbances, she began to squirm, scratching at her skin. Rory had removed the Hagpipe from his neck, and it now hung by its thong on the bedpost, and without its protection, he too began to scratch furiously at his body.

The sheets had been laced with itching powder!

There would be no sleep in that bed tonight or anything else as they washed and dressed in the clothes they had in the room for their departure in the morning. The sabotage had been thorough as all items in their travelling bags had suffered the same fate as the bed, and they began to scratch again. The first argument between the couple started as to whom Rory had trusted with the care of his possessions. Wee Charlie was still laughing as he sneaked away from outside the room as Heather began shouting at Rory, who was determined that he would not trust him again!

The rest of the night was spent cleaning and checking all their possessions until sunrise, when Rory left to check his preparations for the honeymoon transport and, hopefully, the appeasement of his wife.

A short time later, he was fully dressed in his last remaining clean clothes comprising his one-piece highland kilt with his sword Hans strapped to his back and his sturdy boots on his feet. He returned to collect an extremely tired Heather and picked her up, holding her lovingly in his arms where she fell asleep. They left the sabotaged honeymoon suite and went down the stairs past the sleeping revellers.

Only a few diehards were still awake in the great hall, drinking. He moved silently with the power of the Hagpipe activated around his neck, enhancing his natural abilities and walked to the temple.

Rory opened the secret door in the east below the stained-glass windows by pressing the letter G inset in the wall. He made his way down the spiral staircase to the cavern below the castle and walked towards his Maltese fishing boat. It was still on the beach next to the much smaller rowing boat. He had transferred all their possessions, along with supplies for two weeks, into the fishing boat and had modified it to create a comfortable area in its rear, padded with cushions and bedding, where he laid Heather. She moaned in comfort as she snuggled into this makeshift bed and was soon sound asleep.

A silent mental call was sent to his sea friend, Nessie, with whom he had discussed the honeymoon plan. Rory was not surprised to see her friendly smiling face pop up out of the deep water in front of him. He thanked her for coming and pushed the multicoloured boat off the beach, jumping into it, causing it to career away from the shore towards Nessie. He lowered a long rope with a wide loop at its end from the front of the boat into the water. He had repeated this procedure frequently with Nessie, who put her head through the loop, pulling the boat towards the exit from the cavern to Loch Ness. It shimmered in white light as Rory took hold of his Hagpipe, visualising the exit from Fingal's Cave to the Atlantic Ocean.

He was not travelling in time, only moving from place to place, and he encompassed the whole boat and its contents, including Heather, in a protective bubble of power as Nessie pulled them out of the cavern and through the exit from Fingal's Cave into the calm sea opposite the island of Iona.

The unnatural Indian summer weather produced by the effects of the concealed Grail Box continued as Nessie gently pulled the multicoloured boat northwards past the abbey on Iona toward the islands of Tiree and Coll. The strong morning sunlight shone on Heather, cocooned in the gently rocking boat. She quietly awoke, looking up at the clear blue sky and forward at Rory's muscular back, standing with his feet rooted to the boat's boards like a human statue.

Heather looked around at her surroundings in the middle of the turquoise blue sea as a pod of dolphins surrounded and swam along with the gliding boat. She raised herself up to get a better look as a young dolphin swam up towards her as she lowered her hand into the water. The dolphin kept pace with the boat as she stroked its rubbery head, much to its enjoyment. Rory heard Heather's breathing change as she awoke; he felt her move in the boat and turned to see her beaming face as she caressed the friendly sea creature.

Rory said, "If you like that, wait till you see my friend."

The boat slowed to a stop as the dolphins swam past. Heather continued to stare into the sea. Where the dolphin had been, a giant oval-shaped green/blue head topped with two antennae emerged from the water on a long, graceful neck, level with her face. Heather gasped as the creature appeared to smile at her, showing a large mouth of razor-sharp white teeth.

"She likes to be tickled behind her antennae," said Rory, as Nessie lowered her head to Heather's outstretched hand, eager for her touch.

Heather stroked Nessie, who felt very similar to the dolphin, amazed at how close she was to the great Loch Ness Monster.

All this time, a private telepathic conversation was taking place between Rory and Nessie, who was pleased to meet Heather and approved of her. She, too, was just as impressed with Nessie and with this honeymoon surprise. After a short time, Nessie submerged and continued to tow the boat, passing through the channel separating the islands of Tiree and Coll towards Barra, South and North Uist.

As they travelled, all the creatures of the sea, including a huge basking shark, swam with them as if paying homage to Rory, standing at the front of the boat. The sea was full of life as Heather gasped, asking Rory what the name was for each creature. He remembered asking Captain Roddy the same questions the first time he had seen them and smiled as he answered her, seeing the look of wonder on her face.

They carried on along the coast of North Uist as the large mountainous Island of Lewis dominated the skyline in front of them, with its many smaller islands hugging its shore. The castaway, tropical-looking Island of Taransay came into view as the boat turned right past it towards the mainland of the Isle of Harris and the miles of pure white sandy beach of Luskentyre.

Heather was speechless, having never seen a sight like it; to her eyes, it looked like paradise. The tide was rushing to the coast, covering the sandy bay, as Nessie released the boat to drift in on it towards the single white Atlantic cottage sitting at the edge of the beach facing the sea.

They had arrived!

Rory perceived that he was being watched as he secured his boat and unloaded its contents into the cottage. He had spotted Ben, the great eagle, in the sky as they travelled and assumed those eyes were the ones watching him.

Unfortunately, he was wrong!

Heather was behaving like a small child, desperate to get her bare feet onto the secluded beach and paddle in the water. They stripped to their shifts and ran, giggling, onto the warm sand. Heather put a foot into the sea and rapidly pulled it back from the waves, shocked by the freezing cold Atlantic water. Rory laughed and stepped into the water, which began to steam as he expelled heat outwards from his feet.

"Try it now," he told Heather as she stepped into the now warm water, more suited to the Mediterranean Sea than the Atlantic.

They laughed and splashed about, with Rory teaching Heather how to swim. The basking shark was filtering plankton in the bay between Taransay and the beach as they swam alongside the peaceful creature under the watchful eye of Nessie, who was snacking on a plentiful supply of fish, attracted by the now warm water.

The first week went by in a flash as the couple relaxed in each other's company with the Hagpipe secured in its box below the bed in the cottage beside Hans, the sword. They settled into a routine of long beach walks, interspersed with eating, drinking and sleeping as they explored each other, becoming one.

It was only when Rory went to recover the Hagpipe to warm up the sea for Heather's swim that he discovered the box was empty!

CHAPTER 22

Return to Callanish

Sir John Menteith the Younger had been given very specific instructions to follow from Satanic Stan if he wanted to regain the estates of the MacSween's. He left his allies of Clan Campbell on the fastest horse they had in their stables, travelling to the Island of Lewis to wait and watch for Rory and his bride arriving at the cottage. He was a sneaky individual, not prone to fighting and knew how strong Rory was from the time he had reclaimed Castle MacSween from him. He remembered how long it had taken for his broken nose to heal; it was crooked now, a constant reminder of how much he hated the MacSween's.

Menteith watched and waited until the couple arrived in their multicoloured boat, documenting all of their actions and routines. He waited until they had gone for one of their long evening walks on the beach. They were always gone for about an hour, picking a vantage point to watch the sun set as they held hands. The cottage had no locks on its doors. They were not necessary in this remote spot; as long as the door was firmly closed to keep the sheep out, your possessions were safe. No one would steal from another here in any case.

Well, nobody, except him!

He sneaked into the cottage and quickly found the box engraved with the image of a haggis below the bed next to a sword with the image of Nessie carved in its grip. He wanted to be far away before Rory discovered the Hagpipe was gone and put the box back exactly where he had found it. Unless opened, he would not know it was gone as the most valuable looking item for a thief below the bed was the sword, and it was not going to be disturbed.

Sir John was long gone with a 24-hour start on horseback before Rory noticed the Hagpipe was gone. He was stranded in the middle of nowhere and on foot, without his powers.

There was no way he could catch him.

Rory could not understand what had happened to the Hagpipe but believed Heather when she said she had not moved it. The only explanation was that it had been stolen. Without it, he could not mentally contact Ben or Nessie to ask for help, nor could he use his superior sight to look for the thief. He was in trouble and knew it. Feelings of despair and self-doubt began creeping into his normally positive mind. This was the second time he had lost the Hagpipe, and it was his own fault. He wanted to be with Heather and grew old with her, but by taking it off he had sacrificed any chance he had of saving their daughters.

Heather could see Rory's anguish as she cuddled him. His mind was racing. He must get the Hagpipe back, but how? Nessie was still swimming in the sea nearby, but how could he contact her. Ben was also in the sky watching over him, and although he could not contact him, he could see Rory.

He went outside to the beach, telling Heather of his plan to contact his eagle friend. They collected large white stones from the shoreline, laying them out in the dark, damp sand where the tide had just left, writing 'BEN, HELP!'

Rory was not sure if Ben could read, but even when he was young, he had always been able to understand him as he was incredibly intelligent. He looked up into the blue sky, but without his augmented sight, he was not sure if the dot he saw was Ben or not. He peered at it, it was getting larger, and he began waving his arms frantically to attract Ben's attention. Within seconds, Rory's question was answered as the giant

Scottish eagle zoomed towards him, landing on the beach with a quizzical look on his face.

Rory could not mentally communicate with Ben, but he could talk. He told his friend of the theft of the Hagpipe and asked for his help. The eagle nodded his head, and Rory informed Ben that, without the Hagpipe's power, he would not be protected as he flew with him, and he could not go too high in the sky or he would not be able to breathe. The eagle again nodded as Rory recovered Hans, his sword, from the cottage and strapped it to his back. Without his power, he could not jump high enough to get onto the back of Ben's neck, and he had to climb up onto him as he lowered his head to the ground.

Rory promised Heather he would be back as soon as possible. She watched, open-mouthed, as her husband soared into the air holding onto the neck of the huge bird. They flew in ever-widening circles, searching the surrounding area for anyone travelling away from Luskentyre. It was an impossible task, like searching for a needle in a haystack, but Rory could not accept the consequences of failure. He tried to think like the thief.

Where would he go?

He must be an ally of Satanic Stan and be taking the Hagpipe to him.

Where would he meet him?

His brain did not work as quickly as when under the Hagpipe's power, but he was more than clever enough without the enhancement to figure this out. The thief would be heading for a stone circle and a portal to give it to him, and the nearest one was at Callanish, a day's ride away. He may already be too late! Rory leaned into Ben and shouted above the wind, "The stones."

Ben understood and took off at full speed, flying north over the Isle of Harris and into the Isle of Lewis, over the mountain tops and fertile farmland dotted with small lochs. The huge standing stones of Callanish were in the north-west of Lewis and had been used by Ben many times in the past to travel. He pushed himself to his natural limits of strength and endurance, and although Rory could not see ahead, Ben could. A small figure was pushing his tired horse at full speed towards the stones in front of them.

The portal in the centre of the stones was active, with a red-hooded figure beginning to materialise, surrounded by a black cloud.

Ben had no time to spare and went into a steep dive as Rory clung on for his life. The horseman was almost at the outer circle of the stones and safety when he was clutched in a huge talon and snatched from the back of his horse.

Sir John was not a brave man, and this was not the first time he had encountered Ben. He soiled himself for the second time in his life as he was grabbed by the giant bird. Ben wheeled away from the stones and the materialising form of a screaming Satanic Stan, who could only watch as the eagle disappeared into the distance.

Once at a safe distance, Ben dropped Sir John heavily onto a marshy spot of land surrounded by large rocks, where the eagle picked a suitable one to land on. Rory sprung from Ben's back, rushing toward the pathetic dirty man he now recognised as Sir John Menteith the Younger. Hans was out of its sheath and in Rory's hands practically before his feet touched the springy grass as he approached him with a menacing look in his eyes.

Sir John cowered in the mud and, even before he was asked, threw the Hagpipe at Rory, begging for mercy. Rory caught the ivory pipe, which instantly imbued him with its power as it touched his skin, hearing Ben laughing in his head at the pathetic sight of Sir John.

A stern-faced Rory advanced on Sir John with his sword outstretched before him, but he was laughing on the inside in mental communication with Ben, sharing the joke and the plight of the cowardly, weak-willed man in front of them. Both were enjoying making him squirm in the mud and soiled clothes.

Rory was determined not to be troubled by him again and wanted to experiment with his control over Hans, his sword, as he extended his will to it in silent communication, releasing it from his grasp. The easy way would be to kill him now, but Rory had made a vow to himself not to kill if he had any other option available.

Hans floated horizontally through the air towards Sir John's head with its sharp point stopping at the bridge of his crooked nose, making him look cross-eyed as he stared at it. As a baby's nappy cannot contain its contents when left too long, neither could the now brown trousers of Sir John as he filled them again. Rory was feeling sorry for him, but his facial expressions were still ones of unforgiving fury. Ben wanted in on the fun and took to the air, hovering over the trembling man, who was sure he was about to become a snack, whether alive or dead, for the giant bird with its outstretched talons.

Sir John had not prayed since he was a young boy, but he began praying and begging for forgiveness now.

It was not Rory's place to grant divine pardon, but he could personally forgive those who wronged him. He granted that now as Sir John cowered and vowed that he would never cross the MacSween's again. Rory emphasised that the sword and the eagle would find him to complete this sentence, no matter where he was, and carry it out should he ever go back on his word.

The power of this sword floating in the air under its own control, and the massive bird overhead, convinced Sir John to be more afraid of them than the red-hooded demon from whom he would have to spend the rest of his life hiding. A position in a religious order, doing good deeds, seemed very appealing to him, and it would grant him protection from the evil one.

Rory could see the change taking place in the man in front of him.

He recalled Hans back to his right hand as he jumped in the air, landing on the neck of Ben, who was filled with the power of the Hagpipe from his contact with Rory. Ben was exhilarated by it and totally refreshed after all his exertions, flying off at breath-taking speed back towards Luskentyre beach.

The muddy, soiled, sad man looked up in wonder as they disappeared into the distance, determined to keep his promise. He headed to the nearest loch to get as clean on the outside as he now felt on the inside after receiving forgiveness!

Heather was a lonely figure standing on the beach, looking to the sky, left alone on her honeymoon. With the Hagpipe back around his neck, Rory could see as well as his friend Ben now. As they flew towards her, he saw the look of abandonment on Heather's face. Rory was saddened at the trauma he had put Heather through and made a new vow to himself. He would not let the Hagpipe out of his sight ever again until all his enemies had been defeated and his family reunited, whole and safe. Heather looked like she needed cheering up, and Rory asked Ben if he would take her for a joy ride. Ben was pleased to do this as long as Rory held her on his neck, giving him the extra power. He banked in the sky, still too far away from Heather to see them, and flew round behind her, silently landing on the beach behind her. Rory leapt from Ben and sneaked up behind her, cuddling her. She jumped with surprise into his arms, relaxing as Rory whispered sweet nothings into her ear, nibbling at her neck. He took her by the arm, walking her to Ben, helping her up onto his neck and jumped up behind her, holding her around the waist. Ben extended his wings and floated up into the air to gasps and squeals from Heather.

Rory extended the hag power around all three of them as Ben took them for a bird's eye view of the Outer Hebrides, looking down on the pure white beaches, mountains and lochs. Rory pointed out the places of interest he knew to her, from the quarry on the mountain of Roinebhal on the Isle of Harris, where the gold that made their wedding rings came from, to Dunscaith Castle on the Isle of Skye.

He showed Heather the Island of Arran, which was a miniature of the landscape of Scotland, and the Firth of Clyde separating it from the mainland of the West Coast where he had rescued his father. They then flew over Kilwinning, where the new Abbey of the Monks of St Columba was under construction on the land donated by the MacSween's.

They doubled back up the west coast of Scotland, away from Largs and the famous battle with the Vikings that Rory had been involved in, freeing Scotland from their control, and over the Firth of Clyde to Dunoon. They looked down on the tree-covered mountains full of nesting haggis and inland past the Holy Loch, turning left back to Loch Striven and the mountain pass at Loch Riddon.

Rory heard Heather gasp again at the view in front of her in the clear cloudless sky. The Isle of Bute, the home of Rothesay, dominated the channel which stretched to infinity into the sea, back to the mountain of Goat Fell on Arran, pointing to heaven.

It was one of the most spectacular views in the world, known as the treasure of Argyll. They were travelling so high in the cloudless sky that they could look down with a satellite view of the whole of Scotland below them. Heather knew Rory was special, but she was speechless at this display of God-like power. Today, every person with a computer can zoom in from space and over land and sea, but not many have done it from the neck of an eagle.

Ben decided to have some fun on the descent back to the cottage with some rollercoaster moves. He again made Heather squeal as she held onto Rory's arms as he plunged vertically to the ground and did a 90-degree revolution. Even Rory was impressed, holding down his breakfast, but he would never admit that as they landed on the golden sand next to the cottage where a clinging Heather was not going to let her man out of her grasp!

CHAPTER 23

Hag

Hag was a pathetic copy of herself, following her defeat by Satanic Stan, and she would have died quickly if it had not been for the attention Bella gave in keeping her alive by hand-feeding her scraps of meat and spooning water into her mouth. Bella was the only one not taken in by the fake magical glamour surrounding the Red Druid, and she saw him for what he was. Even her own sister, Isa, had been taken in by him, listening to his lying words, which wormed their way into her head. Bella did not know why she was not affected by the hypnotic words he spoke, but she thought it had something to do with the warm white crystal around her neck, which she refused to take off, no matter how many times she was asked.

Hag was lost within a weakening, starving body, with her mind, free spirit and intellect trapped in a cage in a tiny corner at the rear of her brain. She could see through its bars, watching what was happening around her, but she had no control over her own body, which was rapidly failing. If it hadn't been for Bella caring for her, coaxing her instinctive reflexes to eat and swallow, she would be dead!

If she was not released from this cage soon, she would be unable to keep the promise she had made to this very person who was keeping her alive!

The honeymoon was over, and Rory pondered his next move to save his daughters as he loaded his Maltese boat. He had considered travelling straight to Castle Sween with his bride to start his new life, but first he had to find a permanent safe location for the Grail Box, and he needed a convenient portal from which to travel. He instinctively felt that the key to saving his daughters was Hag, his pet haggis.

It was an uneventful cruise home under Nessie-power as they snuggled in the bedding and cushions in the rear of the boat, talking about their future. Heather said she would miss her mother at Castle Urquhart and Rory suggested she and her stepfather Hamish could join them at Castle Sween, where his skills in training new apprentices would be of great use. He was no longer needed at Urquhart Castle, and Rory was sure he would like a fresh challenge. Heather was sure her mother would also enjoy taking charge of a new kitchen, training new lassies as well, and they could all travel together. It was agreed they would speak to them and maybe move before Christmas and the bad weather. Rory was happy with this but said he would have to remain at Castle Urquhart until the winter equinox, and then he would join them.

He had a plan that would only work with the aid of the power of the ley lines unleashed at the equinox.

The newlyweds received a warm welcome home, with Rory's single male friends giving him some strange nudge, nudge, wink, wink, looks and comments about what married life was like. Rory was very naïve, giving an honest answer, which was not what they were looking for. If only Monty Python had been in existence at this time, he would have understood the question!

The abbot approached Rory, who could see by his ashen face that something was seriously wrong as he joined him in his chambers. The *Book of St Columba* was open on his desk as he directed Rory to look at it. He explained he had looked at the book while Rory was away, and two pages at the back of the book that had previously been blank now showed new images.

Rory looked at the book, and the first page showed the completed new abbey in Kilwinning, which Rory had seen from the sky, with a secret circular chamber below it containing the Grail Box. He realised that meant he had to move the Grail Box there for safe keeping.

The second picture was very disturbing indeed. It showed the destruction of Castle Urquhart! It was a ruin, and Castletoun had been wiped off the face of the earth. Rory went as ashen faced as the abbot. The corruption of the Druids by Satanic Stan had changed the course of history, but St Columba had recorded the course of actions they had to follow. Plans would have to be made to evacuate Urquhart Castle without alerting the obvious spies within it. The book was never wrong: The castle would fall, and those who were loyal and loving within it must be saved!

Rory told the abbot of his intention to leave with his bride and her family to Castle Sween and said he would see if any others wanted to go as well. Some would have to stay so as not to arouse suspicion, and Rory had an idea regarding how to save those left behind.

The abbot said he was planning on moving key monks and the book and bank to the new abbey in Ayrshire at a place, now known as Kilwinning, where its construction was being supervised by a young stonemason monk called Winning! (* See Appendix.)

The *Book of St Columba* was indexed to go to him next, and Abbot MacCallum said he had a lot to teach him before he would part with it.

It was a busy two months as people left in small groups with very good excuses to start new lives or to care for elderly relatives who had passed on their land to them. Heather was escorted with her parents by Rory on Jet, his horse, to Castle Sween and her new home. The abbot relocated to Kilwinning Abbey as the normal cycle of Scottish weather changed to autumn winds and storms before the cold Arctic winds and snow hit. This was good news as the attack predicted on Urquhart Castle could not take place until spring.

The population of Castle Urquhart was slowly cut to the bare minimum under the supervision of the constable who was included in the planned evacuation by Rory and the abbot. He was determined to stay and resist the enemy to the end with trusted volunteers and, hopefully, to escape with Rory at the last moment.

The winter equinox was fast approaching as Rory kissed Heather goodbye, promising he would be back in time for Christmas. He left on foot on the road to Kilmartin and its numerous standing stones and cairns. The nearest portal he came to was at the Ballymeanoch stone circle, situated in the secluded, quiet countryside. Argyle was portal central with its large number of stone circles and burial vaults containing the remains of the returning Templar Knights, which were all aligned with the winter equinox. It was a place of great power, and Rory did not even have to reach for his Hagpipe for the doorway between two adjacent large stones in front of him to activate. He visualised the cave of the haggis graveyard below Urquhart Castle.

No one was aware of his return as he stepped through the stones into the cave, which was illuminated in subtle white light from the crystals in the arched ceiling.

The small figure of Bella had cared for her guardian to the best of her abilities and created a rock nest around the old wasting shell of Hag. No one approached the haggis. Even her sister Isa and the Druids seemed unable to come within a foot of the stone circle as if it were emitting a field repelling them. Only she could put her hand inside the circle to feed and stroke the frail creature. Bella knew Hag did not have long to live, and no matter how hard she tried to feed her, the food fell out of her snout. It was the winter equinox, and the Druids were leaving to go up to the new altar above the cave to prepare to kill another village girl. There was nothing Bella could do to stop the killing taking place around her, and now her only friend was going to die, leaving her here alone, surrounded by all this evil!

Rory approached the rock nest in the centre of the cave, past the seemingly empty, rectangular altar of haggis tusks.

The Grail Box was still there, he knew, but 33 minutes into the future. He knelt down at the circular ring of stones, remembering when he had first discovered the haggis egg, which had hatched into his friend Hag. Rory did not have to see the moon to know when it reached its zenith as he felt the power of the equinox flowing through him as he stretched his right hand into the stone circle, holding the Hagpipe with his left.

Bella was sitting beside her friend, watching her waste away as the equinox came. Her mouth fell open as a hand appeared in the circle and began stroking the failing haggis, which moved in response to the touch. The hand lovingly took hold of the haggis, lifting it from the ground and out of the circular rock nest, vanishing before her amazed eyes!

Rory felt the leather skin and wings on the back of his friend Hag responding to his touch. Something was drastically wrong with her as he scooped his hand below her and lifted her out of the stone circle and into his lap. She was emaciated, and he could see she did not have long to live. He was not going to permit that as he carefully placed her back in the stone nest, now in his time.

He walked to the altar of haggis tusks and reached out his right hand, calling the Grail Box back into real time, watching it appear in from of him. Rory reached down to the ivory tusks, which parted in front of his hand, revealing the rods of Moses and Aaron, which he then removed and inserted into the holes in the Grail Box. It was risky, but it had to be done. No one had looked in the box since it had been sealed, but Rory knew it was the only way to save Hag. He prised open the lid of the Grail Box, illuminating the cave in blinding white light.

Rory knew what was in the box and did not need to see to find what he wanted as he shut his eyes tight and put his right hand and arm in the box. He touched stone, parchments, and finally found it on top of folded linen: A wooden cup. It was the Grail Cup used at the Last Supper and made from the same acacia wood as the Grail Box, which caught the blood from Jesus as he was crucified.

It had the power to grant everlasting life!

Rory removed it, rushed to the freshwater spring at the rear of the cave and filled the cup, running back to Hag. He knelt by her and saw she was practically dead as he raised her snout and poured the water into her mouth, emptying the remains over her body. The transfiguration was immediate!

As he watched, Hag became healthy and regained her full stocky figure. She instantly became alert, and her eyes sparkled with a white light as she was released from the mental prison in which she had been placed. She raised her head to Rory with a large smile of teeth and tusks as she communicated in a mental burst of joy at seeing Rory. Hag spoke urgently to Rory; time was of the essence as she informed him how and where to save the twins.

But something was wrong!

Rory watched in awe as Hag began to grow younger as she talked, her wings receding on her back as her body shrunk in size. Only the two tusks on the right and left side of her face remained full size, giving her a very strange look. Soon she was a tartan-pelted infant as she said a rushed goodbye of, "I love you" and turned once again into a black watch tartan-coloured haggis egg with two large haggis tusks lying either side of it in the stone nest.

This was not what Rory had expected when he had let her drink from the cup of life!

He continued to watch open-mouthed as the two tusks and egg vanished to their correct points in time to start the everlasting cycle of the haggis again! He knew where the tusks and egg were going; he had already found them in his own life history. His friend Hag was like a haggis phoenix; she was going to be born again in his past and meet him as a boy. He wondered just how many times this had happened, or was this the first time? He returned the Grail Cup back into the Grail Box, securing its lid, cutting off the blinding white light emitting from it leaving the rods in the holes situated in its wooden sides. The Grail Box had to be moved from Urquhart Castle, it was no longer safe here, and he had been shown where it should go.

He took hold of the rod of Moses protruding left to right through the top centre base of the box and visualised the chamber he had seen in the *Book of St Columba*. The Hagpipe illuminated below his shirt as a white light shone through his clothes, Rory and the Grail Box vanished from the cave of the haggis graveyard, reappearing on top of a black iris shaped raised dot. This was the meeting point and centre of all the worlds ley lines and situated in the middle of a perfect circle.

CHAPTER 24

St Winning's Well

Abbot Malcolm MacCallum arrived in the small town now known as Kilwinning, situated in the lowlands of the west coast of Scotland, slightly inland from the channel of the Firth of Clyde and the Island of Arran. He had travelled with Father Doogan and a wagon full of pigeons trained to return to various important locations, including Urquhart Castle, Castle Sween and the islands of the Outer Hebrides under the control of the Lords of the Isles.

The pair had been soaked to the bone from the autumn storms and horizontal rain lashing them on the trip. They were pleased to see that the stonemason monks had been very busy with a wing of the new abbey already constructed, giving them much-needed shelter.

The land where the abbey was being built had previously been a major pagan centre and Druid site due to it being on top of the main ley line that connected it to the most well-known standing stone location in the British Islands: Stonehenge. It was on the main artery of ley lines travelling from both Kilwinning and Stonehenge, which passed all around the planet. The monks of St Columba knew the location of the new abbey was important, but they did not comprehend how important it really was.

The abbot and Father Doogan were met by Father Christopher Winning, a young man in his twenties with a wiry, muscular frame. He was used to hard labour, having worked with stone all his life, coming from a family of stonemasons. He was uncommonly attuned to the life forces of the planet, and he felt in his bones the importance of the ground on which he was standing.

As he helped dig the foundations of the abbey, a shudder had gone through him as his shovel struck solid rock. It was the backbone of the ley line, 33 feet below the ground's surface. It protruded from the ground like a camel's hump, in a perfect circle, 33 feet in diameter. He briefed Abbot MacCallum on his find, and surprisingly, the abbot appeared to have been expecting this news.

The monks had constructed a circular wall around this chamber in the middle of the new abbey building, which was then built around it, including a concealed trap door in its roof or basement, depending on one's perspective. The chamber now looked like a large well or giant chimney if one had an aerial view of it. The abbot and monks knew it was important, but even they could not guess the magnitude of Father Winning's discovery!

Rory materialised in the pitch-black, lightless chamber; it took him a few seconds before he saw a dim light exuding from the Hagpipe. He took it out from below his clothes and used it like a torch to look around the 33-foot-wide circular room with its high 33-foot roof.

He could see a trap door in its ceiling, but there was no way anyone could get out of this pit unless the trap door had been opened and a ladder lowered. Any normal human being would be trapped here, but he was no ordinary human being.

Abbot MacCallum was above, accompanied by Father Winning, and they were expecting him. He opened the trap door, looking down on Rory below. He wanted a look at the Grail Box before Rory placed it out of time and into safety. A novice monk, Father Jacob, had constructed a special rope ladder 33 feet long to reach down into the chamber, which was hidden in the basement. It was affectionately known as Jacob's Ladder; one's life was in peril as it was so dangerous climbing up and down it. Just like the biblical one that reportedly reached all the way to heaven, that was where one would go if you fell off it!

The abbot gingerly climbed down and warmly embraced Rory, congratulating him and wishing him a Merry Christmas. He told him he would ensure this chamber would remain undisturbed and protected for eternity.

He watched in awe as Rory removed the rods of Moses and Aaron from the Grail Box, which vanished before his eyes as he placed it 33 minutes into the future. The rods remained on the stone floor in real time. Unless the box and rods were reunited, no person could ever open it again!

It would be certain death for anyone to touch the box without the rods correctly inserted, and Rory was certain no one would ever find the Grail Box here. The abbot lifted the rod of Moses, and even he could feel the power emanating from it. This was the same rod that had turned into a serpent in front of the pharaoh as he freed the Israelites and when Moses had commanded the Red Sea to part!

The abbot carefully placed it back on the ground, saying he would initiate a new order to shroud the location of the Grail Box in myths and legends with only three persons, at any time, knowing its true location. Rory knew the rods were far too powerful to be left in real time. Who knows what mankind would do with them? He placed them backwards in time to keep them separated from the Grail Box.

Everything begins somewhere, and the lodge of the perfect circle came into existence. If anyone looks at a circle, you will see that it also is the number zero. This new order continued from all the previous orders of the Knights of St John and the Knights Templar. It had been created as misinformation regarding the location of the Grail Box, with its members becoming known as Masons. (* See Appendix.)

Only Rory, Abbot MacCallum and Father Winning knew the truth, the first three of the newly formed Lodge 'O'.

The abbot bade Rory a fond farewell, wishing him luck, knowing of the ordeal he had to face and the imminent attack on Urquhart Castle. He watched as Rory took hold of his Hagpipe and vanished in a flash of light! He reappeared instantly in the Ballymeanoch stone circle, where he had initially left on a cold, snowy night. He began running with his enhanced speed back to Castle Sween, eager for his first Christmas with Mrs MacSween!

Father Christopher Winning was up at first light the next morning and went out in the cold, in his brown habit, to collect water at the well at the rear of the new abbey. He winched down the bucket, looking forward to a wash and drink from the fresh spring water. He put his cup into the bucket, filling it for a quick drink but stopped suddenly as he looked into the cup before he raised it to his mouth. The water was blood red; in fact, it was blood: the blood of the Messiah, with miraculous healing power!

This was the fabled fountain of life, created by the power of the Grail Box leaking out in a circle from the centre of the ley line mound below the abbey, affecting the whole area. The well would subsequently be filled in to hide it due to the number of people being drawn to sip the blood, causing them to be healed of all afflictions.

The monks did not want any undue attention being drawn to where the Grail Box had been hidden. They created a story of a dead sheep infecting the water supply, and no one would drink the well water after that. Only a few knew the truth with a street being built over its location and named St Winnings Lane.

There would be no sign marking its location, but historic records tell of the humble stonemason monk, now known as St Winning, who discovered a miracle well and had a town named after him called Kilwinning. To many, this small Ayrshire Scottish town has no importance.

A select few have a different opinion, with the first Masonic temple having been built next to the abbey and protected by a police station adjacent to it. The power of the Grail Box, constantly emanating from below the ground, affects all who reside in the area with an effect known to the guardians of law and order as KD's (Kilwinning Disease), as the magic-like power below the ground slowly escapes, subtly changing them. Where else could this worldwide phenomenon of Masonry begin?

To the initiated, with their perceptions altered, it is the centre of the universe!

CHAPTER 25

Destruction

Satanic Stan transformed himself, assuming the physical appearance of his host's body, John Grant, the rightful laird of Urquhart Castle. He amassed an army comprising all the disgruntled clans, including the MacGregors, Campbells and disenfranchised MacDonalds who had split from their wealthier, distant relatives, led by Eoin MacDonald, the Lord of Skye. He wooed and wormed his way into becoming their leader with promises of power and vast riches.

Stan had convinced them that he had the ability to destroy all the mythical beasts that had interfered, backing the MacSween's, changing the balance of power in the Highlands, and making all of them weaker in the process. He told them he had already dealt with the pet haggis of their enemy, and Nessie and the giant eagle were next. He did not reveal his true nature to them as they were deeply religious in their own way and would rebel against him if they knew his true identity and plan. Strategies were completed, vast amounts of arms were collected, and huge amounts of gunpowder was manufactured over the winter months.

The combined troops of the allies of evil totalled 10,000, and it was arranged that they would amass at the estate of the Grants in Glen Moriston, where he, in the possessed body of John Grant, would lead them to Urquhart Castle as soon as winter was over. The forests there would provide the wood to construct a trebuchet siege engine capable of hurling a boulder

200 yards at 126mph to destroy the castle walls. He even had a name for it. "The Wolf", after the wild predator of the Highlands that shows no mercy to its victims!

* * *

Rory enjoyed the calm before the storm with his wife, family and friends at Castle Sween over Christmas and into the New Year, with many parties and feasts arranged to pass the time away on the long dark snowy days. He knew his greatest trial was in front of him, and he was not going to risk any of his loved ones in a futile fight to save Urquhart Castle, which had been preordained to be destroyed.

Spring came far too soon as he set off on foot, dressed in his warm, full highland kilt and sturdy boots, with Hans, his sword, strapped to his back. It was an emotional departure from Heather as they had become inseparable over the winter confined together in Castle Sween. Tears ran down Heather's face as she urged Rory to be careful and return safely to her. Rory promised he would, but deep down inside he was not sure if he would be able to.

He had crossed paths with Satanic Stan several times now, and he or it had increased in power with every clash. Rory knew he had been lucky to escape from him as he fled to Malta through the Azure Window. He doubted that even with the power of the Hagpipe and his sword combined, it would be enough to stop him.

* * *

Bella was growing fast with her twin sister Isa and had sought out any person unaffected by the glamour and illusions and evil of the Red Druid, who rarely made an appearance now, causing his influence to weaken. She found the good spey wives in the area who taught her all about healing herbs and how to administer medicines to help others. Isa, on the other hand, embraced darker evil magic and was forcing people to help her will instead of helping them. Bella was determined to find the owner of the hand that had saved her protector Hag, and as soon as she had learned enough, she was determined to travel the time shift portals to find out who it was!

It would take her a long time. She would be an elderly wise woman before she tracked down young Rory in Urquhart Castle and became reunited with her haggis, Hag. She would be very surprised at the outcome. The reborn haggis remembered everything and, when not in the company of young Rory, was often found cuddled up at her feet. It had the uncanny ability to predict events as if it had experienced all of them before, which of course, it had.

* * *

Rory reached the nearest portal of the Ballymeanoch stone circle in Argyll and passed through it, travelling to the haggis graveyard cave below Urquhart Castle. It was just as he had left it, except the pile of haggis tusks had rearranged themselves back into a pile from the oblong shape of an altar. It was early March. The first signs of spring were emerging with yellow daffodils springing from the ground as he climbed the staircase and out of the temple into the castle grounds. He sought out the giant, six-foot-eight-inch Constable John Gregg in his quarters and offices in the gatehouse. For all his size and invulnerable nature, Gregg had greyed and looked a worried man since he had last seen him. The constable was studying information he had received from a newly arrived pigeon, detailing the imminent arrival of a ten-thousand-strong army marching on the castle with a massive siege engine in tow. He was very pleased to see Rory, warmly shaking his hand with the secret grip they both knew. The constable told Rory this news, and also that he had discovered who the spy was that had been leaking information, and that Rory was not going to like it!

It was his young half-brother, Johnny, the genetic son of the ex-laird, John Grant. Rory was disappointed but not really surprised, as he considered that he had been present at every meeting and discussion and had known his every move.

That was why he had not included him in the secret talks to evacuate key persons from the castle. He had experienced this Judas effect before, in stories told to him by St John. Rory was aware that there was no point in confronting Johnny just now. He would have to learn the error he had made the hard way!

The arriving army would be taking up a position to attack by the next day, and Rory instructed the constable to make it impossible for Johnny to send any more communications out of the castle, which was put into lockdown. All the remaining inhabitants of Castletoun outside the gates were evacuated inside. They were very unhappy at leaving, but the constable was well known and very persuasive.

Rory was determined no one would die because of him and had everyone assembled in groups within the chapel. There were still hundreds of persons within the castle, but with the support of the constable and his deputies, they were ushered into the temple until it was full. He addressed the gathered congregation, explaining he was going to take them to the secret chamber below the castle and send them through the portal to safety in Argyle, where they could make their way to Castle Sween and safety. The option was to remain and face certain death, and no one refused. It was a sombre procession as Rory led them down the spiral stairs from the secret door in the east of the temple.

Only those present who were brothers of HAGI knew of the hidden cavern, and they helped the frightened women and children, some of whom were enjoying the adventure, especially when they saw the huge fully-grown Nessie overlooking the evacuation from the underground lake. The stories of the monster were well known, and they told them to their children at bedtime to make them behave. The fact that she was here now protecting them reinforced their commands for good behaviour from their offspring to follow every instruction. Nessie spoke to Rory mentally, who informed her of the imminent attack and to seek safety in Loch Ness. She submerged in the deep water and gracefully swam out of the entrance with only her head and neck visible to the assembled crowd to exclamations of wonder and amazement from those who had not seen her before.

Rory walked to the cave of the haggis and activated the portal at its entrance in a shimmering white curtain of light, connecting it to the standing stones of Ballymeanoch. He stepped through to confirm all was safe, vanishing to gasps from the waiting crowd and immediately stepped back, reappearing in front of them. This was magic to most, even the brothers of HAGI, who knew of Rory's abilities. It was hard work, but the choice of remaining to die or to walk into the light and a new life convinced the crowd to obey the request. Rory explained they would only feel a tingling on their skin as they passed through, and once a few had gone, they began to pick up pace.

But they were not moving fast enough. This was going to take far longer than Rory had estimated!

The Wolf had been put in place overnight on the high ground overlooking Urquhart Castle, but dawn did not come. The sky was black with a storm cloud that obliterated all daylight. The invaders used the extended blackness to carry barrels of gunpowder to the castle gatehouses, silently putting them on either side, pleased with their element of surprise as they crossed the lowered drawbridge.

The sky rumbled with distant thunder. No lightning preceded it, against all the laws of nature. Satanic Stan channelled the weather to his will, moulding and directing it, creating devil fork-shaped lightning bolts that he fired into the wooden houses of Castletoun. This unnatural fire rained down from the sky, and soon the whole of Castletoun was ablaze. No one could survive this as the 'Wolf' unleashed a volley of giant boulders at the castle walls, shattering them with each impact. No screaming could be heard from Castletoun or the castle over the noise created by the ground-shaking thunder and the castle walls being reduced to rubble. This was because there was no one to scream. The last people to leave were the constable and his deputies, who were already halfway down the spiral staircase with the last of the elderly and disabled as the gunpowder ignited, destroying the matching towers of the gatehouse supporting the drawbridge. The darkness concealed the evil smile on the face of John Grant as he redirected his lightning bolts to the distillery and brewhouse behind the smithy, causing a volcanic explosion as the whisky was hit.

Fire spouted into the air from the burning liquid in the exploding vats as the stacked store of hundreds of barrels of whisky were thrown upwards, bursting open as they returned to the ground and creating a fiery hell.

The whole castle was ablaze as a pair of young, terrified eyes looked out from the top of the Grant Tower. *How could his father do this?* Johnny thought. He was supposed to come back for him, not destroy everything. He looked towards the hillside seeing his robed father illuminated in the light of the raging fires and lightning. The shell of John Grant was looking at him, too, smiling as he redirected the position of the 'Wolf' and the loading of the largest boulder yet into its sling. It was pointing directly at Grant Tower! Johnny waved and shouted for him to stop, jumping up and down on the roof. He was sure his father could see him as their eyes locked on each other, and he heard an evil laugh ringing in his head. He watched as John Grant transformed into the red-hooded 'Satanic Stan' as he signalled the release of the boulder!

Johnny knew the truth now, but it was too late. He watched as the boulder flew towards him, seemingly in slow motion, striking the middle of the tower. His father was evil and wanted him dead. He was gutted inside. Only his mother and Rory loved and cared for him, but this realisation came too late as the tower began to crumble beneath his feet!

Rory helped the constable and deputies with the last of the castle residents through the portal, then ran up the stairs to the temple to see what was happening to the castle and to check everyone was evacuated. John Gregg, the now ex-constable of Urquhart Castle, materialised in the Argyll countryside to see the population of the castle encamped around the standing stones. He was going to return to the city of his birth. The boys from the football teams of the Celtic Warriors and Castletoun Rangers were going with him to start a new life in the green glen of Glaschu (Glasgow). He organised his deputies to relocate the rest of the population to Castle Sween or to nearby relatives as he set off. He had a dream of opening a small pie and pastry shop in his name with his life savings. He would work with the knife gangs of the east and west of the growing city and introduce them to football to stop them fighting, just like he had achieved at Castle Urquhart. He set off with a spring in his step with the founding members of the new teams of Rangers and Celtic, optimistic of his success.

What could possibly go wrong?

Rory returned to the temple to find a boulder had come through the roof, it was now open to the sky, and he saw another one fly past above the gap heading towards the Grant Tower. He jumped up out of the hole onto the roof as lightning lit the sky, illuminating his brother, Johnny, standing on the roof of the tower. Johnny had no chance of survival, and Rory, even with his super-speed, could not save him, but he knew something that could. Rory mentally called out to Ben, his giant eagle friend, telepathically showing him the scene unfolding before him, asking for his help to save his brother.

It was extremely dangerous for Ben, he was frantically dodging the lightning bolts in the sky, but he could not refuse a request from his friend, no matter the danger to himself. He dived for Johnny just as the tower he was standing on disintegrated below him!

CHAPTER 26

Nessie's End

Johnny fell, shutting his eyes, praying for forgiveness for betraying Rory. They were answered as a huge talon gently closed around him, lifting him into the air! He was far from safe; Satanic Stan began throwing lightning bolts at them, furious at being thwarted. Even with Ben's great speed and manoeuvrability, he could not fly faster than the speed of light. Soon he and Johnny would be fried in the sky.

Rory had to help them and, instinctively, raised Hans, his sword, into the air with his right hand pointing it towards Ben and Johnny.

He took hold of the Hagpipe with his left hand and focused the power from it into the sword, using it to direct a beam of energy from its tip towards his brother and eagle friend. With milliseconds to spare, the beam enveloped Ben and Johnny, creating a protective bubble around them as the lightning struck.

The globe of power sparkled with the electricity surrounding it, but it held like a forcefield, protecting Ben and Johnny within it. They were safe, and Ben mentally communicated his thanks to Rory as he flew away towards Castle Sween, out of the storm's range and to safety.

A roar of anger went up behind Rory, who had just revealed his location to Satanic Stan, now mustering all his fury and power into Rory's destruction. He was so focused on his intent that he did not see the surrounding army of now unbrainwashed clans had noticed his true nature. They were fleeing the battlefield to get as far from him as possible before they, too, were subjected to his wrath.

Rory jumped back down into the chapel, landing on the chequered floor next to the boulder that had destroyed the wooden roof, bringing down the huge candelabra light with it. The first bolts of forked lightning were hitting the chapel before his feet touched the ground, setting fire to the remains of the roof. His only chance of escape was to get to the portal below the temple in the loch cavern. As he made his way to the secret door in the east, another bolt hit the stained-glass right window of Nessie, destroying it, showering him in multicoloured glass. Fortunately, his tough leathery skin, similar to that of a haggis, but normal in appearance, protected him, and he was uninjured.

Time was of the essence. Rory rushed to the spiral stairwell and down it as the temple above was ground to dust by the destructive bolts blowing it to oblivion. The rocky roof of the cavern was shaking as the onslaught above gained in power. The skin on Rory's arms tingled with the supernatural forces at work.

Above ground, Castle Urquhart was being systematically destroyed and would never be restored to its former glory. In time, it would be left a ruin grown over with grass and weeds, visited by tourists in search of the famous monster of the loch. For now, Rory had only one thought, and that was to escape. He hurried to the cave of the haggis graveyard and its portal to safety. He looked out over the water to the cavern exit as Nessie spoke to him from the relative safety of the loch. He saw her graceful neck and head raised out of the water, looking in at him on the sandy beach as the mouth of the entrance collapsed in a pile of rocks, cutting it off from the loch.

Rory heard the high-pitched squeal emit from Nessie's antennae on her head as she tried to activate the portal at the entrance to the cavern.

The portal had been destroyed just like the one at the Azure Window and could never be used again! Rory could feel the frustration coming from Nessie. She was trapped forevermore in Loch Ness with the cavern portal destroyed. She could not leave it ever again. If Nessie could cry, she was crying now as Rory heard her sobbing voice say, "Goodbye" to him in his head.

The direct contact Nessie had experienced with the Grail Box as she pulled the ship *Eternity* to the Azure Window had blessed her with a very long lifespan. Unknown to her, near the end of her life, she had the ability to self-produce one grey-blue egg.

Her days of freedom, travelling the seas of the world were over, and she knew it. She was now contained in the giant aquarium of Loch Ness and would forever more be known as 'The Loch Ness Monster'! She would be the last remaining animal of her species, and like the dodo, her days were numbered. The one-egg legacy was a lonely curse, and the solitary existence of any offspring hiding in the black depths of Loch Ness from the attention of mankind hunting the monster was no life at all!

Rory felt the disturbance to the ley line network surge through him following the destruction of the portal. Rocks began to fall all around him. His time was up as he took hold of the Hagpipe, activating the portal in the entrance to the haggis cave, visualising the portal at the Ballymeanoch stone circle and his escape to Castle Sween. He had to concentrate very hard to maintain the contact as the shimmering curtain of power began flashing in multi colours with the disturbance to the ley lines. He had no choice but to step through the portal as the roof came down around him, burying his Maltese boat that would someday confuse any archaeologists finding it in Scotland!

Rory felt something was wrong as he tumbled through time with the sound of Satanic Stan's cackling laughter ringing in his head! He could feel Stan's joy at his victory over him as he landed on a rocky surface in a confined space in the pitch black!

Stan looked down on the flaming remains of Castle Urquhart, a burning inferno that made him feel content and, somehow, at home. His victory was complete: his enemy was lost in time, and the Grail Box was buried and lost forever below the castle ruins. The creatures were all either dead like the haggis, trapped forever in torment like Nessie, or lost without leadership like the eagle. He was pleased with his work and could feel no movement in the ley lines from anything capable of disturbing his plans. He was looking forward to travelling back in time to sacrifice the last threat to him: the 16-year-old daughter of Rory, the sweet Bella!

Bella was a star pupil of all the wise women. She was a human sponge, learning all the powerful good lore and was approaching her 16th birthday and the winter equinox when she decided to leave the Druids at Castle Urquhart and her corrupted, evil twin sister, Isa. She had learned enough to know that to remain there was certain death. At her first opportunity, when the stone circle in the haggis graveyard cave was unattended, she took hold of the white crystal around her neck, stepped into it and vanished. She would have to keep moving randomly from portal to portal, blocking her thoughts and leaving her mind blank to avoid her sister seeing her location. It took a lot of willpower, but she was highly motivated to find her father and to save both herself and her sister!

She escaped just in time as the Red Druid returned to enforce his control over the Urquhart Druids and kill her. He was furious at her escape, interrogating Isa to find out where Bella had gone but to no avail. The link between them was blocked, and he had underestimated Bella's power to conceal herself from him. Stan was supremely confident of his dominance now and knew that he was stronger than Rory. He would crush him! The extra pleasure of making him watch the slaughter of his daughter, Bella, would be nice, but the conversion of his other daughter Isa to evil and making her hate her father enough to kill him would torment Rory forever!

CHAPTER 27

The Eglinton Trophy

Rory raised his head and banged it on a rocky roof above him. He reached out with his hands to either side and above him, discovering that he was in some sort of a tunnel, which was not wide enough to turn his large frame.

Fortunately, he was as one with his Hagpipe now, which suddenly and protectively burst into life without any prompting, enveloping him in a protective bubble of power. He lay still in the tunnel as it illuminated in crisscrossing lightning bolts so bright and powerful, he had to close his eyes and brace himself against them. If the Hagpipe had not automatically activated, he would have been electrocuted to death and left a pile of bones, with all his flesh fried off. The lightning arched around his protective bubble but did not penetrate it.

The Hagpipe had saved his life again, but Stan could obviously find him anywhere he was in contact with a ley line. Rory realised this tunnel must be connected to it as the unnatural lightning passed along in front of him and dissipated. It left a static charge in the air, making his hair stand on end, reaching up to the roof like that on a toy troll.

Rory began to crawl forward. Where was he?

Archibald, the 12th Earl of Eglinton, had the foundation stone of his new castle laid by the youngest Provincial Grand Master of the perfect Circle Lodge in 1797. Alexander Hamilton was the laird of the Grange Estate and very proud of his grandson who was named after him. Alexander Hamilton would be recorded in history as one of the founding fathers of the now USA, which gained its independence on the 4th of July 1776. He would become the first secretary of the treasury and the main author of the economic policies of this new country's first president, George Washington. They were great friends and brother Masons, building this new country on its principles and hiding signs and secrets in the very fabric of society, even in the design of the new currency, the dollar, and in the architecture of the capital city, named after its first president, and called Washington.

Rory was unaware of his place in time as he appeared 42 years later from the laying of the foundation stone on Thursday the 29th of August 1839. He was trapped within the secret tunnel leading to Eglinton Castle to the Circle Lodge and totally unaware of his involvement in the historic events which were about to unfold.

Archibald William, Earl of Eglinton, the 13th Earl and current Grand Master of the Circle Lodge, was proud to have the now elderly Alexander Hamilton as one of the 40 knights present for the last joust the British Islands would ever see; a competition to win the now priceless 4 foot 8 inch (140 cm) high Eglinton Trophy he had commissioned. It was a magnificent prize weighing in at 1600 ounces (45 kg) of solid silver, made in a medieval Gothic style and had taken four years to complete. Its side shields bore the coats of arms of the 14 knights of the tournament with a fifteenth shield that was blank. The three-tier trophy depicted the knights on horseback, taking part in the joust around the centre piece, depicting Eglinton Castle. The height of the trophy was doubled when placed on the ornately carved three-tier wooden bases. The first stood around 2 feet and 10 inches (85 cm) in height. The dedicatory shield reads 'Presented to Archibald, Earl of Eglinton, by the Visitors to the Eglinton Tournament held at Eglinton Castle MDCCCXXXIX'. The bottom eight-sided tier is never seen in public as it makes the trophy too high to be viewed.

Or is it because of what's carved on it?

The 13th Earl of Eglinton was also honored with the presence of Louis-Napoleon Bonaparte, soon to be Prince Louis Napoleon, the future Emperor of the French, as one of his knights. He was the nephew and heir of Napoleon I (Napoleon Bonaparte), who took Malta on 9 June 1798 from the Hospitallers and the island Rory had saved along with the Grail Box in 1565. The Turks and the Ottoman Dynasty had been defeated, but Malta still fell to Napoleon Bonaparte and the French in a bloodless coup 233 years later. Louis knew his uncle Napoleon had never found the Grail Box on Malta and regretted his failure to find it. Napoleon considered the box to be the world's greatest prize. Louis wanted to prove his worth, be more important than his uncle, and do something that he had failed to do. He had heard rumors that the Grail Box was here, and he wanted it!

Thursday the 29th of August 1839 dawned clear and fine. The knights and their entourages struggled to organize the parade comprised of 40 knights, each with his own entourage. They were to ride to the castle, pick up a lady, officer or knight, and return to the lists. The drive of the picturesque estate was lined with thousands of spectators when the parade finally began as Lady Somerset, the Queen of Beauty, appeared heralded by trumpets. An unnatural storm burst from the ley tunnel in a fiery display of lightning bolts from its concealed exit under the waterfall at the rockery. It struck the ornate white castle bridge crossing the River Garnock, illuminating it in shimmering sparks which lightened up the spectacular gardens of Eglinton Castle, similar to a Christmas display of white lights. The electric eruption then surged to the sky, turning it as black as night, filling it with rain clouds. The sky was soon irradiated with flashes of lightning at the same time as the ground shook and rattled, vibrating with each great clash of thunder. A deluge began as if a tap had been turned on, flooding the ground below, trying to wash away the evil that had just emerged!

Lord Eglinton immediately ordered the ladies into carriages, but the knights and their entourages were soon soaked in the squall and covered in mud. They marched into the lists down a parade route lined by the umbrella-bearing audience. The torrential rains flooded the lakes of the Lugton Water, which ran around the castle estate on three sides. No carriages could cross the raised roadway which crossed the shallowest part of the river back to the castle. The lakes swelled, filling the Garnock River, which surged along, full with the unexpected downpour. The entire audience, apart from Eglinton's personal guests, were stranded without transportation. They had to walk miles through the rain and the mud to nearby villages, where only the first people found any food, drink, accommodation or transport.

It was a total washout!

Rory stuck his head out of the hidden tunnel as a torrent of water flowed down from the waterfall above him to the rockery below and onward to the River Garnock. It was speeding past, carrying tree trunks and debris of all sorts in its rush to the sea. He was patient and saw no point in leaving the dry tunnel until the storm passed. The sky was already beginning to clear as his hair fell back to his shoulders as the static charge from the tunnel dissipated. The lightning receded as the storm blew away into the distance, the thunderclaps becoming further apart, counting from the flash from 10 seconds to 20, then to 30. This translated into the number of miles away the storm had moved and safety from the lightning bolts. The sky began to clear, with hints of blue appearing as rays of sunshine burst through, and as quickly as it had started, the rain stopped. Rory squeezed out of the tunnel, hugging the rock wall so as not to get wet, past the edge of the waterfall, onto a raised hill overlooking the gardens of the Eglinton Estate. They were separated into adjoining squares of high-cut hedges containing various flowers and stone sculptures of people and animals and a large hedge maze. The sun burst through the clouds as the sky became a kaleidoscope of colour. A giant rainbow arched across the sky, finishing in the middle of the Lugton Water.

Young, slim-built, dapper Louis-Napoleon Bonaparte had been soaked to his bones as he made his way back to the castle when he saw the heavenly sign of the rainbow appear, ending in the Lugton Water in front of him. A story is recorded of him throwing a stone into the Lugton Water and a bell shape coming to the surface; it remained there for some time, which he interpreted as a good omen for his future. In fact, the upside-down shape did appear, and Rory saw it as well as he silently walked up behind Louis-Napoleon. Rory recognized the shape immediately because he had held the object in his hands when he had fed water to Hag, his pet haggis, giving her eternal life. It was the Grail Cup, a true treasure at the end of the rainbow and a sign that evil could be defeated. The French coat of arms on the tabard worn by Louis was not missed by the keen sight of Rory as he startled him by his presence, speaking to him in perfect French. They both admired this wonder in the lake until the rainbow faded and the cup disappeared. Louis was surprised at how fluently this giant, dry, tartan-clad Scotsman with red hair could speak his language. In no time, Rory knew exactly where and when in time he was.

The now completed abbey in Kilwinning was very near, and following the appearance of the Grail Cup, Rory deduced that the tunnel he had been in must go to the abbey in the opposite direction. It would lead him back to the location of the Grail Box, hidden below it and to the portal back to his own time. Rory introduced himself to Louis as Knight Rory MacSween, who had come to take part in the joust. They were soon best friends, with Louis inviting him as his guest at the castle. Their joint experience with the vision of the Grail Cup appearing before them had changed and inspired the future Emperor of France. He was in the company of the most highly influential members of society, all of whom were members of a very special club that had influence all around the world, including the current President of America. Louis had spent some time in the company of Andrew Hamilton, who had inducted him into the Circle Lodge, joining these illustrious members.

On shaking hands with Rory, he knew that he, too, was a member and promised that he would introduce Rory to the rest of the group tonight at the castle. Louis had a great vision for the future of France and vowed to himself someday to repay his friends, both here and in America. He had an idea of a gift to cement the friendship between France and America, a statue of a beautiful woman welcoming all visitors to New York, the main port he had visited. But first he must become the leader of his country, and he had the very friends to help him!

Rory was also filled with hope for his future after seeing the Grail Cup vision. He had memorized the *Book of St Columba* and remembered an entry of him with a magnificent trophy surrounded by armor-clad knights. He remembered the picture well, and if it was correct, he was about to meet an old friend, but first he had to win that trophy!

CHAPTER 28

Joust for Life

Rory walked with Louis, deep in conversation about the current and past events in his own country and the persecution of the Knights Templar by King Philip IV. Louis trusted Rory as a brother and happily discussed his plans to restore the honour of the Knights Templar as soon as he took back control of his country for the Napoleon dynasty. (* See Appendix.) Louis was going to be a man of great power and influence, Rory realised, and he had a vision to remake his country that had been enforced and welded into his being, following his experience of seeing the Grail Cup.

The weir was still in torrent following the overflow from the Lugton Waters after the torrential downpour. They had to cross the river to reach the castle, but they would be washed away in the flood if they attempted to wade through it. Rory could jump it easily, but he did not want to reveal his powers to Louis. He did not have to as Louis walked past the raised crossing and up a small hill covered in high oak trees which hung over both banks of the river. Built into the branches, above the raging river, was a narrow wooden bridge crossing over it. It had a rail on both sides to hold and was designed for the breadth of one person to cross the river in one direction at a time. If anyone met another person in the middle going the other way, someone would have to back up or get wet. Both Rory and Louis walked up the slippery wooden ramp onto the bridge in single file to cross the river. With the waist-high rails supporting them on either side, it was not difficult to cross, and they stopped in the middle to enjoy the view of the estate and the magnificent Eglinton Castle. It truly was a wonder with its Gothic castellated style dominated by a central 100-foot (30 m) large round keep and four 70-foot (21 m) outer towers. It was second only to Culzean Castle in appearance and grandeur, which still stands on the Ayrshire coast.

The storm had passed, and the hot sun shone down, evaporating the pools of water lying on the ground in spiralling mists of steam. It was a pleasant afternoon for a walk, and Rory asked Louis if he could visit the jousting arena. They walked up a small hill, away from the castle, towards a flat grassed area of the large estate. There, a three-floored wooden viewing stand had been erected overlooking two straight racecourse-like tracts, separated by a sturdy wooden partition about five foot high. Colourful banners depicting the crests of the knights taking part in the joust adorned the large viewing stand, capable of seating a thousand people. Rory laughed to himself, seeing one of the largest banners was white, displaying the cross of St John, identical to the tabard he wore on his quest for the Grail Box. They must be expecting him, he thought, as they walked to the brick stables and smithy behind the stand. It was a hive of activity with the noise of hammering as several blacksmiths made final adjustments to the suits of armour to be worn by the knights.

Rory was very interested as he watched the new techniques and tools being used by the blacksmiths. He needed a suit of armour if he was going to take part, and he wanted to make it. He approached the head blacksmith and shook his hand, introducing himself as a blacksmith and a knight. The head blacksmith, a squat, muscular man, returned the special grip, and both talked about the systems being used in the forge and Rory's need for armour. This caused a panic with the blacksmith with the amount of time it would take to construct a new suit of armour to be ready for the next day. Rory said he would do it if the blacksmith had any spare metal available.

The head blacksmith pointed to a pile of rejected armour in the corner of the smithy and a spare forge ready for use, telling Rory he was welcome to have a go. The scepticism was soon forgotten as Rory stripped to his waist, showing his rippling muscles and measuring the spare armour against his body, he began adjusting it to fit him. In practically no time, he had constructed a full suit of armour as the rest of the blacksmiths and Louis stood, open-mouthed, watching him.

A quick coat of black paint finished the armour, and the legend of the black knight was born. A mystery knight would be taking part in the tournament the next day, but he needed a horse! Rory redressed and walked to the stables next to the foundry. He noticed an overflowing supply wagon containing fruit and vegetables bumping along the access road past the stables, heading to the castle. It was trying to find a path through the flooded road and was shedding handfuls of large carrots, with their long green stems still attached, onto the road. This was a good omen to Rory as he picked them up. He knew carrots and horses went together as he walked to the paddock at the rear of the stables.

It was full of the largest horses Rory had ever seen. They had to be big to hold the weight of the knight and his armour. All were either white or tan coloured, except for one huge lone, jet-black stallion standing at the far end of the paddock. It was the double of his own horse, Jet, and to Rory's keen eye, he was convinced it must be descended from him. The head stableman, an elderly balding, slim man, walked up to Rory, who was staring at Jet and said, "He is a beautiful beastie but quite untrainable; no one can go near him. He is kept only as breeding stock."

Rory introduced himself again with his special handshake, which was returned, and cheekily asked, "If I could train him, would you let me ride him in the joust?"

The stableman laughed, knowing just how violent the horse was and readily agreed, looking forward to seeing this stranger humiliated in his attempt.

Louis was standing watching this exchange, and after seeing Rory make the armour, he did not discount him succeeding as readily as the stableman. Rory looked directly at the black stallion, letting out a piercing whistle as he called out to the horse in his mind. The stallion raised his head, and his ears stood up, listening to the source of the whistle and began walking meekly towards Rory. For the second time that day, jaws dropped open, this time by the stableman, as the horse peacefully began eating the carrots offered by Rory without biting him. Everyone stopped working and stood in stunned silence as Rory whispered into the horse's ear and blew gently up his nose. This was the first horse whisperer the stableman had ever seen, and he was even more surprised when Rory leapt gently onto the horse's back and took off on a flying run around the paddock, followed by every other horse in it.

The stableman was still standing like a statue with his mouth open when Rory returned and leapt off 'Jet 2', landing beside the stableman, saying, "I will be back for him tomorrow."

Louis was amazed as he talked to Rory, looking for answers as to what he had just witnessed. He was overwhelmed with the miracles he was witnessing today, but Rory only replied that he had a gift with horses. Louis could not argue with that, but he had already made his mind up that he was not going to face the black knight in the arena tomorrow!

Rory and Louis walked back to the castle, past the well-drained, short-cut lawns where several lords and ladies were bowling with wooden bowls towards a smaller white ball called a jack. They were competing in a smaller, less violent tournament for the Eglinton Jug, which had been commissioned at the same time as the trophy and was also made of solid silver. Unknown to them, this was the beginning of the oldest lawn bowling tournament in the world that continues to this day. Representatives of all the bowling clubs in Glasgow and Ayrshire meet annually on the first Thursday in July. They compete in teams of four to win this very Jug, donated by the Earl of Eglinton. It is also unofficially the oldest drinking competition in the world.

Louis was anxious to introduce this mysterious highlander to his fellow knights and leaders of the Circle Lodge; Archibald the Earl of Eglinton, Alexander Hamilton the Laird of Grange and the Knight Marshal, Sir Charles Montolieu Lamb.

They may know something about this stranger that would explain him, Louis thought to himself. The three did indeed know something and seemed to recognise red-haired Rory when they saw him in his green and black MacSween tartan, with a very special sword strapped to his back. Louis was not qualified to know their suspicions, and they found a quiet spot to talk with Rory well away from curious ears. The mystery deepened for Louis, who was not invited to be party to this conversation!

The next day began bright and dry, perfect for the joust, except for the water-laden ground. Elaborate rehearsals and training in the nearby St John's Wood had not prepared the participants for the crowded and already sodden conditions for the re-enactment of the medieval joust and revel on Friday the 30th August. As a result, the opening parade took three hours longer than planned to marshal. The second attempt to have the parade began with a smaller audience of spectators than the day before, many having been scunnered (unimpressed) following their soaking the previous day. The Knight Marshal, Sir Charles Montolieu Lamb, led with his squire and a halberdier (a guard who carried an axe-like blade and a steel spike mounted on the end of a long shaft) and his escort. He was followed by the presentation party, headed by Archibald, Earl of Eglinton, in his carriage, followed by the Queen of Beauty, Lady Seymour, Jane Georgiana the Duchess of Somerset in her carriage with her lady in waiting. Accompanying her, outside the carriage, were two pages holding two large hunting dogs on long leashes, and they took up position at the end of the estate drive. Rory decided not to join the parade, standing with the artisans allocated to record the day's events for inclusion on the bottom wooden tier of the trophy. He wanting to keep the black knight a secret for the joust itself and watched from the castle lawns where the 40 knights were riding to pick up a lady, officer or knight and return with them to the start of the parade and proceed along the estate drive to the arena stand for the joust to be opened.

It is well recorded that you should never work with children or animals, and the two young pages should never have been put in charge of two large, strong hunting dogs as they did not have the strength to restrain them. The dogs had caught the scent of a very strange animal indeed. In fact, she had been travelling through time looking for her eight-year-old master ever since he had left her, so long ago now, on the banks of Loch Ness. The dogs pulled free and ran into the heather and bracken undergrowth, hunting out the young haggis which burst from cover, running down the estate drive towards the scent of her master, screaming in Rory's head for help. The crowd lining the drive had never seen a creature like it. A haggis; they thought they had all been hunted to extinction. The knights on horseback, armed with their jousting poles, did not want to miss claiming this rare creature as a prize and broke ranks, joining the chase.

Haggis can move very fast when they want to, even with their uneven legs, and Hag was easily outpacing the heavy hunting dogs, leaving them behind. However, the horses were speeding up, overtaking the dogs, with the nearest knight lowering his pole to stab the haggis in the back of the neck, killing it. Rory saw the events unfold before him as if in slow motion. He moved with incredible speed, grabbing a croquet mallet and some white bowling jacks from the lawns. He hit a jack with the mallet in a swinging motion, firing the stone jack through the air with perfect aim, striking the first knight on his metal helmet and knocking him from his horse. The second nearest knight was no luckier and soon joined the first, flat on his back in the mud. The remaining knights decided the prey was not worth it and pulled up their mounts, not wishing to suffer the same fate as their colleagues.

The haggis ran straight and jumped into the outstretched arms of Rory as the artisans watched, expecting him to have his head bitten off by the razor-sharp teeth it was displaying. It was not to be as Rory mentally talked to Hag, his pet, explaining that he was an older version of the master she was looking for. He tickled her behind her ears as she squealed with excitement as the artisans furiously scribbled down notes and diagrams of the events that had just occurred. Rory explained to Hag where and when to find him when he was a sixteen-year-old to reunite him with the Hagpipe. She smiled up at Rory and replied, "I know. I can speak freely to you now. You rebirthed me with the water of life, and I retain all the memories from our adventures in the past and some that have still to happen for you. We will meet again when you need me. Have faith and continue to love; you will not fail!" He was intrigued by his friend's words and wished her goodbye as she ran off to the ley tunnel and the portal back to the past to help a young Rory.

The artisans had grouped together to compare notes, and one was swinging a mallet, hitting a jack through the air. His surname was Dunlop, and innovation ran in his blood. A descendant of his from a nearby village called Dreghorn would in the future revolutionise travel by inventing the pneumatic tyre. Currently, Rory had given him an idea as he removed one end of the mallet and curved the remaining part, shaping the wood so that it would elevate the jack higher into the air. He would, in the future, experiment with many clubs and change the size of the jacks, calling them balls. Everyone would want a shot of this new game; it could finish like croquet, with the ball going through a ring or into a hole in the ground. Golf had been invented!

Order was restored, and the procession eventually made its way to the arena where Archibald, Earl of Eglinton, escorted the Queen of Beauty, Lady Seymour, to the royal box in the stand where she pronounced the joust open. The 40 knights had been reduced to 38 following the withdrawal of two rather dizzy but otherwise unharmed knights. The crowd filled the stand, enjoying the event, desperate for more entertainment which came when a mysterious knight, all in black armour, on a massive black stallion, entered the arena and rode up to the Queen of Beauty, handing her his rolled-up pendant. The crowd gasped as she unfurled it, revealing the Red Cross of St John. No one gasped more than those in the box: Archibald the Earl of Eglinton, Alexander Hamilton, the Laird of Grange, and the Knight Marshal, Sir Charles Montolieu Lamb.

They knew the truth now and the identity of this mysterious black knight. The facts were in front of them: he was a red-haired highlander with a sword on his back, played with a wild haggis, and possessed all the signs and secrets. Notwithstanding that, he could do miraculous things.

He was the Pure One, talked about in all the rituals!

The black knight began his first joust and, within a very short time, no knight wished to face him, as each one facing him fell to the ground in a heap. It was not lost on his opposition that he was riding a horse that could not be ridden, according to the head stableman. They also knew that Louis-Napoleon had withdrawn from the competition with a mysterious injury prior to his joust with him. The black knight walked up to the royal box to lift the trophy, bowing to Lady Seymour. It was her turn to gasp as Rory removed his helmet, shaking loose his long red hair framing his handsome square-jawed face. No single man could lift the Eglinton Trophy as it was far too heavy, but this giant knight lifted it to the crowd as if it were an eggcup to cheers from all assembled. He then gifted the trophy back to the people to be kept safe for them within Eglinton Castle, on condition that the fifteenth shield on it was left blank to represent the mystery knight. The story of the Black Knight was now well and truly embedded in history's records. The artisans had been busy carving the dark wooden base of the trophy, which has, even until today, been kept hidden from view, under lock and key in a secret storeroom.

Well, who would believe a chaotic carved story depiction on eight wooden panels of a haggis being chased by dogs, knights struck from their horses by a ball hit by a long red-haired highlander with a stick, leaving them all scrambling about in the mud?

CHAPTER 29

Circle's Centre

Lady Seymour was very excited to get to know the most sought-after male at the grand feast and ball within Eglinton Castle that night. All the ladies-in-waiting were gathered around the tall, handsome, red-haired highlander like a gaggle of geese, swooning at every word from him. Lady Seymour wanted him for herself and quickly ushered them away, much to their frustration; she wanted to get a dance with Rory. He was not comfortable with all the feminine attention he was receiving and was still naïve, not understanding how his physical appearance and abilities affected the fairer sex. The only woman for him was his wife, Heather, much to the disappointment of all the beautiful women, fervent for his attention.

Rory was relieved when Archibald, the Earl of Eglinton, Alexander Hamilton, the Laird of Grange and the Knight Marshal, Sir Charles Montolieu Lamb, took him aside to a private room for a chat. They withheld no secrets from Rory, now recognising him as their superior and ultimate Grand Master, foretold in the secret book to which only they, as the three Grand Masters of the Circle Lodge, had access. They confirmed to Rory that the ley tunnel, hidden behind the waterfall, did indeed go to the concealed circular chamber below the original abbey building in Kilwinning. The premises of the first mother lodge had been built where the abbey had once stood. They had discovered the secret vault, and the trapdoor to it, on building the lodge. Their own members had secretly excavated and constructed the concealed entrance built into the wall of the chamber and the tunnel leading to the Eglinton Estate.

Archibald, Alexander and Charles were the only three members at present who knew about the book of ultimate knowledge that had been discovered wrapped in clean linen on top of the marble altar within the chamber. It had the secret symbol, which had been lost and had now been found again, sitting on top of it, showing its importance. Rory was intrigued. What book was this, and what was this symbol? He had to find out, and it was arranged for him to pay a private visit to the temple the next day with the three Grand Masters. They would go the comfortable way, by carriage, to the new temple to save the long crawl through the tunnel. Alexander was getting too old for this type of exertion in any case.

They were very interested in Rory's sword, which he called Hans, and wanted to know if the stories about it were true. Rory could see no issues with this as they knew all about him by what they had already divulged. He raised his right hand above his head, calling Hans to it. With a hiss, the sword flew into it from its Nessie-embossed leather scabbard strapped to his back. The three Masters gasped as Rory spun it in the air at breath-taking speed and planted it point-first and up to its hilt in the stone floor in front of them.

Hans slipped into the floor like a knife cutting through butter as Rory watched the faces of the three Masters, who all turned to their left, raising both hands in the air between them and the sword. They had obviously been working on some new signs, Rory thought, amused at their antics. Each one took it in turn, trying to pull the sword from the ground, but it was stuck fast, and they looked at Rory, assessing his power in a new light. No one would believe the stories about what Rory did next, but very few believed any of the rituals of these Free Masons in any case. A mental call was sent out from Rory, and Hans slowly raised itself out of the ground into the air. The three Masters were astonished and absorbed by this display as the sword floated through the air above Rory and replaced itself into its scabbard. All three crossed their body with their arms creating the cross of St John, bowing to Rory, who raised his right hand in recognition of their gesture of submission and fidelity, into a position that looked similar to that of Moses with his raised hand, holding his staff of power.

Rory was escorted by the three most influential men in the castle back to the ball, to the top table where the Earl of Eglinton relinquished his chair to Rory, sitting on his left, giving him the most exalted seat in the castle. Only the three Masters and Rory knew the true reason why.

Only a few people in the world got to be in the company of the Pure One!

Rory awoke the next morning after a luxurious sleep in the soft duck-feather-filled mattress in a huge four-poster bed. It was the best bed he had ever slept in, easily accommodating his large frame. He was just awake when servants entered with a three-course breakfast, starting with freshly squeezed juice and porridge, followed by a full Scottish fry-up, kept warm on a hot tray and covered by a metal dome. His every need was attended to, and no king could be served any better. He was embarrassed by all the attention but had to accept it as he did not want to offend the servants who were so eager to please him. He put his foot down, though, when they wanted to assist him regarding washing and dressing in the adjoining toilet suite, much to their disappointment.

He walked down the right side of the magnificent two-sided marble staircase to the location of the ball the previous night. It was now an empty space except for the cleaning servants and the senior butler, who was waiting for him. Rory was escorted to the main door, where he was informed that the earl and his guests were waiting for him. The Scottish autumn weather had resumed its normal rhythm, and a grey overcast sky awaited Rory as he stepped out of the castle to its long drive and manicured lawns.

It was lined with all the castle guests, knights and servants, including Louis, who seemed motivated to get back to France to proceed with the great work he had in front of him. He had received his sign, accepting that he was part of the group protecting the Grail Box, and that was sufficient for him. He knew who the guardian of the Grail Box was now and classed the black knight as his friend. He certainly did not want him to be his enemy. The earl had informed him that time and circumstances would reveal the exact location of the Grail to him, and he looked forward to that day.

A black carriage pulled up in front of Rory, and a coachman opened the door for him to join the earl, Alexander and Charles within. Everyone wanted one last look at the black knight and winner of the Eglinton Tournament as the coach was pulled along the drive past the stables. Rory watched the old stableman having an impossible task trying to control his jet-black horse, causing him to laugh. The stableman was trying to blow up its nose and feed it carrots, but the horse was having none of it, nosing the carrots out of his hand to the ground, then eating them and running off. Jet's ears pricked up as the carriage passed, and he briefly ran alongside it, looking in at Rory and, with a toss of his mane, said goodbye to his true master.

It was a short trip to Kilwinning, which had grown in size since the last time Rory had been here. The carriage crossed the stone bridge over the Garnock River and along the main street towards the former abbey. It had fallen into hard times and was nothing but a ruin in places, surrounded by a graveyard. The monks of St Columba had long since moved from the area, with a new church having been built on the site, following the religious revolution in Scotland implemented with the teachings of John Knox. (* See Appendix.)

The carriage carried on up the road past the Celtic cross dedicated to St Winning. Rory remembered him very well after just recently meeting him. He would be very surprised that a town was named after him. They arrived at a small rectangular building made with the reclaimed heavy masonry from the larger demolished monastery building that had stood on the same spot. It was the first Masonic temple in Scotland MKO (Mother Kilwinning Zero) or, as it was called by its three Grand Masters: 'The Circle Lodge'!

It was aligned perfectly with the cardinal points of the planet, north, south, east and west and the summer equinox. It was built on top of one of the most powerful meeting points of ley lines on the planet. Rory's skin tingled with the power radiating from the ground beneath his feet. It was not only coming from the ley lines but emanating from the Grail Box still within the chamber!

Rory walked with the three Masters to the double front doors, supported by a large stone pillar on each side. Above the doors in the middle was a carved symbol of a triangle containing an open eye. It was the same as the brass symbol he had made and taken to St John!

Archibald, the earl, unlocked the door, and they all entered a bright hallway lit by high windows on either side, shining down on two small rooms situated on the left and right. The floor was covered with shiny white and black tiles in a chequered pattern like a chess board. Built into the wall in front of Rory off centre to the left and right were another two single doors. Archibald locked the front doors behind him, lit oil-burning lamps and handed one to each person. Rory watched as he unlocked and opened the left-hand door facing him and walked through it. Rory followed Alexander and Charles through the door into a large, windowless rectangular room.

The door was again locked behind him. No one was going to disturb them!

Even in the gloom of four lamps, Rory could clearly see he was standing in a replica of the temple of the now destroyed Urquhart Castle, minus its stained-glass windows. The three Masters lowered a huge candelabra on a pulley from the ceiling and lit its oil-burning lamps. They raised it back to the ceiling, illuminating the temple in an orange-white light. Rory looked down and saw that he was standing on the same chequered floor as the hallway; raised wooden seating was on his left and right and in the space between the two doors at the entrance to the hall. In front of him, in the east of the temple, was a raised area with seating on both sides and two smaller wooden chairs either side of a large one in the middle; they all faced west towards him, past a marble altar on the level floor. Just as with the Urquhart Temple, the walls on the north, south, east and west had the letters A, I, G and H.

Rory smiled to himself, remembering his own initiation in the temple at Urquhart Castle and the explanation he received of the meaning of the letters, which represented Animal, Invisible, Great One and Haggis. He looked around the room, but even with his enhanced eyesight, he could not see any other exit or entrance other than the way he had come in. It was the turn of the three Grand Masters to smile, enjoying the puzzled look on Rory's face.

The Knight Marshal, Sir Charles and Earl Archibald walked to the centre of the chequered floor and kneeled opposite each other, one at a white tile, the other at a black one. Simultaneously they pushed down on the side of the tile nearest them, and there was a loud click as the tiles popped upright on a lever. Two large metal rings were exposed in the false section of flooring, which lifted away easily on pulling the rings. A large square hole, big enough to accommodate the largest man, was revealed when the hatch was put to one side. Rory came forward and looked in to see the vast improvements since he had last been here. There was no need for a dodgy rope ladder now. A wooden staircase had been built around the wall of the circular chamber.

He followed his companions down the stairs by lamplight, looking at the walls as he went. All around the dome-shaped vault were nine brass letters W, F, E, N, O, W, H, E, O, the exact same letters as on the symbol he had made for St John. Rory knew their meaning when the letters were rearranged.

After all, he had created it. They read HOW, NEW and FOE, representing the battle between good and evil and creation. Rory spoke them out loud as he walked down the stairs. The Grand Masters turned and looked at him; he was the only person besides them that knew the secret words.

More lamps were lit at the bottom of the stairs as Rory passed an area on the wall that concealed the exit to the ley tunnel. He could feel the power in the chamber pumping through him in time to his heartbeat as he turned to face its centre. A rectangular marble altar had been placed there, which was about five foot in height and the same in length and breadth. On top of it was a linen-wrapped parcel with an item sparkling on top of it in the oil lamplight.

Rory walked over to it to get a better look. It was the triangular symbol he had made for St John all those centuries before. It was well worn, but he could still see the marking he had put on it quite clearly. That was really good brass, he thought.

He set it aside and unwrapped the protective linen from the book as the pulsing surging through his body intensified. He identified the heavy leather-bound book embossed with a picture of St Columba immediately. It contained Rory's life history, detailing all the things he had already done and would do. Rory turned the pages as the pulsing in his chest increased into the vice-like grip of a heart attack.

All the pages in the book were blank!

CHAPTER 30

Circle's End

The three Grand Masters were powerless to help Rory as he dropped the *Book of St Columba* onto the top of the altar; gripping his chest and the Hagpipe with his left hand, he held onto the altar for support with his right. Rory was in trouble, and he knew it. According to the book, he did not even exist. His life history had not been written! Rory needed help and fast, or he would blink out of existence, just like his history in the book. He focused on the Grail Box, sitting in this very spot but displaced in time 33 minutes into the future. With the last of his strength, he willed it back to the present. The three Masters looked on in disbelief as the ultimate prize of humankind materialised on top of the marble altar with the rods of Moses and Aaron at its side.

The *Book of St Columba* vanished as it joined all the holy texts comprising the whole history of religion and the two stone tablets marked with the Ten Commandments within the Grail Box. The wooden, deep Grail Box, marked with the Red Cross of St John on its top, sat centrally on the altar, overshooting it at either end. The three Grand Masters could not believe their eyes. They were standing in the presence of the gateway to God, which contained the Holy Grail cup and the death shroud of Jesus. They quickly prostrated themselves on the floor, averting their eyes from the box of power in front of them.

The pain in Rory's chest stopped at the containment of his life's history within the Grail Box. His future was like the blank pages in the *Book of St Columba*, still to be written. It was up to him to write his own story now, and he knew what he wanted, and that was his wife, Heather, and his daughters.

The Hagpipe was still vibrating next to his chest, but the speed of it had changed. It was going fast like an alarm clock, trying now to warn him of something. Rory brought his focus back to the circular chamber and noticed it was getting cold, very cold indeed, as he saw his breath plume from his mouth as he exhaled. Condensation was collecting very quickly on the stone walls, running down them, beginning to puddle on the stone floor and turn to ice. The oil lamp light was changing colour from its yellow-orange glow to a deep red as Rory ordered the three Grand Masters back up the stairs to the lodge, instructing them to close the hatch. The three men, including the elderly Alexander Hamilton, moved incredibly fast, driven on by adrenaline and fear, and soon the hatch was shut, enclosing Rory within the vault. They made it just in time as Rory saw figures beginning to materialise around him. All were robed in white with pointed hoods raised over their heads and drooping at the front, covering their faces. They stood side by side with their backs to the walls, facing the centre of the chamber and Rory. They were standing as still as statues, looking inwards to witness the events about to unfold. Rory recognised them. He had seen them before. They were Druids, but not free-willed ones.

They were possessed!

A smaller figure about four-foot-high, wearing a sackcloth dress and with shoulder-length jet-black hair, began to materialise in front of Rory. He recognised her instantly; it was one of his twin daughters. It was Isa whom he had last seen on the Island of Malta, playing with her twin sister Bella and his pet haggis, Hag. Rory's heart leapt, he could save her. Isa raised her head and looked up at Rory, who saw her dirty matted hair and ashen face with a pair of the blackest eyes he had ever seen. His heart dropped, and he was filled with sadness. She, too, was possessed, and an evil smile split her face, showing a mouthful of rotten teeth. She smelt bad, very bad, and raised her right hand towards Rory. It was holding a long, very sharp dagger. She had only one intention, and that was to kill her father, Rory!

What was he to do?

He could easily defend himself against her, but would that mean hurting her, if not killing her! He could not do that to his own daughter; he was filled with despair. How did matters get to this stage? He wanted to save his family, not do them harm! Then the thought came to him, just let his daughter kill him, put an end to it all!

Rory recognised this evil working into his mind and knew where it was coming from. He had felt it before when attacked by Satanic Stan at Jerusalem. He would not give in to despair. He would fight it. He took hold of his Hagpipe with his left hand, surrounding himself in a protective bubble of white Hagpower.

Isa began stabbing at him in a robot-like fashion, but she could not penetrate the protective shell which sparked with each contact as evil collided with good.

Rory could see each blow was causing Isa pain, which etched across her face. This, in turn, was hurting him inside. She could not keep this up without doing herself real harm. Despair began creeping into his mind again like a thief in the night as he heard a familiar laugh vibrate around the chamber.

It was the source of all the evil at work: Satanic Stan was here!

Rory looked up from Isa to see his fully solid form standing in front of the Druids, dressed in his red robe, with red glowing eyes staring at him. His power dominated the chamber, filling it, but he was keeping his distance from the Grail Box behind Rory. Rory knew he had a chance to beat Stan still. He held that thought, driving the despair again from his mind. In its place, he filled his thoughts with love for his daughter standing in front of him.

The protective bubble grew whiter and brighter, and with every blow from Isa's dagger, some of it clung to the blade and began to work along it. Soon it was on her hand and began working its way up her arm. Rory concentrated, extending all of his love towards Isa until the light expanded and fully engulfed her. Isa dropped the dagger as the greyness fell from her face, giving way to a healthy pink glow as her eyes changed from black to a green-brown colour with a yellow fleck. She reached forward and cuddled Rory's legs as Satanic Stan let out a howl of frustration.

It was Rory's turn to go on the offensive as he commanded Hans from the sheath on his back to kill Satanic Stan, causing it to fly through the air towards Stan's chest at breath-taking speed. One cannot defeat evil with evil; this was a major mistake. The sword possessed awesome power, but Stan had more, gained from the cumulative evil stored within mankind. It lives and grows within everyone, and to defeat it, one must stop feeding it!

Stan laughed loudly as he extended his will and struck the sword from the air, shattering it! The magic sword was broken and lay on the ground in front of the Druids. Rory understood now. This was how it had been broken and why the Druids had possessed it in the past. The answers to all the unexplained experiences of his past were being revealed. The chamber vibrated with the aftershock of the power that had just been used, shaking the chamber, and knocking the Grail Box from the altar to the ground behind Rory. Satanic Stan was supreme in his power, feeding off the evil intent from Rory, who was now his to possess. With a wave of his hand, Stan sent the Druids and Isa and the broken sword back in time, wanting to savour the pleasure of his defeat of Rory alone. He grew in size, taking on his true form, complete with horns on his head. Satan reached the ceiling, looking down on Rory, surrounding himself and filling the vault with blackness. The oil lamps went out, the only light left in the chamber being the light of the protective bubble around Rory. Satan's giant red hand reached down to the bubble, pinching it between thumb and forefinger, and began to squeeze!

Rory knew he was beaten. Despair washed over him like the tide on a beach, growing stronger as each new wave came into the shore; Satan's evil laughter reverberated in his head. He was transported back in time, becoming that little eight-year-old boy again; good for nothing, worthless, useless. His only purpose was to be the toy of his stepfather, to be abused, torn and beaten by him. The vision of John Grant stood over him again, smirking and aroused at the pleasure he was receiving at Rory's torment. Hidden visions of the past flooded through Rory's mind as Satan tortured his soul as cruelly as his stepfather, John Grant, had physically abused his small body every time he was alone with him. The evil revealed that John Grant had never wanted or loved Rory's mother, Mary. All his manipulations in dispossessing them of his father were to gain control of Rory for his unnatural urges and pleasure. He had beaten Rory's mum just to make Rory comply with his depraved wishes and left her alone as long as he obeyed.

Rory was as powerless now as he had been as a child. The light of the bubble surrounding him began to change, growing dimmer, darker, becoming black. The only remaining light was the glow of the Hagpipe he clung to in his left hand. Soon even it would be extinguished, and Rory would be the slave of Satan forever.

Anger and hate were not the answer; they only made Satan stronger, increasing his ability to possess Rory. The Hagpipe was not strong enough to fight this unearthly evil, and Rory collapsed to his knees before him. Rory could feel that he was going to be lost forever, the same as his pet Hag, lobotomised, a puppet for Satan to play with. He felt the last of his conscious thoughts in his head. Had he endured all the experiences on his journeys and adventures for it all to mean nothing?

All the humiliation and abuse he had suffered as a child were not his fault. He was as innocent then as he was now, burnt clean of all sin in the fire of the Hagpipe. He was determined that his last thoughts were not going to be of his stepfather or possessed by Satan but of those he loved.

Rory forced himself to think of his beloved Heather, twin daughters, parents and all that he loved. His body might get defeated and broken, but the innocence of his spirit and the love he had never would. The fightback began. He remembered what Hag had said, "Have faith and continue to love. You will not fail."

The glow in his hand from the Hagpipe became stronger, turning into a white light, but it still was not enough to defeat Satan. It was strong enough, though, to clear his mind as it drove away all the despair, filling it instead with love. Rory knew he did not have the power to defeat Satan, *but* he refused to be possessed by him. He would die filled with love, not hate.

Satan was furious at Rory's resistance. He had always resisted him, and he really wanted the pleasure of seeing him break; however, his death would suffice as he began again to squeeze!

The pressure was unbearable, but Rory resisted. His body convulsed in a fit as he stretched out on the stone floor as if crucified, reaching toward the four points of the globe in the same shape as the cross of St Andrew on the Scottish Saltire. His left foot struck the side of the unprotected Grail Box lying on the ground behind him without the rods inserted into it. Screaming filled the room, along with a blinding white light as all discomfort and pain fled from Rory.

The screaming was coming from Satan!

He was the one who was in control, trying to possess Rory, and he was the one that had caused the contact with the Grail Box!

You cannot totally destroy evil, but you can diminish it!

Rory kept his foot firmly against the Grail Box, the source of everything that was good, as he held the Hagpipe with both hands. He focused the Grail power up his leg into his torso, arms and through his hands, melding its divine power with that of the Hagpipe. He cast this combined force at the giant red image of the horned demon.

The blackness in the chamber was replaced with white light as Rory focused his thoughts on love and everything that was good. He watched as Satan reduced in size, turning back into the red-robed Druid of Stan as the light compressed him. He squealed in pain and shrunk again, transforming into the human form of John Grant. He held his hands outstretched, begging and pleading, crying out to Rory to stop, just as Rory had cried and pleaded with him to stop when he was a boy. It was not hatred or vengeance that made Rory ignore John Grant's pleas as he continued, willing this great power towards him. It was love for his fellow man to diminish this evil and the hatred that Stan represented in the world. The pleas of John Grant had no effect on Rory, just as his had been ignored when he had cried out in pain as a child.

The human form of John Grant changed again into that of the red-robed Stan but consisted of a black cloud in a human shape, its head comprising solely two red hate-filled eyes that looked directly at Rory. The evil glared at Rory and shimmered as the white light shone like the sun filling the chamber. The human, robed shape changed again, turning into a cloud of blackness as the light penetrated it, causing it to dissipate, clearing it away like the steam from a kettle until just a pair of malevolent red eyes were left floating in the air before Rory until they too blinked out of existence.

The battle had been won. Good had triumphed!

Rory relaxed and let go of his control of the Grail power, moving his foot away from the box, but the light in the chamber remained on as he lay exhausted on the floor. His senses were still acute, and he felt as if he was floating, not lying on hard rock. A peaceful calm voice was in his head talking to him, and he had heard that voice before. He opened what he perceived to be his eyes. He had been here before when he touched the Grail Box. It was the afterlife, a pure white space travelling to infinity full of floating, star-like twinkling balls.

The soothing voice spoke, "You have done well, my son. My enemy will take a long time to recover his strength but recover he will. However, for now, mankind is safe. You have earned your reward. Your path is now yours to choose, but you must choose wisely. You are no longer guided by me in your actions which were recorded in the *Book of St Columba*. The pages are blank, and it is up to you to write your own history. That was the limit of my influence to advise you without breaking the arch of time and allowing my enemy to escape his prison. Heed these words carefully as you choose your path, especially if you move through time. Your route is like a tree with many branches with new shoots waiting to grow. Every action you take involving other people starts that new shoot growing and puts you on this new road connecting you to the lives you have touched. This is the same for all my children, and it only takes one wrong decision to change the direction you are taking on your path through life. You have the unique ability to travel to any of these life-changing moments to change your destiny and that of those around you. Of all your abilities, this is the most important one; you must consider the consequences of changing history.

"I have set some points in mankind's history that cannot be changed, and you will instinctively know what they are as they affect the whole human race. There is no limit to the number of paths which overlap into multiple realms created by the actions of all the beings on Earth, but only you can change the direction you take. Be warned, though, there are others who have great power, like you and your creature friends, who I am forbidden to interfere with.

"What do you want as your reward?"

Rory did not even have to think about it. He wanted his wife and family!

"SO, LET IT BE!"

CHAPTER 31

The Twins

Rory opened his eyes again; he was lying on the rocky floor in the secret chamber below MKO. The oil lamps were burning again, and the Grail Box was sitting on the altar in its centre next to the rods of Moses and Aaron. Had he been dreaming?

No. His sword was gone, and the concealed trapdoor to the lodge above was still closed. He could hear the three Grand Masters above, getting ready to open it. He quickly approached the Grail Box, which was open and now contained the blank Book of St Columba, which was the appropriate place for it, he thought. He inserted the rods and replaced the lid marked with the cross of St John on it, and removed the rods. Rory took hold of his Hagpipe with his left hand and placed the Grail Box and the rods of Moses and Aaron 33 minutes into the future to keep them safe forever!

He lifted the brass symbol from the floor and placed it in the middle of the altar for the Masons above to remind them of their rituals. The trapdoor opened, letting in light from the lodge above, and the three Grand Masters came down the spiralling staircase to join him. They all looked at the altar and at Rory with quizzical looks on their faces. Rory asked them what they remembered. They could only recall leaving after the Grail Box appeared and shutting the door to give Rory privacy. They could recall no more as their memories had been subtly altered. Rory smiled and instructed them that they were the guardians of this chamber and to keep it safe. The secrets of the Grail Box had been lost and would only ever be found again if the time and circumstances were right.

The three Masters nodded their understanding, promising that the ritual would be altered accordingly to keep the secret safe. Rory was happy with that and considered that sometime in the future, he might return to see how things had worked out.

He told the Masters he was leaving by another route and wished them well as they returned to the lodge and closed the trapdoor. They obviously thought he was leaving by the ley tunnel. They were not far off the mark as Rory chuckled to himself, taking hold of his Hagpipe. The entrance illuminated in a sparkling sheath of white power as he stepped into it. He had an appointment with his own destiny and had his daughters to save. He knew where he was going as he had been there before. This time he wanted to be 30 minutes earlier and to reset all the damage Stan had done.

It was the 22 December 1541: the winter equinox.

It was time!

Heather was waiting at the entrance to the Grant Tower, with a concerned Hag looking up at her. She planned on heading to the most remote communal privy for privacy away from her mother. She intended to deliver the baby herself but was woefully out of her depth. Her heart leapt on seeing the frail, stooped figure of Granny Grant carrying her large medicine basket, walking towards her. Granny had lived a long time, looking for her mother and father and was now going against all the lore she knew to deliver herself from her mother. She did not know what would happen but knew she would be no more at the end of it. Another contraction doubled both Heather and Granny Grant over as she reached her in the doorway. Heather was more concerned for Granny Grant than herself. She was young and strong; Granny was old frail and looked very weak! The contraction passed, and both recovered, panting heavily. Granny took Heather by her free right arm, holding her basket in her left and propelling her towards the nearby temple with Hag at their feet. The contractions were 15 minutes apart but rapidly progressing as they entered the temple, making their way to the east and the G on the wall.

The full super moon of the winter equinox was beaming in the stained-glass window, illuminating them in the blue colours of the loch and purple of St Columba's robe as they neared the altar.

Hag knew where they were going and ran ahead, jumping up on the altar and upwards off it, pushing the G on the wall with her snout and opening the secret door.

The next contraction came and passed as Heather and Granny reached the door. A few deep breaths later, Granny took a candle from her basket and lit it as Hag ran ahead and down the spiral staircase. Heather did not know where she was going, but she knew she was being helped, and that was all that mattered to her just now. Moonlight was beaming in from the cavern entrance to the loch, bouncing off the still water in the huge cave below the castle. Granny and Heather walked from the stairs towards the smaller haggis graveyard cave. Hag was waiting for them and let out a high-pitched squeal as a shimmering white curtain illuminated its entrance. The contractions were minutes apart now, and Granny Grant visibly struggled with the pain she was feeling and was now being supported more by Heather than the other way around. They passed through the curtain of power into the cave's interior, illuminated with light from the reflective roof crystals which fed off the candle's glow.

Granny sat the candle down on a rocky shelf to keep it safe as she would need her hands. She didn't know how she would find the strength to complete her task, but she must!

Heather looked around and saw a gleaming mountain of haggis tusks next to a large circle of stones on the sandy floor. Granny took a quilt out of her basket, placed it in the stone circle, and asked Heather to lie down on it. She just made it in time as the strongest contraction yet racked her body, forcing her legs apart as a concerned Hag cuddled into her in the circle. Heather looked up at Granny Grant as the pain coursed through her, looking for help. She was horrified at what she saw; with each pulse of pain, Granny was flashing in and out of existence!

Heather let out a mighty scream which vibrated around the cave. First one and then another baby was born in quick succession as two pure white crystals fell from the shimmering reflective ceiling into the stone circle next to the twin girls who were floating in the air!

Neither Granny nor Heather could believe what they were seeing as two large hands began to appear below them, carefully holding the twin girls. As they watched, the hands were followed by the rest of Rory as he brought himself back to normal time from 30 seconds in the future.

Rory stood smiling at Granny Grant, who smiled back as she vanished. He looked down at his two blonde-haired twin daughters smiling up at him. One had green-brown eyes with a yellow sparkle, and the other the eyes of the purest sky blue. Heather looked confused but smiled as Rory wrapped their daughters in blankets and handed them to her.

They were safe!

Rory carefully carried his future wife and daughters back to the castle and the Grant Tower with his pet haggis Hag at his ankles. He had a second wedding to Heather to arrange and a christening with a lot of questions.

Epilogue

Thousands of years in the past, the Druid chief stood with his oak staff at the bonfire heating the cave below the now Urquhart Castle as the spey wife attended to his wife in childbirth. His Grant-born wife screamed as she gave birth to two healthy raven-haired twin girls at precisely the same time on the winter equinox as the birth of a set of blonde twins so many centuries later.

The omens were good!

Urquhart Castle would be destroyed by natural forces in the future but not just now. Nessie was still free to roam the portals, and Rory could write his own future history.

His daughters were loved and safe, and the Hagpipe was going in its box after he checked on the ancestor of an old friend. After that, he could think of no reason to use it again, but he had not considered the challenges of rearing two girls with the power of the haggis coursing through them.

In the distant past of China, Yror, the first and greatest Shaolin monk, materialised on the peak of the extinct volcano in the land of the dragon. The order of the Shaolin was created, and his huge grey-robed frame would soon be replaced on this spot by the original Shaolin Temple. All the displaced and orphans of the wars would soon fill it, trained in the mystic arts and science and placed on 'The Path to Enlightenment'. Yror reappeared many times over the centuries, remaining as unchanged in appearance as if seconds had just passed for him. He was pleased with what he saw and appeared for the last time on 19 March 1279, holding a sleeping seven-year-old Zhao Bing in his arms. He handed him to the Grand Master of the temple, giving precise instruction as to his training.

The future of Bruce Lee and all that his life would affect depended on it!

Appendix and Source Notes

Ley Lines Explained

These magnetic lines of power were created at the dawn of the creation of the planet when the molten magma connected to the earth's core spewed out by volcanic activity and cooled over millennia. The oldest ley lines are found in the colder northern hemisphere, where they cooled first and got buried below topsoil and water. There are fewer ley lines in the southern hemisphere, especially within the active volcanic ring of fire and seismic activity. It takes a very long time to create a ley line, and they do not operate if they have any breaks. The continuous connection joins them to the central point of control, which in their case is the molten spinning core of the planet. When connected and boosted by the magnetic and solar power of the sun and moon at their equinox, a doorway is created. Those in tune with this ancient power can travel in time and place along this ley line network.

The Grail Box

It is a 6ft by 3ft by 3ft deep wooden coffin-shaped box made from the acacia wooden cross used in the crucifixion of Jesus and marked with the Red Cross of St John on its top panel. This shape was made from the blood seeping from the crown of thorns pressed into his head. Over time every religious artefact, starting with the stone tablets of the Ten Commandments given to Moses from God and all the original religious texts, were contained within it. The Grail Cup was made from the same acacia wood as the crucifixion cross. It and the death shroud that wrapped the body of Jesus were included in the box along with the original copies of the new testaments written by four of the surviving disciples. The box could not be handled unless the staff of Moses and its sister staff, the rod of Aaron (Aaron, the brother of Moses), were inserted into the holes in the Grail Box, which had been created by the nail holes that pinned Jesus to the cross. These rods were the only objects powerful enough to make contact with the Grail Box and fitted through the holes on either side near its top and into a hole at the bottom, allowing it to be carried.

Chapter 2

HAGI. The meaning of which is Haggis, Animal, Great and Invisible and its significance to the storyline is fully explained in Book 2: *Rory MacSween and the Rescue*.

Chapters 3, 5 and 12

The Book of St Columba.

The full version depicts the life story and historic events experienced by Rory MacSween. At this point in the story, it is in the possession of Abbot MacCallum at Urquhart Castle. It relates to the premonitions recorded by St Columba referred to in Books 1 and 2 in this series: *The Secrets of Urquhart Castle* and *The Rescue*.

St Columba's journey to Southend on the Mull of Kintyre in Scotland. The malevolent storm that attacked him as he travelled to Scotland was a tactic used on several occasions by the incarnations of John Grant/Evil Stan. This would also prevent his historic meeting with 'Nessie', detailed in Book 1: *The Secrets of Urquhart Castle*. The full story of the saving of Rory's parents is also contained within Book 2, which also details the remaking of Hans the Sword.

Without the guidance of the *Book of St Columba*, Evil Stan can only travel in time using the ley line portals at the height of their power at an equinox. With the power of the Hagpipe, Rory has no such restriction and had already travelled back in time to deal with this threat. These events, including the retaking of Castle Sween and Rory's first encounter with Sir John Menteith, are revealed in full in Book 2 of this series: *The Rescue*.

Granny Grant and Hans the Sword

Only those with the same genes as Rory can handle Hans, the magic sword. It has a handgrip made from the left tusk of the first haggis. The details of how Granny Grant handled it are detailed in Book 2: *The Rescue*.

Keystone

A Keystone is a wedge-shaped stone used in the construction of all arches and bridges to complete the structure and provide stability and strength. This method of construction is still used today and can easily be seen if you look up as you pass under a stone bridge.

Brief history of the Old Testament

The history of the Old Testament details one of the main starting points of the split between Judaism and the start of the Arab tribes, which would later develop into the Islamic religion. It can all be traced back to a family fallout following the death of Abraham between his son Isaac and his twin sons, Esau and Jacob, over jealousy, money and property (Genesis 25, 19 to 34 and Genesis 27), which resulted in Jacob changing his name to 'Israel'.

If this sounds familiar, the human race is still doing this today. As a stone thrown in a pond starts a ripple, it expands and becomes a tidal wave that can't be stopped, as do the actions of every human.

St John

St John the Evangelist is usually depicted as a young man in Christian art. He is symbolically represented by an eagle, one of the creatures envisioned by Ezekiel (1:10) and in the Revelation to John (4:7). The use of the chalice as a symbol for John is sometimes interpreted with reference to the Last Supper. (Excerpts from Wikipedia and the Bible.)

Christmas Day

The modern date for Christmas Day is celebrated on 25 December, but this may be due to the date of the winter equinox being celebrated on the 27th, which coincidently happens to be the feast day of St John in the Roman Catholic Church and in the Anglican Communion and Lutheran Calendars. Surely this is just a coincidence?

The Beatitudes are:

Blessed are those who mourn, for they will be comforted; Blessed are the meek, for they will inherit the earth. Blessed are those who hunger and thirst for righteousness, for they will be filled. Blessed are the merciful, for they will be shown mercy. Blessed are the pure in heart, for they will see God. Blessed are the peacemakers, for they will be called children of God. Blessed are those who are persecuted for righteousness's sake, for theirs is the kingdom of heaven. Blessed are you when others revile you and persecute you and utter all kinds of evil against you falsely on my account. Rejoice and be glad, for your reward in heaven is great, for so they persecuted the prophets who were before you.

The Battle of the Milvian Bridge

This took place between the Roman Emperors Constantine I and Maxentius on 28 October AD 312. It takes its name from the Milvian Bridge, an important route over the River Tiber. Constantine won the battle and started on the path that led him to end the tetrarchy and become the sole ruler of the Roman Empire. Maxentius drowned in the Tiber during the battle, and his body was later taken from the river and decapitated. According to chroniclers such as Eusebius of Caesarea and Lactantius, the battle marked the beginning of Constantine's conversion to Christianity. Eusebius of Caesarea recounts that Constantine and his soldiers had a vision sent by the Christian God. This was interpreted as a promise of victory if the sign of the Chi-Rho, the first two letters of Christ's name in Greek, was painted on the soldiers' shields. (Excerpt from Wikipedia.)

The Battle of Arsuf

This battle took place just outside of Arsuf (Arsur) when Saladin attacked King Richard's army when it was moving from Acre to Jaffa. Following a series of harassing attacks by Saladin's army, the battle was joined on the morning of 7 September 1191. Richard's army successfully resisted attempts to disrupt its cohesion until the Hospitallers broke ranks and charged; Richard then committed all his forces to the attack. He regrouped his army after its initial success and led it to victory. The battle resulted in the coastal area of southern Palestine, including the port of Jaffa, returning to Christian control. (Excerpt from Wikipedia.)

A report of the Battle of Arsuf says, "In truth, our people, so few in number, were hemmed in by the multitudes of the Saracens, that they had no means of escape, if they tried; neither did they seem to have valour sufficient to withstand so many foes, nay, they were shut in, like a flock of sheep in the jaws of wolves, with nothing but the sky above, and the enemy all around them." (Sourced from Wikipedia.)

History records this on the Battle of Arsuf: "There the king, the fierce, the extraordinary king, cutting down the Turks in every direction, and none could escape the force of his arm, for wherever he turned, brandishing his sword, he carved a wide path for himself: and as he advanced and gave repeated strokes with his sword, cutting them down like a reaper with his sickle, the rest, warned by the sight of the dying, gave him more ample space, for the corpses of the dead Turks which lay on the face of the earth extended over half a mile." (Sourced from Wikipedia.)

The Battle of Hattin

This took place on 4 July 1187, between the Crusader Kingdom of Jerusalem and the forces of the Ayyubid Sultan Salah ad-Din, known in the West as Saladin. It is also known as the Battle of the Horns of Hattin, referring to the shape of a nearby extinct volcano. The Muslim armies under Saladin captured or killed the vast majority of the Crusader forces, removing their capability to wage war. As a direct result of the battle, Muslims once again became the eminent military power in the Holy Land, re-conquering Jerusalem and several other Crusader-held cities. These Christian defeats prompted the Third Crusade, which began two years after the Battle of Hattin. (Excerpt from Wikipedia.)

Cliftonite

This unusual metal alloy is not naturally found on Earth and can only be sourced from meteors that were large enough to survive burning up on entering the atmosphere. Scientists have recently found living bacteria in this metal, proving life exists outwith our planet. A vital ingredient in Hans the Sword, giving it life.

King Richard the Lionheart

The return of King Richard to England. If it wasn't for the actions of Robin Hood and his Merry Men, he would have had no home to go to, but that's another story.

Divining

This is the ability to find water underground and the position of the magnetic ley lines. It is usually with the use of a forked twig of wood held between the thumb and forefinger, which will involuntarily jerk up and down over the position of the underground water or ley line. This is caused by the arm muscles involuntary contracting. The more accomplished diviner can accomplish this by merely holding their arms at an outstretched 90-degree angle to the body.

Bruce

Zhao Bing was born on 12 February 1272 and reportedly died on 19 March 1279. He was also known as Emperor Bing of Song and was the 18th and last emperor of the Song dynasty in China. He was also the ninth and last emperor of the Southern Song dynasty. He reigned for about 313 days from 1278 to 1279 until his death, aged 7. (Excerpt from Wikipedia.)

The Tower of Blois

Named after Adela Blois of the house of Normandy, who filled in as regent for her husband's duties during his extended absence as a leader of the First Crusade (AD 1095–1098).

Cyprus

In 1191, during the Third Crusade, Richard I of England captured the island from Isaac Komnenos of Cyprus. He used it as a major supply base that was relatively safe from the Saracens. A year later, Richard sold the island to the Knights Templars. (Excerpt from Wikipedia).

Fort St. Elmo

A ravelin is a triangular fortification or detached outwork located in front of the inner works of a fortress comprising the curtain walls and bastions.

St Elmo's fire. An observation by the author when carrying out research for this book in Malta. Travelling about the island, I noticed an insurance company called St Elmo's. Do you think they specialised in 'Fire Insurance'?

Kilwinning

It was named after a St Winning, who is well documented in historic records. He had a well named after him located at the rear of the abbey, which reportedly supplied water with healing powers. It has since been filled in and hidden somewhere under houses on the street called St Winning Lane.

Free or Speculative Masons

Famous authors like Dan Brown wrote many books including them and connecting historic links between Kilwinning and Roslyn Chapel or the rose line as it is known, trying to connect the location of the lost religious artefacts or the blood line of Jesus Christ. The inquisitive human race love secrets and are always looking for an answer to their existence. The answer could be found if one knew where to look, and millions of humans worldwide, on the circular planet Earth, are still looking.

Only a few find the secret to the meaning of life, including the members of this first Lodge of Masons who call it number 'Nothing' in reference to it being before one, or perhaps, is it because it was the same shape as a circle?

The answer to the meaning of life is 'One' thing. Each of us has to find the answer to this, the greatest of all questions.

If you embrace charity and have faith and hope then you will find your answer, in your Centre!

Napoleon

In 1853 Louis-Napoleon Bonaparte (Napoleon III) officially recognised the Order of the Knights Templar when he became the Emperor of France. Their great wealth and power would never be restored, but their good name was.

The Religious Reformation in Scotland

John Knox c. 1513 – 24 November 1572 was a Scottish minister, theologian, and writer who was a leader of the reformation and is considered to be the founder of the Presbyterian Church of Scotland. This split from Roman Catholicism created the new dominant religion in Scotland, which no longer followed the Pope as their religious leader. The followers of the Presbyterian religion refer to themselves as Protestants. A religious split continues to divide the population of Scotland and Northern Ireland between the Protestants and the followers of the Roman Catholic faith to the present day.